"I loved this delightful gem of a novel: a deeply satisfying, unique reading experience. If you're passionate about reading I know you'll be passionate about this book."
— Liane Moriarty

No Two Persons

A Novel

Erica Bauermeister

New York Times bestselling author of The Scent Keeper

Spectacular Praise for *No Two Persons*

"I loved this delightful gem of a novel: a deeply satisfying, unique reading experience." —Liane Moriarty

"A breathtaking novel about the power a book can have." —*Newsweek*

"Moving . . . There's plenty of charm to this thoughtful take on a book's impact on its readers." —*Publishers Weekly*

"I loved the power this plot gives to reading itself, that dear and vital realm of our experience." —Joan Silber, National Book Critics Circle and PEN/Faulkner Award Winner, and author of *Improvement*

"A gloriously original celebration of fiction and the ways it deepens our lives." —Nina de Gramont, *New York Times* bestselling author of *The Christie Affair*

"A wondrous ode to the power of fiction, *No Two Persons* will linger with its readers in much the same way its fictional novel remained with its characters." —Marie Benedict, *New York Times* bestselling author of *The Mystery of Mrs. Christie*

"As perfect a depiction of the power of story as one could ever find, or need." —Natalie Jenner, bestselling author of *Bloomsbury Girls*

"Immensely satisfying. Storytelling at its best." —Alka Joshi, author of *The Henna Artist*

"Beautifully written and inventive."
—Diane Chamberlain, *New York Times* bestselling author of *The Last House on the Street*

"A beautiful and haunting love letter to the redemptive power of stories."
—Kim Michele Richardson, *New York Times* bestselling author of *The Book Woman of Troublesome Creek*

"Beautifully explores . . . the power of words and story to heal us." —Marjan Kamali, author of *Together Tea*

"Almost unbearable truth and beauty and depth . . . The perfect book."
—Louisa Morgan, author of *A Secret History of Witches*

"Wondrous and moving . . . a love letter to every writer, reader, and human who has ever opened their heart to the transformative power of story."
—JoAnne Tompkins, author of *What Comes After*

"Gorgeous, nuanced, and intimate, *No Two Persons* will stay with you well after the last page is turned."
—Anna Quinn, author of *The Night Child*

"A very tender, very true book about the power of stories. Bauermeister creates a kaleidoscope of beautiful, unexpected ways of seeing the world."
—Yara Zgheib, author of *No Land to Light On*

No Two Persons

ERICA BAUERMEISTER

ST. MARTIN'S GRIFFIN
NEW YORK

Published in the United States by St. Martin's Griffin,
an imprint of St. Martin's Publishing Group

NO TWO PERSONS. Copyright © 2023 by Erica Bauermeister.
All rights reserved. Printed in the United States of America. For information, address
St. Martin's Publishing Group, 120 Broadway, New York, NY 10271.

www.stmartins.com

Designed by Jonathan Bennett

The Library of Congress has cataloged the hardcover edition as follows:

Names: Bauermeister, Erica, author.
Title: No two persons / Erica Bauermeister.
Other titles: No 2 persons
Description: First edition. | New York : St. Martin's Press, 2023.
Identifiers: LCCN 2022056023 | ISBN 9781250284372 (hardcover) |
    ISBN 9781250284389 (ebook)
Subjects: LCGFT: Novels.
Classification: LCC PS3602.A9357 N6 2023 | DDC 813/.6—
    dc23/eng/20221202
LC record available at https://lccn.loc.gov/2022056023

ISBN 978-1-250-86902-9 (trade paperback)

Our books may be purchased in bulk for promotional, educational,
or business use. Please contact your local bookseller or the Macmillan Corporate
and Premium Sales Department at 1-800-221-7945, extension 5442, or by email at
MacmillanSpecialMarkets@macmillan.com.

First St. Martin's Griffin Edition: 2024

10 9 8 7 6 5 4 3 2 1

For Holly

No two persons ever read the same
book, or saw the same picture.

The Writings of Madame Swetchine, 1860

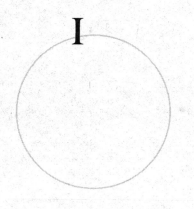

I

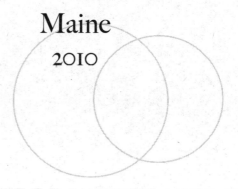

Maine

2010

The Writer

The story on Alice's computer screen had been finding its way into words for more than five years, or maybe forever. Over that time, it had grown, changed, creaked, flown, gone silent, and then gained its voice again, its plot taking unexpected paths, its characters turning into people she hadn't thought they would be, just as she had. This glowing screen, the one constant. This story, in all its iterations. Now awaiting the last step. Someone to say *yes*.

She was young for a writer, barely twenty-five, but in some ways Alice had always been old. Always been watching, learning, searching for the things that people were not saying. Truth lies below the table; she knew this even as a child. If given the choice, she would have taken her dinner plate down into the cool, dark space beneath the tablecloth, where she could watch her mother's fingers tighten along with the conversation. Watch her older brother's shoes point toward the exit even as their father interrogated him about his latest swim meet. Medals he did or didn't get, effort he did or didn't expend.

Children, of course, did not eat under the table, so for Alice, a tendency toward napkin-dropping had to suffice.

Why can't she keep that thing on her lap? her father would say to her mother.

But you could learn so much more, keeping your gaze down. Just as well for Alice, who had never liked meeting people's eyes. It always felt like looking into a jam-packed closet—or opening the door to your own.

In any case, her father preferred children who were respectful.

When Alice had learned how to read, she'd discovered her own world, far from their house and their eastern Oregon town. Her brother called it hiding, but as he'd read the entire *Lord of the Rings* trilogy three times by that point, he was hardly one to talk. After Alice brought her choices home from the library, she'd open their covers, smelling other children's meals and lives in the pages, and she would put her face in and blow, like a human smudging to make the stories hers.

Her brother caught her at it one day. Peter was eight years older than Alice, and ever so much taller. He was like a great and gentle horse in her life. When she confessed what she was doing, he just smiled.

"Ah, Alice," he said, switching into his Bilbo voice. "Just

a plain hobbit you look. But there's more about you than appears on the surface."

The year Alice turned nine, an author came to visit her school. It was on that day Alice understood for the first time—in a way that was both slightly depressing and terribly exciting—that books were written by people. Real people, with mascara that flecked down onto the soft pale curves of skin under the eyes, and a sweater that was a bit too long in the sleeves. This woman at the front of the class, this not-quite-finished-looking woman, had written the book she was holding in her hand. Before this point, Alice had never met an actual author, and so it had been possible to pretend that they were no more real, and thus as magical, as the characters inside. But here was this woman, telling the class that she wrote every day, during these hours, using this ordinary pen. That the characters were her friends.

"I live in their world when I am writing," the author said to the class.

Yes, Alice thought, the breath catching in her throat. And in that moment, she changed her allegiance from magic to magician.

"I'm going to make my own worlds," Alice told her brother.

Peter was getting his things together for a swim meet. He was always swimming—or running or lifting weights in preparation, his weekends spent traveling to swim meets with their father. Their father said children needed to have goals, by which he meant, win. By which he meant, Peter. Alice wondered what their father would say about her new goal, but it was not something she would tell him. She had learned that being a girl was a little like going under the table, out of the line of sight. And that could be beneficial.

Peter was the one she told things to. He would make a secret picnic—peanut butter and jelly sandwiches, with double jelly the way she liked, and potato chips he'd bought on the sly from the corner grocery store—and they would sit in the leafy refuge of the tree house he'd made in the woods, and he would listen to whatever she wanted to say.

Now, in his bedroom, he glanced over at her and smiled, just a bit, and she looked for a moment into his eyes.

Too much in there, Alice thought.

"Peter," their father yelled from downstairs, and Peter startled.

He looked at Alice and shook his head. "You get the world they give you, Alice," he said, reaching for his backpack. "I'm sorry."

But he was wrong, Alice told herself. He had to be. Books, by their very existence, proved that.

The year Alice turned ten, Peter went to college on a swimming scholarship, leaving her alone. It had been clear for a while that Alice was not a social creature, never inclined toward sleepovers or witty notes passed in class, caring little for Girl Scouts or clubs. She'd always been that kid—you know the one—reading by herself during lunch or on the bus. A small animal, not weak enough to attract attention, just alone.

It was perhaps not surprising then, that while she was disappointingly average when it came to math and geography, she was always at the top of her English classes.

"She could be a teacher someday," her teachers said, year after year.

Why don't they ever say writer? she wrote to Peter.

Because you're the one with the imagination, he said. *That's your door out, Allie girl. Use it.*

So Alice decided to train herself. If writers were magicians, she figured, then there were tricks you could learn. She was old enough by that point to know that magic in the real world was just a series of illusions, carefully crafted to distract you from what was really going on. A wall of medals. A fresh pie every Sunday. A father home for dinner every night. *Look there, not here.*

People didn't see reality because they didn't want to, not because it wasn't there. It stood to reason that writing was no different. Look carefully and all the tricks would become clear.

After that, while some girls spent their allowances on clothes or lip gloss, Alice bought books.

What's wrong with the library? her father demanded. But

Alice needed the books to be hers, so she could write in them. Notes in the margins. Arrows drawn from one page to the next. Marking the clues that tipped you off to what was coming, the one detail that told you all you needed to know about a character.

When she had to go out in the real world, she watched for what people didn't know they were telling you. She noted a hand playing with a necklace. An eyebrow, as an interrogative or a dismissal. The way little kids' shoulders would turtle up near their ears when a bully was near. She listened, as well. To the pauses. The falters. The emotional floods of surprise or warmth or anger. She collected the stories she witnessed and wrote them in notebooks that she kept under her mattress. Once in a while, she would send one to Peter.

Maybe you can make worlds after all, he wrote back.

Alice was fourteen when Peter quit college, four months before his graduation, taking off for parts unknown.

You see? their father said to their mother, *this is what happens when you insist upon naming your child after a boy who wouldn't grow up.*

For a few years, he sent her postcards. A rocky coastline in Maine. A market in Egypt. Mono Lake, its limestone formations rising out of the blue water like castles. *Allie girl, you would love this.* Alice would hold the postcard close to her face, inhaling to see if she could smell her brother on the paper. Sometimes she thought she could. But as time went on, the cards became fewer, the words on them more and more vague until they seemed to disappear even as she read them.

And then there was nothing at all.

Alice's father said he had wasted enough money educating his children, but the eloquence of Alice's application essay helped get her a scholarship at a small, tree-lined college in Maine, a whole continent away from their eastern Oregon town. That first semester, Alice signed up for two classes in science and one in economics. The last item on her schedule was a creative writing course—small and innocuous as a white rabbit, a minor prop on a well-appointed stage.

Core requirement, she said to her parents, when they asked.

Now things will start to happen, she thought.

Alice took a seat in the third row, on the right side near the door. Closer to the front than she would usually choose, but she was excited. The creative writing professor was already there, standing behind the podium, making conversation with a few students. An older man, tall, but with a kindliness that surprised her. She'd been expecting something more along the lines of Jack Kerouac or James Joyce, all tortured soul and swagger. But Dr. Roberts was neither of these things—although he did seem absent-minded, one side of his button-down shirt collar still stuck underneath the neck of his sweater. Alice wondered how long it would be before he noticed.

"I know," he said, as he started up the class, "you're all dying to be published. But it can take a long time, and sometimes it doesn't happen at all. That's not the point, though. The point is what you'll learn on the way."

Alice could almost hear her father: *That's what people who failed say.*

"Let's start with the basics," Professor Roberts said. "If you think about it, every story—even the most fantastical—is grounded in things we already know, and every book is about questions that have already been asked."

Alice leaned forward, waiting for more explanation. She'd waited years to be here, with someone who could open the doors she needed opened.

"Bilbo may be a hobbit," the professor continued, "but we were all small at some point. And if you want to be a writer, chances are you've also experienced what it's like to be an underdog."

"What about serial killers?" interjected a young man in the second row. Alice looked over, observing the sprawl of his body in the chair. *No underdog there,* she thought. She could already see his future. Fifty books with his name emblazoned across the front in sans serif type. Probably in red.

"Well," Professor Roberts said, "of course serial killers do exist, although in far fewer numbers than your average airport bookstore might have you believe. But more relevant to this discussion"—and here, for a moment, Alice thought that Professor Roberts might be more formidable than his appearance suggested—"the serial killer genre asks one of the most common questions of all: What are we humans willing to do to each other? Or for each other? It's actually the same question you'll find in *The Iliad* or *Pride and Prejudice*. Or, perhaps, any night around a family dinner table."

Alice looked up.

"The trick for a writer," the professor continued, "is to take those eternal questions, those known bits and pieces, and put them together in a way that helps us see our world in a different light. That's where you come in."

He looked out at the class and smiled. "Easy, right?" he said. "So, let's start at the beginning. Write me a story."

Alice had been waiting her whole life for someone to say that.

Back in her dorm room, she took out a pen and a pad of paper, and let the words race out of her. She worked all weekend, ignoring economics, science. The night before the story was due, she stayed at her desk until dawn, typing up the handwritten pages and checking for misspellings, grammar mistakes. She wanted it perfect. She turned it in with a feeling of complete and utter satisfaction and waited to see the response.

It was a simple one, written across the top of her first page: *Let's talk. My office hours are Tuesdays, 12–2.*

Professor Roberts's office was just as it should be, bookshelves from floor to ceiling, a desk of dark wood, covered with neat stacks of papers. He motioned to the chair across from him.

She put down her backpack, and sat looking at him, expectant.

"Alice," he said, "you've got incredible talent. I've never had a student with such a command of details."

This is where it happens, Alice thought. *This is where it starts.*

"Thank you," she said. Then she saw it, the way his fingertips reached for his pen, brought it closer. "But?" she said.

He smiled. "You see? Details. That's what makes you good."

She waited. *It's going to be okay. Whatever it is, you can learn it.*

"Alice," he said, "the world you've created on these pages is extraordinary—but reading this feels like watching a beautiful movie from the back row. I suspect that's because you're doing that, too." He paused, then continued, "If you're going to write the book you're meant to write, you'll have to let it in. You'll have to let us in."

"I don't know . . ." she said, but inside her, the sentence was shorter, instinctive. *No.*

"I understand," he said, nodding. "And I'll teach you everything else I can, but that one's on you."

Alice knew there were some boxes whose lids were meant to stay closed. She would do anything else, though. Learn anything else. Over the next three years, she took every course Professor Roberts taught.

"I want you to go to a coffee shop," he said in one class.

"Close your eyes and listen. Write down what the people around you are feeling. Not saying. Not thinking. Feeling. Ask yourself: How do you know that? Is it a dip in a sentence? A scrape of a chair? The snap of a plastic lid onto a cup? Use the details to take us inside."

"I see what you're doing," Alice said later in his office.

"Is it working?" he asked.

She shrugged.

"Do you want it to?" he asked.

And then, Peter came home.

Not home as in their parents' house, but home to their eastern Oregon town. He'd gotten a job as a cook in a restaurant, and an apartment—a small basement place on the other side of town—before they even knew he was there. It was August; Alice was home for summer break and one day he just walked into the kitchen.

It had been seven years. He was thinner now, a lot. Their mother fluttered, trying to feed him. His hair was longer, and Alice thought it suited him, even though their father would hate it. But none of that mattered, because he didn't stay for dinner, slipped out before Alice could get him alone, ask any of the questions that had filled her mind.

Where have you been? Why would you come back?

She saw him three more times before she went back to college, always in that basement apartment. He cooked her dinner on a small two-burner stove. A curry. A pozole. A pasta Bolognese. They ate sitting on the floor. Between bites, he told her about climbing a flight of five hundred steps to a temple. About a train ride across Russia, the rumble of the wheels on the tracks. Of hitchhiking across France, the car accident, the family who took him in for a week while he healed. Got better.

"They laughed together, Alice," he said. "At the dinner table. Can you imagine?"

Being there was like their picnics in his tree house, only not. There was something about Peter now—not new, but more so. Once, while he was cooking, she closed her eyes and listened. Heard the vibration in him. Too fast, even though when she opened her eyes, there he was, standing like the calmest thing on the planet.

She would have stayed with him if she could. She tried once, saying she'd sleep on the lumpy sofa. But the apartment was small, and she could feel how much he wanted to be alone in it. How these evenings were his gifts for her, dearly bought.

The last time she saw him before she went back to college, it seemed as if something had loosened, unraveled, but she thought that might have to do with the bottle of wine he'd brought home from the restaurant, almost completely consumed.

"Sometimes I wonder," he said, his back to her as he did the dishes, "what it would have been like, just to be in the water by myself. Nobody else in my head."

"Peter," she said, standing up, moving toward him, "I'm sorry. I should have . . ."

"What?" he said, not turning around. "What could you have done?"

I could have loved you so much that nothing else would matter. I could have made you a world, hidden you under the table. I could have run away with you.

"It's okay, Alice," he said. "I'll be okay."

Because he was her big brother, and because she wanted to, she believed him.

Alice got the news three days after she returned to college that fall. She listened, silent, to her mother's voice on the phone.

"Peter died of an overdose. They found him in the bathtub."

"He chose a way that wouldn't make a mess," her mother added. "He was always a neat child."

"Was there water in the tub?" Alice asked.

"No," her mother said. "What an odd question."

But Alice knew it was the only one worth asking. She hung up the phone, went into her closet, and closed the door.

She flew home for the funeral. In the church, she stood pinned between her mother and father as the pastor spoke. Her father's back was straight; her mother curled over like a pill bug. Alice closed her eyes, breathed in the smell of anguish and guilt, one on each side of her. Neither from the person she expected.

Too late, she thought, and took the night flight back.

She stopped going to her classes, even the one with Professor Roberts. She couldn't write—how could you with only one word at your disposal? It banged in her thoughts like a ball against a wall. *Why. Why. Why.* It was there when she dreamed, when she woke up, when she stood in the shower or tried to read her textbooks. She gave up on classes and walked all day, across and off campus, through the town, as the weather started to change and the leaves got ready to turn and fall.

She knew there was a pool in town; she'd seen it, but never gone inside. Now, at the end of each day, she found herself standing in front of the door.

Finally, she bought a bathing suit, and walked in.

It wasn't like the Olympic-sized aquatic centers Peter had competed in, with their blasts of chlorine and shining lights. This one felt more like the multipurpose room in an old elementary school. There was a group of older women in a water aerobics class, a few swimmers in the lanes. But the air was warm and the ceilings tall, the sounds of voices and splashing bouncing off the walls and up into the air. Alice found an empty lane and sat at the end, her feet in the water, stretching the cap over her head as she had seen her brother do so many times. She knew the resemblance would end there; she had always been a half-hearted breaststroker, frog-kicking her way across the pool in spasmodic little bursts.

You're lucky, Allie girl, Peter used to say. *Your talent is quiet.* And Alice always thought that was just one of those things people said, like *you've got a good personality* when what they meant was *you'll never get a guy.*

But she was rethinking that now. Sitting at the edge of the pool, she positioned the goggles over her eyes, and the world narrowed, a strange and blinkered vision. She ducked underwater, and all the sounds turned into a booming silence. It was just her and the water and the blue line down the center of the lane, stretching out to an end she knew would be there.

She pushed off, reaching her arms out, then drawing them back. The *why* was not gone—she could hear it with each stroke—but by the fifth lap, the word started to change, its hard surface beginning to dissolve in the water, until it was the rhythm of her arms and legs and nothing more.

She could only manage about ten laps that day, but it exhausted her in a way that felt good. She found, however, that as soon as she was out of the water, the *why* came back, as strong as ever. And so, she returned to the pool, every day, adding laps to her count until she was up to twenty, then thirty, then fifty. As her breaststroke became more assured, her rhythm smoothed out, arms and legs propelling her forward. She didn't even realize for a while that the word in her head had become two.

You know. You know. You know.

Professor Roberts was standing outside the pool one afternoon when she exited.

"I heard you were here," he said. "My wife's in the aerobics class. She was talking about a young woman who couldn't stop swimming. Described you to a T."

Alice nodded.

"It's been a month. Are you coming back to class? Are you writing, at least?"

"I can't," she said.

He looked at her for a long moment. "It doesn't have to happen in my class," he said, "but it's time. Write the thing you're meant to write, Alice."

It happened on the second half of her twenty-fifth lap on her thirty-third day of swimming. She had just pushed off the concrete wall, still underwater, her arms pulling back on the first stroke, when an image came into her mind. A young boy, sitting in a field. Tall grass, huge sky, the boy at the center, but shifting, changing, getting ready for something.

She thought at first it might be Peter, but this boy was blond, while her brother had been all dark hair and eyes. And unlike Peter, this boy was scared of water; she could feel it.

Still, there was something about the boy that felt familiar. Necessary. She took another stroke, wanting to get closer to him, knowing that couldn't happen physically, but drawn forward anyway. At the same time not wanting to rush, and lose the image. Because he was the door; she knew it. The beginning of a book.

Don't be scared, she said. But whether it was to him or herself, she didn't know.

She swam, but slower now.

It's okay, she said. *I'll take care of you.*

At first, he only came to her in the pool—*Strange,* she thought, *for a boy who hates water.* But who was she to question? All she knew was that she wanted to be with him, discover his story.

It wasn't love. Well, it was, but not the way that love was described in books. More like encountering a path, winding off into the woods. How can you not want to see where it goes? How can you not love its twists and curves?

She started going to the pool earlier and earlier, arriving as it opened, swimming as long as her body would let her. She found if she let her thoughts wander, meld into the rhythm of the strokes, the boy might give her something new—the image of a garden. A boat. The clink of glass against a tabletop. A mother, looking back over her shoulder at her son. Each image a seed, seeking soil. *I'm here,* she said, and opened her mind to them.

One day she was standing in the shower in the locker room, the hot water running over her, her muscles still twitching from exertion, when she heard the door to the pool open and then a bustle of noise—women laughing. The aerobics class. Alice usually timed her exit from the pool so she could have the locker room to herself, but she'd been so deep in her head that she'd lost track of time. Now she stalled. After a few moments, she realized they might need her shower, so she came out, and encountered a forest of old women, all naked. One of them looked over. A tall woman, her arms and legs lean, her stomach just slightly paunchy.

"It's our little mascot," she said to the others. And then, to Alice, "You've been getting better."

The women turned, smiling. Alice nodded, slightly confused, and tried not to look at them too much—what else did you do in a room full of old naked bodies? But the women seemed not to care. Greetings over, they continued on, breasts swaying like pendulums as they walked to the shower, stomachs rolling into soft mounds as they leaned over to dry a foot, a crotch. Everywhere she looked were the gnarled roots of varicose veins, the shining ropes of scars—across abdomens, chests, along the sides of knees.

Alice had never seen her mother without clothes, or even in a swimsuit, for that matter. Her experience with naked bodies had been confined to high school locker rooms, where the breasts were fresh as new apples, buns tight with exercise. Too much perfection. She'd always tried to change in the stalls, wait until the other girls were done to come out.

But this was not that. This was all that fruit gone over-ripe, going back to the ground it came from. She suspected those perfect high school girls would be horrified. And yet, there was something so gracelessly graceful about it all.

"See you tomorrow, Flipper," said the tall woman as she hooked the strap of her bag over her shoulder.

When Alice got back to her room that day there was a message from the dean of students, requesting her presence. She went to his office. He told her what she expected to hear: at this point, there was no chance she could pass her classes. He needed an explanation, a reason to help, to save her scholarship for the next year.

"I heard you've had a loss," he said. "How can we assist you?"

"You can't," she said. "But thank you." Her mother had taught her to be polite.

She went into town, found a job washing dishes in a restaurant. The last guy had just quit, saying he needed to study harder for finals.

"Four to eleven P.M.," the owner said. "Can you do it?"

"Yes," she said.

She had her dorm room for another couple weeks. The dean said he was giving her every chance to turn things around, which was nice of him, she supposed, especially after he'd said it wasn't possible. When school was over, she'd find a place to live off-campus. She didn't need much—a chair, a bed. An electrical outlet.

Her parents called.

"What are you doing?" her father said. "We got the notice from the college. This is just like your brother."

"No," Alice said. "It's not."

"Are you coming home?" It wasn't a question; her father didn't ask questions. But Alice answered it anyway.

"No," she said.

When there was only one week left in the semester, Alice went by the local bulletin boards on her way to the pool. She checked the notices—*rooms for rent*—and pulled down five slips of paper with telephone numbers on them. In the locker room, she spread them out along the bench, like a bunch of Chinese cookie fortunes.

The door to the pool opened and the aerobics class started coming into the locker room. Alice still found it strange being around the older women, but not for the reasons she'd expected. Over the weeks, as she'd tried to tactfully ignore everything below chin level, she'd ended up looking into eyes. Inquisitive, tired, filmed over, occasionally filled with a desperate pain or sorrow that had

Alice diving into her backpack, pretending to dig for an elusive hairbrush. And yet, she'd found the exchange of glances leading to words. A *hello*. A *how are you?* Nothing earth-shattering. *Nothing to write home about,* her father would have said. Now Alice wondered if he was wrong about that, too.

"What you got there, Flipper?" The tall woman, Kat, was standing next to her, water dripping from her braid. "Looking for babysitting jobs?" she asked.

Alice almost laughed. It was the second-most prevalent use of the bulletin boards, but she couldn't imagine anything she was less prepared for.

"No," she said. And then added, without thinking, "A place to rent."

Kat looked across the locker room. "Gracie," she called out. "Isn't your renter leaving?"

Gracie walked over. She was shorter, rounder, her hair gray and curling, her smile kind.

"Yeah. In a couple days, actually."

"Flipper here is looking for a place. How about yours?"

Heaven, Alice thought a week later, was a wood-paneled studio apartment, set above a garage that smelled of sawdust. She put down her suitcases next to the pull-out couch and went over to the desk in front of the south-facing window. She looked out, across the neatly tended garden to the field beyond, its grass tall and wild.

She pulled her laptop from her backpack and opened a new document.

Here we go, she said to the boy.

Over the weeks, then months, life turned into a simple rotation of dishes, pool, laptop. The writing was different this time—before she had been a magician in charge of all the tricks. Now she was a listener. A follower.

She knew that this boy lived only in the confines of her mind, and yet there was something about looking through his eyes that made her go to places in herself she hadn't known existed. He lived through her and she through him, a symbiotic relationship that was nourishment and companionship and sometimes abject loneliness. Because some mornings the boy was not there when she woke up. She worried he had given up on her. Or perhaps he wanted a sharper, deeper insight to make him feel fresh and true. She would do it for him, to lure him back—crater out her past, her emotions, her thoughts.

Sometimes what she wrote felt more real than truth. But maybe that's what writing was, in the end—a way to get to the bedrock, the oxygen. To search out the possible. *What humans are willing to do to, and for, each other.* Wasn't that what Professor Roberts had said?

At the restaurant, the waiters came and went; at the pool, Alice swam and made conversation with the women. Sometimes, when she had written through the night, she'd look over in the early-morning hours to see Gracie and her husband drinking coffee in their kitchen, the scene lit like an illuminated diorama: "Domestic Life." *It looked nice,* Alice thought.

"Are you ever coming home?" her mother would ask on the phone.

Alice listened for what her mother might not be saying, but the connection wasn't good and what could have been a catch in her mother's breath was probably just the sound of a kitchen drawer opening.

"I'm fine," Alice said. And in a way, she was.

Every so often, Professor Roberts would invite her over for dinner. The first time, Alice was surprised, but then not, by the woman who opened the door.

"Hello, Flipper," Kat said. "I'm glad you could join us."

The food was simple—grilled pork chops, corn on the cob, a salad. It was August, and they ate outside, the conversation comfortable.

"How's the writing?" Professor Roberts asked.

"Slow," Alice said. "But I think that's good." He didn't ask anything more, and for that she was grateful. She wasn't sure what would happen if she let the story out before she was done.

Later, Alice helped Kat with the dishes. On the refrigerator, Alice saw a child's drawing. She looked at it, head cocked.

"Our grandson's," Kat said. Her voice dropped, almost disappeared on the last *s.*

Alice had seen the other women at the pool talking about their grandchildren, their faces lit, happy.

"Is he all right?" Alice asked.

Kat shook her head. "Hard to say. We don't see him much. His father—our son—well, maybe we'll just say life isn't always easy."

Alice, who had spent much of the evening fantasizing about what it would be like to have these two people for her parents, was silent.

"The world's a complicated place, Alice," Kat said, handing her a plate to dry. "But I think you know that."

Alice nodded, but later back at her apartment, she found herself going over the evening again and again. She'd always prided herself on her ability to see things in people they might not see themselves, but now she was realizing that was still only her view, which was itself limited. She hadn't thought, hadn't wanted to think, that there might be a yet more complicated way to see. Another side, or two, or ten. Sitting at her writing desk, she thought of all the life lived by those old women in the locker room, of the sadness in Kat's eyes. Considered the fact that she hadn't even known Professor Roberts was a father, a grandfather, not because he hid it, but because there are things you can't see until you are ready to look.

The months passed. On the pages, the boy—Theo, she knew now—grew up. There were times when what she wrote shocked her, broke her heart. But she realized that didn't matter anymore. What mattered was the story.

And then one day, almost four years after she sat down at the desk in the tiny apartment for the first time, Theo's story was quiet in a way that meant finished. She spent another nine months polishing the scenes, reading the sentences aloud over and over, changing a comma, a word, to make the music in them true.

Until, at last, it was done. She knew it, felt it like a full and calming breath. She clicked Save for the 40,458th time. She printed out the small mountain of pages, put a long green rubber band around it, and placed it in her backpack. The weight of it was solid and exhilarating.

She walked out into the world, which seemed exactly the same and utterly different. She wanted to tell someone, tried even—the barista at the coffee shop where she ordered a latte to celebrate. But she got only a breezy "I've thought of writing a book, too!" and a question on whether she wanted a single or double shot.

So Alice took her coffee and walked across town to the campus, and into the red brick English building, where she climbed the stairs to Professor Roberts's office. The door was open, but he wasn't there, and Alice couldn't decide if she was relieved or not. She left the manuscript on his desk with a note: *I wrote it.*

One week later, he sent her an email:

You did.

There had been more work, of course, months and months of it. Clarifying and elaborating. A side plot cut for the sake of the story. The ending given another beat, two.

"How do you feel about that opening line?" Professor Roberts asked.

"I don't want to change it," she said. It was the closest thing to a dedication she would ever write. He must have seen her expression because he let it stay.

Then, finally, it was time. She'd done everything Professor Roberts and the internet sites and the books and articles about publishing had told her to do. She'd buffed her query letter to a high gloss, double-spaced her manuscript, set the font at twelve-point Times New Roman. She'd researched literary agents, and the emails were ready to go.

Still, she paused, waited. One week, two. Because what that list of agents' names made suddenly and undeniably clear was that if, by some miracle, this story did make it out into the world, it would cease to be hers. The prospect filled her with an almost overwhelming desire to grab the book back, keep it safe with her.

"What if they don't see him the way I do?" she asked Professor Roberts. They were sitting in his office. It was supposed to be a celebration of her finally sending off her queries, only that hadn't happened yet.

"I guess I come at it a bit differently," he said, settling back in his desk chair. "I think each story has its own life. In the beginning, it lives in the writer's mind, and it grows and changes while it's there. Changes the writer, too, I'd bet." He smiled at her, then continued. "At some point it's written down, and that's the book readers hold in their hands. But the story isn't done, because it goes on to live in the readers' minds, in a way that's particular to each of them. We're all caretakers of the stories, Alice. Writers are just the lucky ones that get to know them first."

It was an interesting concept, but Alice wasn't sure she agreed. Maybe because she had thought—back when she heard that author speak in elementary school, back when she was learning the tricks of a good sentence or scene—that the books she'd write would stay somehow separate from her; perfect, beautiful worlds she could hold in her hands, easily passed on to be admired. She hadn't expected this story, this one that felt like a heartbeat.

"I don't know . . ." she said.

"What is a story if we don't tell it?" Professor Roberts asked.

A secret, she thought. And Alice knew what a secret could do to you.

So she sent the emails. Waited for responses.

No.

No.

No.

No.

No.

No.

It was astonishing, she thought, how much it could hurt. Those blithe, generic dismissals—*sorry, not for us . . . needs perspective . . . I just didn't love it . . . remember this is only one opinion . . .*

"You'd think they'd be more original," Alice told Professor Roberts.

Not saying how each response, landing in her inbox, waiting to be opened, made her feel like the other Alice. *Drink me* and grow tiny, inconsequential, invisible. *Eat me* and feel the rejection grow so big it becomes the world.

Month after month, until all her queries were quashed or would simply, obviously, never earn a response.

"It's never going to happen," she said to Professor Roberts.

"I believe in you," he said, and gave her one more name to try.

And so now on the screen in front of her was a new email, addressed to a woman named Madeline Armstrong, someone Professor Roberts had gone to college with, centuries ago.

A Hail Madeline pass, Alice thought.

But the only other option was giving up.

"Okay," she said to the room, to the boy, to herself. She moved the cursor to the small paper airplane icon in the upper left corner of the email. Closed her eyes.

Please, she said to the universe. *Please.*

Then she clicked Send, and it was gone.

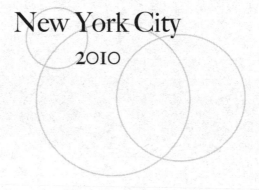

New York City
2010

The Assistant

Lara was tired. Swamp-tired, the kind so thick and murky it makes your bones rot and your brain sludge over.

I am a swamp monster, she thought as she stood over her screaming baby's crib at 2 A.M. And then, oddly, musingly, *Maybe that's where nightmares come from*—babies, feeling that looming, almost inhuman presence standing over their beds—*It's just your mommy, honey. She's just tired.* But maybe babies know it's not you. Not really.

It was funny; the fairy tales always talked about baby changelings. They didn't talk about the mother versions, not quite themselves, not quite there as they changed a diaper, popped a pacifier in their own mouths to clean it after a two-second journey to the floor, the sidewalk, a dog's mouth. How do you trick the fairies into giving the mommies back after they're stolen?

She reached down and lifted her baby to her chest, feeling the heat radiating off his body into hers. Four months they'd been doing this dance, this heat-to-heat, back-and-forth shuffle, love-and-loss. *Part of me, not part of me, part of me, not part of me.* There were times when she felt his emotions so cleanly, so clearly, it was as if she and he were still one thing. And then she would look into his howling, balled-up face and think she knew nothing about him at all and never would.

His screams were quieting now. He could sense the comfort that was coming. Her nightshirt would open and there would be peace and sustenance. But mostly peace. He'd nursed an hour before; he didn't actually need food. Not that kind.

She circled the room once, joggling him slightly, pondering. Bed or living room? That was the 2 A.M. question. Bed meant she could fall asleep if he did, just slip on down the pillows until everyone was horizontal. She knew it was wrong, got in the way of sleep training. In the morning Leo would wake up and see them and shake his head, just a little, as if he thought she couldn't see. Sometimes she didn't, but she felt it all the same, that shift in the air as he went to the shower, to work, to life. Leo was a good husband and a loving man, but they'd both agreed they needed his income, so he got to sleep. She was a barely paid reader at a literary agency. Not what she'd said she was going to be when they met.

Lara had been heading toward grad school back then. She'd taken the GREs and was applying to PhD programs in literature—and then there he was. Sitting next to her at a bar. Tall and lean and brown-eyed, an electrical engineer who also read books. They started a discussion on *Infinite Jest* (no) and Isabel Allende (yes), an infinite sky of shared words, and all she wanted was to fly forever. They went to bed, and when she woke up a few months later, the deadlines for grad school had passed and she had to wonder—if she'd really wanted that, would she have let this happen? Or had it just been a thing to do, a road to follow that was clear and lined with billboards that said things like *Good Job!* And *Wow!*

Lara's twin sister Saylor never seemed to worry about those billboards. She looked for street signs instead, new places to go. She was a traveling nurse, her life light on its feet. But things had always been like that for Saylor. Effortless. And you couldn't be jealous, because after all she was a nurse, doing good things—even as she went wherever she pleased. Even if, most recently, what pleased her was the Caribbean and a moody but beautiful free diver named Tyler. All of which sounded a bit too much like a romance novel for Lara.

It was Leo who had encouraged Lara to try for the assistant job at the agency. Madeline Armstrong Literary. The job involved the usual laundry list of tasks, but among them was reading submissions. *The slush pile*, as it was oh-so-tactfully called in the industry.

"You'd be brilliant at it," Leo said. "I've never met anyone with better instincts about writing."

"But I'm not a writer," she said.

"You don't have to be a farmer to cook," he said. Which was obscure, but she liked that about him, too. They were living together by that point, in his small but perfect apartment, with its alcove off the living room. An extra space, necessary for nothing, waiting for dreams. They'd painted it a warm, deep orange, and being in there felt like standing in sunshine. Sometimes she wondered if it was the alcove or Leo she had truly fallen in love with, but then he smiled at her, and she knew.

She'd gotten the job, a gift landing in her startled hands. She would make less than nothing, but Leo's work paid well, and he said he was happy to be a patron of the arts. Living off her boyfriend wasn't the scenario she'd imagined in college, when she was taking Feminist Literary Theory and binge-watching old episodes of *Sex and the City*. Back then, she'd told herself she was going to be bright, bold, never dependent on anyone else, certainly not a man—but then, it had never made sense how Carrie could afford her life, either.

Lara and Leo popped open a bottle of cheap prosecco to celebrate her new career. "Let's make memories," Leo said, grinning, and they'd had celebratory sex, free-ranging about the apartment, young and happy, reveling in the glorious arc of their lives.

The baby was no longer crying, calmed by her pacing. Lara thought about putting him back in the crib—it was a long shot, but sometimes it worked—and made a move toward it. He sensed her shift in direction and his screams returned.

It was going to be a long night, she thought.

Bedroom or living room? she asked herself again. *Living room,* she decided, and headed there, grabbing her laptop from the kitchen counter with one hand as she went. Maybe she could at least get some reading done.

On her first day of work, Lara had ridden the subway to an office in an old brick building in the middle of bustling New York City. Entering the door was like going back a hundred years, to a time when the world believed in paper and stairways were wooden and narrow and smelled of old ink. It turned out the other assistants were all hot out of college, too, most of them living packed four to a tiny apartment. Almost all female, except for that one guy who couldn't stop talking about how he went to Brown. The fact that Lara lived with her boyfriend set her apart a bit socially, but it was soon clear that when it came to work, they all faced the same insurmountable task.

"Find the needle in the haystack," Lara's boss had told her that first day. "The One. I don't have time for the others."

Madeline Armstrong was a powerhouse of an agent, in the business for decades. When she wasn't out at lunches that were never about food, she sat in her office, her white hair perfect, phone to her ear, soothing authors, cajoling or bullying publishers, a conductor in a symphony of words. Her shelves were lined with books, every author name recognizable. Many of them women. Lara could have watched Madeline for hours, mesmerized, but there was no time. The assistants sat in a maze of desks outside the agents' offices, their eyes flying across pages, fingers scrolling through queries. Looking for The One.

No.
No.
No.
No.
No.

It was astonishing, Lara thought, the sheer outpouring of human desire. The need to record, to create, to be acknowledged. *Read me read me read me.* The queries tsunamied her inbox, twenty to thirty a day. Girl-meets-boy. Poor-kid-gets-rich. Rich-kids-go-bad. Boy-saves-the-world. Boy-writes-a-bestseller-then-gets-writer's-block-but-lives-in-a-gorgeous-condo-while-his-girlfriend-helps-him-figure-it-out. Girl-meets-girl. Dog dies. First love. First fuck. Bad parents. Bad husbands. Bad habits. War. War. War. Robots. Fairies. Vampires. Dragons. Change centuries. Tell-alls. Tell-nothings. *Pride and Prejudice* on a ranch, at a mall; swap out the sisters for men, dogs, parakeets. Change countries. Add zombies. Repeat.

But Lara had loved it, even though the work was its own kind of flood, breaking the banks of office hours and submerging the rest of her life. She read manuscripts on the subway, on the toilet; she even used a cookbook holder as a stand to prop her iPad as she made a quick stir-fry.

Come on, baby, she said, each time she opened a document. And sometimes, it almost happened—a character blossoming like a flower, a scene that made her forget to blink. A few manuscripts she passed along to Madeline, but so far, Lara had yet to find the needle, the story that took the familiar and turned it into something profoundly new.

She would, though. She had to—because more than anything, those brief transcendent moments had taught her that she loved this work. Loved the chemical change that could happen when a story started to lift off a page, or a writer turned a small detail into an insight that shimmered. And more than any of that, she loved the idea that she was seeing it first.

This, she thought, *this is what I was meant to do.*

She had not intended to get pregnant—but apparently her son was a determined little soul, the sperm half of him vaulting hurdles of latex and chemicals to land with a delighted squeal on a mistimed egg. She hadn't even noticed for more than eight weeks, so secure was she in their Fort Knox of contraceptive protection, so caught up in the manuscripts that she missed the passing periods. It was Leo who'd asked; Leo who had schedules at work, not haystacks.

"Oh my god," she said, staring at the stick. She counted back to the night of the prosecco—and she couldn't decide if it was the irony or the cliché of it that was worse. *My life is a bad book,* she thought.

But then Leo had proposed, so sweetly, and they were married. A quiet ceremony, just the two of them and their parents at city hall.

I am so happy for you, Saylor wrote on the back of a post-card that featured a flamingo in Florida.

"I still want to work after the baby comes," Lara told Leo, and he agreed.

"We'll figure it out," they said, and Lara was thrilled at their use of the plural pronoun.

She waited until the size of her belly made waiting counterproductive, then told Madeline, whose frown was both legendary and suddenly much in evidence.

"These are coveted positions," she noted, as if, perhaps, Lara didn't know.

Lara had proven herself to be an astute reader, however, and so Madeline gave her four weeks of maternity leave. Another assistant (not happy about it, but eager to make herself invaluable) took over Lara's office duties of answering Madeline's phone and overseeing her calendar.

"You'll still read manuscripts from home, though, right?" Madeline asked.

Lara imagined herself working while her baby slept or nursed or lay blissed out in a patch of sun, a symbiotic relationship of words and milk and blankets.

"Yes," she said, "of course."

And she'd tried not to be offended when she suddenly became the go-to reader for every manuscript that had anything to do with motherhood. The mommy memoirs all seemed so snarky, she thought. So exhausted. *Needs more perspective,* she wrote in her editorial reports, confident in her literary acumen.

Oh, she said to herself after the birth. *Oh.*

While her baby was still in utero, Lara had filled a bookshelf with tales of daring girls defying dragons and rules. She declared she would read them to her baby, regardless of its sex, secretly believing it would be a girl. It had to be. She'd grown up with a twin sister, gone to a progressive girls' high school, then college. She had no idea what one did with a boy. When the doctor asked, ultrasound wand in hand, if she and Leo wanted to know the sex of their child, she had declared no—which sounded deliciously politically correct. The reality had more to do with superstition. If she acted as if she would accept anything, she would get the result she needed.

And then they had Teddy. She wondered sometimes if the name choice had been appealing because it was a stuffed bear, something more comprehensible than a small human male. But the name was also for Leo's grandfather, so there was that.

In the hospital, she'd held the baby in her arms and panicked: *How do I do this?* Books, she understood. Their words stayed on the pages, patiently awaiting your interpretation.

People said books clamored for your attention, but that verb was only metaphorical. This baby-human in her arms was its living definition, full of his own needs, his own noises. And she didn't know how to read any of them.

She looked down at him, his small face bunched and confused.

"Me, too, little guy," she said.

Hours later, a nurse had come to take him. *Circumcision,* she'd said. Lara knew that she and Leo had agreed to this (not her choice, but also not her body part)—but Leo had gone back to the apartment to pick up a forgotten something, and the nurse was here, and Lara couldn't let the baby go without a parent, not for that. And so, she had stood in an appropriately small operating room, a closet, really, holding her baby's hands above his head while a doctor cut part of him away and he had screamed and she had sobbed, *I'm so sorry I'm so sorry I'm so sorry,* and she realized that all of this was far more complicated than she'd thought.

Madeline had been disappointed once again when Lara had asked, at the end of her maternity leave, if there might be a way she could work from home. She would have to give up the office part of her duties, which meant a drop in her already pitiful salary, but it didn't make sense for her to go into the city for a job that paid less than half the cost of day care.

She couldn't imagine Teddy in day care, anyway. He was not an easy child. His idea of a nap was a semicolon at best, never a full stop; a paragraph break. The only way to quiet him at night was to nurse or walk. Most days she had clocked the exercise goal on her Fitbit before 4 A.M. Throwing the wrench of day care into the mix seemed questionable. The caregivers would take one look at her howling child and deem her a bad mother, foisting her difficult offspring onto others.

"What do you want?" she asked her baby, looking into his eyes, checking the tension in his hands, doing all the things the how-to-parent books had suggested. And Teddy had cried.

Madeline agreed to a new arrangement, with Lara as freelance reader. It reminded Lara of the piecework women used to take in a century before—pennies for a finely stitched shirt. Madeline said they'd try it on a six-month probationary basis. Which really meant *Find the needle. Now.*

So Lara dug into the stack whenever she could, reading whatever they sent her. In addition to the mommy material, she now seemed to be assigned a significant number of manuscripts about boys. Apparently, he-who-had-gone-to-Brown had moved on to a PhD program at Harvard, leaving Lara the expert in boys simply because she had one.

"Doesn't it make you more sympathetic to our masculine plight?" Leo had asked.

Lara looked up from the dinner she was eating with one hand, the other supporting Teddy against her chest, his little face hot against her shoulder, and saw Leo wink. Which, whether he knew it or not, saved their marriage.

Because honestly, it was beginning to get to her, the way men (okay, Leo) were allowed to add feminism to their identity like a fancy font in the book of their life, while for women it seemed to be viewed more like the plot line—once established, any straying from the path viewed as a fatal flaw.

"How's it going?" the other assistants would ask when she called in, the familiar sounds of work behind them. "How's the baby?"

Lara could hear it in their voices—*Remember to be supportive!*—while underneath ran the other narrative—*Thank god I'm smarter than her.* It was her job, after all, to read subtext.

"Great," she said, and tried to pretend that she didn't miss the discussions among the assistants, the disagreements and bonding over manuscripts. Didn't miss the way Emma from Montana advocated for the cowboy books and Julie leaned into fantasy and Christy loved food fiction because her new boyfriend was a chef. Didn't miss the *Oh my god, listen to this sentence,* the lines no one could resist passing along to the assistant sitting nearby, because it didn't matter how many manuscripts you read, there was still a thrill when one of them turned all the lights on, even if only for a moment.

More and more these days, Lara thought, *working from home* just seemed to mean doing neither well. "You can have it all," the newest self-help manuscript declared, causing Lara to close the document with far more vigor than was necessary.

"It's not unusual, honey," her mother said, when Lara called her, crying. "You're just a little lost."

Her words made Lara want to cry harder. Because her new life felt like walking through dark mountains without a map. A rabbit hole without an end. A name she did not fit. There was nothing *little* about this, except perhaps the size of her son.

"You just need a break," Saylor said on the phone. But Lara's twin was a woman with her hand on the tiller and no anchor below. She had no idea how heavy seven pounds and eleven ounces could be.

There were times—when Teddy was sleeping, or nursing, his small fingers soft against her skin—that Lara was filled with love for this child, this thing she and Leo had created that was warm and physical and human. And ever since that surreal moment in the operating room of the hospital, she had felt a connection to and responsibility for him that sometimes seemed like the only solid thing she stood on.

But that experience also made clear what she had long suspected: she had no idea how to be a good mother, and especially, no idea of what to do with a boy. She was supposed to have a girl who would read *The Paper Bag Princess* and wear onesies that said "future feminist." Where did this boy in her lap, at her breast, fit in? What if he wanted toy guns? To play football? Wear a dress? Watch porn as a teenager?

At night she would pace the small apartment, Teddy in her arms. Those hours, spent in the company of a baby whose needs were elemental, inarticulate, took her mind to places she would rather not explore. Night after night she'd walk, feeling the back-and-forth shuffle within herself. *I am me, I am not me, I am me, I am not me.*

Now, laptop and baby in her arms, she made her way to the living room. It was 2:20 A.M. dark, the kind where even the shadows have fallen asleep. A streetlight shone outside, illuminating the path to her reading chair by the window. She and Leo had always loved the tree in front of their apartment, the way it clocked their seasons, back when time was measured in months, not minutes.

In the chair, Lara set up her command station: laptop and a glass of water on the small table to her right, Teddy in her left elbow. She opened her laptop. There were forty manuscripts in her queue.

"Okay, team," she said. "Let's get to work."

She settled Teddy onto her left nipple and clicked on the first manuscript. The title appeared on her screen, black letters against the illuminating white. One word: *Theo.*

She shook her head. Another boy-book. But as Madeline would say, the only way out was through, and this one had come with an outside recommendation. Not that that was ever a guarantee of quality. Lara took a drink of water, ready to give the manuscript five pages, then go on to the next in line; she didn't have time for more. She clicked to the first page.

Wandering is a gift given only to the lost.

Nine simple words, but they wrapped around her like her mother's arms, holding her when she was little. Like Leo, sitting across from her in the bar the night they met, his eyes containing worlds she wanted to explore. *You're not crazy,* the words on the page said. *I know you.*

Did you write this for me? she wondered. And she felt the tightness inside her begin to loosen.

She'd fallen into stories before. It was why she'd wanted to do this job in the first place, that experience of opening a book and feeling it reach out and grab you.

Now she read on, knowing she should be standing back, analyzing, considering craft, market appeal, defects. She tried, but in the end all she could do was dive in.

Four hours later, Leo came into the living room, groggy with sleep.

"Hey," he said.

Lara looked up, shocked, uncertain who he was. For a moment, she was still the boy in the book, her thoughts turned new colors through his eyes. She could feel the roughness of his denim jeans as if she was wearing them.

Shaking her head, she looked down to see her son, crooked in her completely senseless arm, knocked out with milk, his mouth dropped open around her nipple.

"You been here all night?" Leo asked.

"Yep," she said, although night was a foreign concept. It was midday in the book; the sun hot in the field where the boy was working. He was a teenager now, hormones pushing through him like corn toward the sky.

"Want to get some sleep?" Leo asked, holding out his arms for the baby. "I can be an hour late."

Again she nodded, grateful, and went to bed, where she plugged in her laptop to save its failing battery and kept reading.

It was something she would tell her son later, when he was learning to read himself—how your first read of an extraordinary book is something you can only experience once. The most fitting analogy might be losing one's virginity with the perfect partner—but that wasn't a comparison she was going to use with a four-year-old.

"It's like eating the best ice-cream cone of your life on a hot day," she told him. "You want to eat it fast, but have it never end."

He'd looked up at her, those freckles of his just showing in the first days of summer. She knew what he was going to say, knew, as always, that her literary insights were falling on ears that were too young—and yet, kernels could turn into stalks. She could wait.

"Are we going to get ice cream now?" he asked.

"Sure thing, buddy."

But in this moment, her boy was still a baby, with his father, and she was in bed with the book, reading as if her heart would break and mend and beat all at the same time. Knowing that each word she read was one less left. Still, she couldn't stop. She had to know what happened. She had to know that the boy on the page, a young man now, would be okay. She could feel the story, rising under her like a wave. The perfect swell of water, arching, cresting, aiming for the shore, and she let it take her until she landed on the beach, the last word sinking into the sand. There.

Oh, she thought. *Ohhh*.

She sat for a moment, feeling herself come slowly back into her world. Then, without thinking, she pulled up a new email and addressed it to Madeline, including the manuscript and two words.

This one.

It was midmorning. Leo had gone to work. The apartment was quiet, and she went into their tiny kitchen and made herself a cup of coffee. She took it to the chair by the living room window and sat, watching the tree, still seeing it through the boy's eyes. A thing to climb. A place of safety in a hard life. A challenge he did and did not want.

She thought of her own child, climbing future trees. What would they mean to him? And it was in that moment that she truly comprehended the precious, terrifying fact of her son's singularity. His life—a part of hers, but not hers. Not *a* boy, but *this* boy. The one who slept in the alcove and would grow up to make his own world. His life a book she would, with any luck, get to read for the first time.

As she sat there thinking, Teddy stirred in his sleep, a slight whoosh of noise. Lara put down her coffee cup and went to stand by his crib, looking down at his small, sleeping form, the thumb that was not quite in his mouth, the knees drawn up near his chest, his breath quiet, but there. There.

You are my wandering, she said, and he opened his eyes and looked at her.

British Columbia
2011

The Actor

I t was a strange thing, Rowan thought, to disappear a bit at a time.

It had started long before he even realized. A white spot, about the size of a quarter, below his knee, a location he couldn't remember injuring. He was a junior at Yale then, studying classical theater, but he was also a deeply physical human—racing down a soccer field or free climbing a rock face. A scar was plausible, if not optimal, for such a handsome young man. He forgot all about it, especially after a movie director from LA, on campus to visit his daughter, happened to see Rowan leaping to catch a Frisbee, blond hair flying, muscled arms outstretched. A Lana-Turner-at-the-drugstore-counter moment, only with more physical exertion involved.

After that, Rowan moved to the West Coast. He aspired to movies with complex characters, but the audience fell for his golden-boy looks. One small bad-boy part, and he was the hot new thing. Within a year, he was spending his days under the steady gaze of a movie camera, his evenings lit by the flashes of the paparazzi.

"Poor Rowan, objectified for his body," his sister Hadley said with a grin.

They were sitting together in his local bar. Hadley was two years older than Rowan, and the one person who'd never let him get away with anything, no matter how cute he'd looked holding that broken toy or, later, hearts. She always said they had to stick together—their parents having divorced and remarried so many times it took an Excel spreadsheet to figure out where they were or who they were with. Hadley lived in LA, too, teaching English to eighth graders.

"Hey," he said, "you know I can do the serious parts."

"I do," she said. "And you will. But Rowan, you were discovered playing Ultimate Frisbee. Did you honestly think they were bringing you out here for a screen version of *Hamlet*? Take the money and run. Or at least pay for my drink."

They walked outside and the cameras went off.

ROWAN'S NEW LOVE? the tabloid headlines screamed the next day.

Two years into Rowan's movie career, the second spot showed up, this time on his ankle, the diameter of a Ping-Pong ball rather than a quarter. If asked, he blamed an old biking accident, embellishing the story with a large Rottweiler, a cute female owner. He was learning the value of spin.

Soon after, he started doing his own stunts. Small things at first—vaulting onto a horse, sliding under a fast-lowering door. The public was thrilled, which led to the precarious chase along the tiled rooftops of Venice, the martial arts fight scenes, the dash across the rotting rope bridge. But it was the base jump off a thousand-foot building, the ground below shrouded in fog, that sealed his reputation. By the time Rowan was twenty-six, he was the go-to guy of the action movie squad. It was yet another step away from the career he'd imagined, but when you were moving fast, people looked at the movement, not you, and in the end, he found that he loved the rush as he leapt, his body flipping and flipping again, hurtling toward the waiting mat below. The one the audience would never see.

ROWAN CAN FLY! *People* magazine declared.

And he did. Up so high he lost track of the ground. It didn't matter, though, because money made the best wings.

When the third spot showed up—a sprawling patch of pallidity where his inner thigh met the family jewels—time stumbled, stalled. This one could not be passed off as a manly scar with a good backstory. Rowan applied the makeup himself and in secret before his next obligatory sex scene. Traces of color remained on the sheets after, but people attributed them to his preening costar. Rowan quickly threw a towel around his hips, deeply grateful that groin shots were generally avoided for men.

He went to doctors, of course. Was told he had vitiligo, a progressive loss of pigment, and that apparently there was nothing that could be done.

"But you're white," the doctor said, shrugging. "Just don't get tan, and you'll be fine."

Sure. Because everybody wanted a pale action hero. Rowan could see his future roles already. The terminally-ill teacher in an English boarding school. The romantic vampire. A Bond villain.

"The good news is, it's not cancer," the doctor said.

"I'm done," Rowan told Hadley.

They were sitting on his deck in Malibu, looking out at the Pacific Ocean.

"That's crazy," she said. She leaned over and tugged up the right leg of his jeans. "Look, you can hardly see this one. But even if you're right—there're plenty of ways around it. I mean, they Benjamin-Buttoned Brad Pitt. And they can do anything with makeup."

"Great," he said. "And eventually I get to play Chewbacca, right?"

"Come on, Ro," she said. "It's no big deal. Just tell people. Be a poster boy."

Rowan loved Hadley, but she was a teacher who taught her kids that everyone was special. Rowan worked in an industry premised on the exact opposite belief. Sure, he could keep covering the spots on set, dye his hair when the encroaching white reached the point that it was no longer ruggedly attractive. But there was more to it than that. An actor like Rowan didn't just exist in a movie. He lived in a world of fans who wanted his impossible perfection to extend into reality—and a world of magazines that sold more copies when it didn't.

"I'm the guy that jumps out of airplanes without a parachute," he said.

"You still would be."

But Rowan knew that wasn't true. It didn't matter that what he had was only skin deep. He'd be the guy with the hole in his armor. The Achilles' heel. No way that guy would survive the fall.

He went to see his agent. "I want to try something different," he said.

"What, you want to go all indie? Now?" She dismissed the idea with a flick of her Brazilian blowout.

He got a couple more good years. Earned the admiration of women by requiring that all sex scenes be filmed with a minimal crew in attendance. He even managed to widen his scope to period dramas, where his ass was shown to great advantage in the tight white pants of a pale British officer. But then the tide started coming in for real—legs first, then hands—and Rowan's world began to narrow.

He found a sympathetic makeup artist and insisted on her presence for every movie, paying her extra on the side for her silence. He stayed away from pool parties and shirtless volleyball games, stopped the indiscriminate dating.

IS ROWAN GROWING UP? the tabloids asked.

Some days, it felt as if his skin was a timer he couldn't stop checking. He'd never actively grabbed the spotlight; it had always just gone to him, moth to flame. Now he dimmed that glow, pulled back.

"Look at you, sharing the screen," his costar joked at the end of a day of filming. Rowan and Terrence had been in four films together by then—buddy pics of the ivory-and-ebony variety.

"Maybe I'm getting more mature," Rowan said with a smile. The tabloid story about his new lifestyle had made the rounds on set, accompanied by the usual jokes.

"Uh-huh," Terrence said, and his eye caught on Rowan's right hand, where the makeup had rubbed off. Someone else might have missed it, but Terrence was one of the most observant people Rowan had ever met. So observant Rowan had worried this might have to be their last film together.

"What's that?" Terrence asked.

And then—because they had shared four films and swapped sweat and stories and bourbon, because the desire to tell someone, anyone, was like a phone that wouldn't stop ringing in his head—Rowan told him.

And Terrence laughed.

"Fuck me," he said. "The Sexiest White Man Alive is going to get even whiter. Only you, Rowan."

"It's not funny," Rowan said.

"Oh, I'm well aware of how pigment can get in the way," Terrence said.

Rowan stared at Terrence. "Are you going to use this?"

Terrence shook his head. "You're already doing it to yourself, man."

That was the worst of it—the daily grind of concealment, of being constantly careful. Being exposed could hardly be worse, Rowan thought.

Then a woman—a one-night stand that shouldn't have happened, but god, he was tired of being a monk—dropped a coy hint on Facebook. Something about an emperor and no clothes. And Rowan realized that he'd been wrong.

"It'll blow over," Hadley said as they sat in his living room. "It's just a rumor. You can't even tell what she's talking about."

But Rowan could feel what was coming.

A neighbor went to the press saying Rowan's new fence was too tall—what was he hiding? Past girlfriends started selling stories about his questionable love life, most of them untrue, but suddenly no one was questioning them. Before, his superhero persona had been a shield, rumors bouncing off. Now former costars insinuated that he didn't kiss—or fight—as well as it appeared on-screen, and suddenly Twitter was asking: Was that an ass-double in those tight white officer's pants? Had he really base jumped off that building? And why *did* he always insist on using the same makeup artist? Before it had been assumed that she was a romantic liaison, or a lucky charm. Now, anything was possible.

At one point he was on the cover of three different magazines at the same time.

WHAT IS ROWAN HIDING?

IS THE GOLDEN BOY MADE OF LEAD?

I DID ROWAN'S STUNTS!

The director for his next movie called, apologetic. Rowan had made him a lot of money in the past, he said, and he appreciated it, but maybe this wasn't the time. The incredibly expensive watch company canceled his series of commercials. And the paparazzi, who had long been ubiquitous, became relentless. The first one to get photographic evidence of whatever Rowan was hiding would be in the money.

"Who knew there could be a bounty on whiteness?" Terrence joked. But he and Hadley were the only two who had really stuck around. Terrence would show up at Rowan's door, six-pack in hand. Not implying that Rowan should hide, but never asking him to hit the bars, the waves, the spotlight, either. They'd talk or watch old movies that weren't theirs. A heaven of the ordinary.

The first image hit the front page of a major tabloid—an old photo, doctored so that Rowan looked leper-like, cringing back from a flash.

IS THIS THE REAL ROWAN? the headline screamed. And all bets were off.

It stunned him, the glee of it, although he'd certainly seen the same causticity aimed at others. Had even enjoyed watching it, on occasion. But he knew fires like this didn't stop until all the air was gone—and there would always be air. Just ask Jennifer Aniston.

"You should have told me." Rowan's agent was furious. "I could have done something."

"What?"

She sat back in her chair, one hand touching her surgically smoothed neck, and shrugged one shoulder.

"They're looking for a voice for the new Disney movie," she offered.

"Tell me it's not a frog."

At least she had the good grace to blush.

During the time when he was perfect, Rowan had found it almost amusing, the way people would assume he was the image they saw on the screen. Now, they saw a photo and assumed something completely different, no more him than the other.

He understood that the same force that was bringing him down had sent him skyward in the first place—but that didn't mean he wanted to stick around for the crash. Didn't want to pick up the pieces. Play the roles he was being offered—the paraplegic, the burn victim, the masked sociopath. Complicated parts, for uncomplicated reasons.

Rowan had shot a movie once outside of Vancouver, BC, and he remembered the beauty of the green and the gray, the relief of not having to worry about getting tan. Now he bought a house on a remote island up there and disappeared for real. Even the paparazzi wouldn't chase him that far. If they were going to travel, they preferred the Caribbean—catching a tryst on a yacht, a flash of cellulite escaping the boundaries of a bikini.

On the island, Rowan took up kayaking. Trail running through the woods. He grew a beard, because the whiteness had slipped halfway up his cheek, a permanent caress. The opposite of a slap, at least in terms of color. He had his groceries delivered to his doorstep and cooked for himself. Living like that, he wouldn't run out of money for several lifetimes. He told himself he was lucky, and he was. The place he lived in was deeply alive, the air so clean it felt like he was drinking it. Deer wandered through his acreage, and raccoons passed by the house in the evenings. He told himself to bond with nature, but for all that his new surroundings soothed his soul, he was lonely.

He called Terrence. "Come visit," he said.

Terrence just laughed.

"They don't call it the Great White North for nothing," he said. "But you can call me any time you want to talk."

It wasn't the same, though.

Just go out, Hadley emailed. *Don't cover it up; just go.* But the few times he tried, he either saw that first moment of giddy recognition turn to pity—or, for those few that didn't know who he was, the half second of confusion when he reached out with payment for something and they saw the bleach-white splotches on his hands, the blue veins underneath. He'd watch as their own hands pulled back, allowing the money to land on the counter.

"For fuck's sake; I'm not contagious," he wanted to yell.

It was funny, he thought later, how, back when he was handsome, no one ever seemed to treat beauty as something they could catch.

Hadley came to visit in the summer.

"Hey, Grizzly Adams," she said when she arrived. She'd driven the fourteen hundred miles from LA by herself, but that was Hadley.

"Hey," he said, and pulled her into a hug. She was the first person he'd touched in half a year, and it felt both completely real and utterly unnatural at the same time.

"Don't let go," she said, and held on for a full minute.

She stayed until September—"The upside of being a teacher," she said. They spent hours collecting mussels from the shining black rocks. Trying to fish. He'd bought an extra kayak for her, and they would go out in the mornings, sticking close to the shore so she could look down and see the starfish. In the evenings, they sat around the firepit, glasses of wine in hand, talking about her students. Not talking about his work.

"You could just stay," he said at the end of August.

"You gotta figure out what you're going to do, Ro," she said.

"I have no bloody idea."

"You can still act."

"I can't be that guy. The one who overcomes the almost-fatal injury to find success again."

"Because it's not actually an almost-fatal injury?" she said, smiling, not letting him off the hook.

But the problem was, in Hollywood you were known for particular things. A smile. A skill. Your skin. A tweet. And when that thing became too big, too *you*, good or bad, there was no acting your way around it. The fact that his thing wasn't life-threatening ironically made it worse, in a surreal sense that could only be true in Hollywood. There was no drama to his situation—it was just a flaw. And thus, fatal in its own way.

"Okay," Hadley said. "Let's try a different approach. What if there's an upside to this?"

"If you start talking about silver linings, Hadley, I will never refill your wineglass again."

"Hey," she said. "Think about it. You wanted serious roles, but nobody could see past that ridiculously gorgeous body of yours. Even you, sometimes. Well, now . . ."

He glared at her.

She continued. "You know what's always been more gorgeous than your body? Your voice."

"So, I should do the Disney frog?"

She laughed. "Well, I mean you could, but I was thinking more like audiobooks."

"That's a thing?" He tried to imagine simply reading a book aloud. No action. No sets. No actors to play off.

"Geez, Ro—yes, it's a thing. I listened to a great one driving up here; I'll leave it for you."

"But you're not leaving, remember?"

"Right. Well okay, let's just say I'll leave it when I don't leave on Friday, how about that?"

It was so utterly quiet without Hadley that the fourth evening after she left Rowan played the first disk of the audiobook in his CD player just to have some company. The novel was about three siblings and their mother, each with a different perception of the past. Rowan listened to the voice of the reader, changing with each character like a jazz ensemble passing breaks. This was not just reading aloud. Not even close.

After that, he started listening to books every night. He gave up renting movies, heading instead to the Adirondack chair by the firepit, or, if it was raining, the couch in the living room. He'd close his eyes, let the book take him. When he was a child, he'd read a lot; loved books, in fact. After he'd started acting, he switched to plays, then movies, scripts where dialogue took center stage. Now he found himself entering a strange hybrid world, where action was words and books turned into voices.

It wasn't easy; he could tell that just by listening. In movies, a single actor was almost always chosen for a single role—unless you were dealing with psychopathic twins or something. In most audiobooks, one voice covered it all. A narrator had to be able to inhabit a myriad of ages and accents, both genders and all their various permutations, without ever relying on the visual of a crooked eyebrow, the mood enhancement of a musical score. And, unlike screenplays, where stage directions were generally clear and directors stood at the ready, a book required the narrator to hunt for clues.

It had been a long time since Rowan had had to dig for a character. He was known for playing The Guy, rough on the edges but good underneath, if the woman could find it there. The dehydrated hero—just add water/bourbon/tequila, depending on the script. Now he listened to every character, regardless of age or sex or nationality, knowing each one was a possibility, a challenge. What would the world feel like in their bones? And how could you inhabit that character with only your voice?

It was like being back in college, where the excitement of his roles had kept him up at night.

He started buying a print copy of each audiobook, so he could listen and read at the same time, highlighters at hand. With orange, he marked pauses, shifts in tone. He noted the slight slur in a character's voice, then underlined when, three pages later, the book mentioned a half-drunk bottle of wine. He used yellow for a character's physical descriptions, highlighting when the narrator made him hear height or weight along with the slow sprawl of a Southern accent, the swirling rapids of a Scottish one.

In a separate notebook, he wrote down comments about the times when a narrator's voice didn't work, and why. When character contorted into caricature, or when a verbal tic—a fade-off at the end of each sentence, a pause between ... each ... word—became a dripping faucet in the experience.

It was a puzzle his mind could play with whenever his thoughts started to head in bad directions. He walked his acreage, the rocky beaches, trying out voices and accents. After a few months, he built a recording studio in one of the guest bedrooms, buying equipment and soundproofing the walls. Then he started practicing, figuring out techniques. He learned to breathe without sound. To keep water handy. To choose a position—sitting or standing—before he began, and maintain it through an entire book, so his voice would stay consistent. He got a printer so he could work with loose pages, slipping each one soundlessly to the side as he was done, his feet rooted to the ground.

At first he, whose acting had been so active, found the not-moving strange. His first fencing coach had always talked about *stillness in motion,* the inner calm within the outward movement. This was the opposite. Motion in stillness. Everything held in the voice.

I contain multitudes, he wrote to Hadley.

Sure thing, Walt Whitman, she replied. *When are you going to put yourselves out there?*

For now, however, all he wanted was that feeling of possibility. The sense that he could find, in the nooks and crannies of his thoughts, or soul, whatever he needed to make the characters come to life.

After six months, though, he was ready. He contacted an agent he'd once met at a party. Not the big leagues, but young and hungry. Through him, Rowan scored his first audiobook gig.

It was for a thriller—not that different from some of the parts he'd played on the big screen, but Rowan didn't mind. He gave extra care to the minor characters: the girlfriend, the taxi driver, the detective's mother. Took his time with the descriptions of setting and the rising moments of tension, not rushing toward the resolution the way some narrators did, as if solving the mystery was the literary equivalent of a quickie.

The audiobook company was thrilled—*An immersive experience,* they said—and sent him another book. Then another. He started waking up each morning with a feeling of anticipation. He still missed people—their laughter, their bodies, the joy of a shared drink in a bar or a pickup volleyball game on a beach. But his mind was awake now, and he liked the feel of it.

Rowan's eighth assignment arrived in the mail one afternoon in October. The title, *Theo,* unwinding across the cover in a handwritten font, with *Advance Reading Copy, Not for Sale* emblazoned along the bottom.

As a general rule, the assignments Rowan received were soon-to-be-published books, read at that point by a limited group of people. Agents. Editors. Marketing. A few reviewers. For Rowan, getting an advance copy felt like someone telling him a secret while still holding a finger to their lips. The experience made more exciting by its exclusivity—although Rowan sometimes wondered what he was supposed to do with the ARCs afterward.

"Are you kidding?" Hadley said. "Send those suckers to me." His sister was taking full credit for his new career, although she hadn't given up on the idea of getting him out of the house.

But Rowan was happy where he was, and happiest inside that small recording studio, where, if he did it right, there were no walls at all.

It became apparent almost immediately that the new book was not a thriller. For one thing, no one died in the prologue. There was just a boy, sitting in a field. Rowan skimmed the opening pages, waiting for the shoe, the machete, to drop. But it didn't. Not at first.

Some twenty pages in, he realized that this book was a slow burn, its pacing completely different. The tension twisting in microturns; in pauses, not words. A shift of light. The twitch of a lip.

The boy, Theo, had a secret, that much was clear, and keeping it was pulling him under. Rowan didn't need to dig too deep to know what that felt like, the persistent weight, the desire to tell, the fear of the consequences. He recognized it in every sentence Theo didn't finish, although it didn't take more than fifty pages before Rowan understood that this secret went far deeper than vanity, or a career.

That first read-through, Rowan didn't touch the colored pens. He just read, letting the words flow through him. He spent the next day walking, thinking. Trying to process. The day after that, he took out the highlighters and got to work.

It was only then that the second contrast between this book and his previous assignments became clear. The thrillers he'd done up to this point had generally been told through a point of view that saw and knew all. A few times, the book had been the exact opposite, relayed in an *I* voice, and he'd enjoyed the challenge of using that personality to color the story. But the point of view in *Theo* existed somewhere in the murky in-between, its focus tight on Theo, but still always from the outside.

"It's tricky," Rowan said to Hadley on the phone. "I mean, remember when we were kids and we used to sneak out at night and stand on the street and watch other families through their windows? Like—you'd feel like you were there with them, but you knew you never could be?"

"You always were a perv, Rowan," Hadley said. She was teasing; he could hear it.

"You know what I mean," he said.

"Yeah," she said quietly. "I do."

"Well, this book feels like that."

Actually, Rowan thought as he made his dinner later, the lighted window concept applied equally well to the relationships between most of the characters in *Theo*. The feeling that there was a piece of glass between them. A distance they couldn't overcome. The whole book seemed . . . what was the word he was looking for? Haunted.

We can never truly know another person, the point of view said.

It breaks my heart, said the voice.

What was he supposed to do with that? Rowan thought as he spooned chili into his mouth. The holy grail of acting was the seamless unification of actor and character. The Oscar went to the guy who *became* the stuttering king or the serial killer. But the point of view in *Theo* basically told you that complete empathy was impossible, while still, in every sentence, yearning for it.

He wanted to call the audiobook company, get the author's contact info. Write her and ask what the hell she was doing, messing with his head. But he wouldn't, he realized as he washed his dishes, for two reasons. One—this was the first literary book he'd been assigned, and he damn well didn't want them thinking he was asking for help. And two—as the author didn't know him and likely wouldn't care if she did—none of this was actually about him. This was about the author and her character. A character she obviously loved with all her soul, with every word at her disposal. A character whose pain she felt on a syntactical level, while still being unable to stop the events that were happening to him.

And the voice that wound them together, like two strands around a stick, over and around each other.

How the hell do you turn that into sound? he wondered.

He started by doing some basic research. He wouldn't contact the author, but he could find out about her. He started with her photo on the back page of the book. She was young, pale, and thin, with dark hair curling around her face. The photo was taken on some beach—rocky; maybe Maine?—her eyes avoiding the camera in a way the photographer tried to make artistic. But Rowan knew those types, the ones who couldn't look you in the eye. Sometimes it was because they were hiding things. Sometimes it was because they couldn't.

Did this book come from your life? he wondered. She had to have some personal connection; Rowan didn't know how you could write a story like that out of thin air. But as Theo had no sister, that left the option of the author having either been Theo (a clever gender switch) or the girlfriend who showed up later in the book. Neither felt right.

"Why do you think the author has to be in it?" Hadley asked. She was getting deeply curious about the book. *I haven't seen you care like this in a while,* she'd said. "Maybe you should stop being so literal."

But he wasn't done. A Google search of Alice Wein brought up a notice in Publishers Marketplace, stating that *Theo* had been bought by a reputable-enough publisher for a mid-five-figure price. Nothing by movie standards, but not too bad in a publishing industry that was still heaving itself out of the 2007 economic crash.

There was a second hit, a link to a literary review, but Rowan had been put under a critical microscope himself enough times recently, and so he passed it by.

That was it. A photo, and a book of words.

Sitting on his couch, laptop on his legs, Rowan remembered how Hadley would sometimes read to him at night when he was young and had trouble going to sleep. She wasn't that much older than him, so their choices were necessarily elementary, but she loved the book about the little bear who keeps wanting to go outside in the snow but finds it too cold. His mother gives him coats and scarves, layer after layer, but he is always cold, until finally she reminds him that he's had a fur coat all along. He takes off all the layers and runs outside, happy.

Rowan had focused on the mother taking care of her child, but Hadley had seen something different—and ever since, she'd had an infuriating tendency to remind him of her interpretation.

You don't need more, little bear, she'd say. *You've got all you need already.*

Maybe, he thought, *he did.* Maybe all he needed was the book.

For the next three days, he went out in his kayak. He couldn't have said why; it just felt right to be on the water. As his paddle dipped, first one side, then the other, he could feel the story settling inside him.

In the evenings, he started working with the pens again. He picked out a new color—green—which he used to note punctuation. Commas, semicolons, em dashes. Highlighted, they became like notes in a musical score, the author as conductor, leading his voice, slowing it down, once, twice, speeding it up in a single sentence that ran like a glorious horse all the way to the bottom of a page.

It wasn't just punctuation, either; he was seeing that now. The words themselves had rhythms and sounds that added color to their meaning. He started reverse-engineering some of the choices, looking in a thesaurus to see other options the author might have used. At one point, about two-thirds of the way through the book, Theo's father called out his name. Alice had chosen the word *agonized* to describe his voice. Rowan looked it up, saw the synonyms *distressed, tortured, hurt.* And yet, it was *agonized* that made you feel the scene— the hard gulp of the *g,* the way the rest of the word pulled you under.

"It's incredible," Rowan said on the phone to Terrence.

"You're really getting into this," Terrence said. "Are you finally having an actual relationship with a woman?"

Rowan laughed and said no. Because it wasn't the author he was interested in; it was the voice on the page, which somehow—and this was odd but also true—felt more honest and human than he could ever imagine the young woman in the photo feeling free enough to be.

Still, in a way, Terrence was right. After years of letting his celebrity or money take the place of any actual effort, Rowan was finally reaching out. The fact that it was toward a fictional voice seemed ironically appropriate for a man who had, with the rare exception or two, forgotten how to be with real people.

He was getting close; he could feel it. He started practicing passages in the recording booth. He'd never done that before, had always launched straight in, made corrections as necessary. Now he tested his voice on various sentences, tried it lower, rougher, calmer. Searching for the sound.

His producer called him, making sure he'd meet his deadline.

"Of course," he said. He was a professional. And yet, part of him waited, wanting to get it—not perfect, but *right*.

Then it was time, or maybe he had just run out of it. In any case, he went into the studio and laid the stack of color-coded pages on the table in front of him.

"Here we go," he said to the air, and turned on the microphone.

It always surprised him—he who did his own stunts, who could do an entire motorcycle chase without sweating up a leather jacket—how exhausting it was to record a book. Usually, he was wiped out after a couple hours, the strain of standing, of focusing so as not to miss a word or make a single extraneous sound causing his body to tremble, his mind to balloon and grow heavy. But on that day, he just kept reading, the highlighting on the pages like whispers guiding him, the sentences drawing him in deeper and deeper until all he wanted was to feel, in his bones, what it was like for Theo as he left his childhood home and went out into the world, as he made a life that was somehow more whole for having been broken.

He kept recording, day after day, sometimes even at night, when everything outside was as dark and quiet as the inside of his booth. When he finally stopped and slept, the author's words became his dreams.

One afternoon, he found himself with a single page left to read. He stood in the silence of his studio, the words in front of him. He knew that when he was done the book would go silent as well—and Rowan could not make it continue, no matter how hard he worked to make his voice and the voice of the book into one. He wondered at the unfairness of this impending loss. Because he had touched that lighted window, felt the warmth of a hand on the other side.

Is it always like this? he wondered. *Can we never truly connect?*

But this was his job. So he kept reading, until he reached the last sentence and the voice spoke quietly to him, through him.

All that matters is that we try.

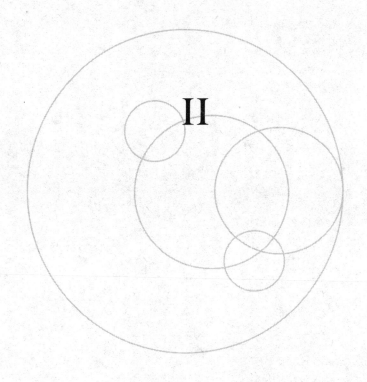

II

The Internet

2012

Cultus Reviews

THEO By Alice Wein

Release date January 25, 2012

Get ready to swim in some murky waters.

From its opening line—a dime-store plagiarization of Tolkien—to its platitudinous closing sendoff, *Theo* is the heartfelt and obviously debut novel by author Alice Wein.

Theo, the eponymous main character, has a tough life. His father is horrible, his mother watches passively from a puddle of guilt, the rest of the world doesn't know or care. It's up to our hero to save himself. When his plan goes horribly awry, Theo flees his small town, guilt-stricken. Will he be able to mend his soul and find the beauty in his brokenness? The answer is a foregone conclusion, particularly when an appropriately sensitive and beautiful young woman appears on the scene.

Wein does her best to throw in a twist or two, but the waters this book swims in are well traveled. You could drown in the symbolism—but we'll avoid the spoiler alerts here.

Booklover 451
Amazon Top 500 Reviewer *****

You're going to want to take this boy home

Get the Kleenex ready because *Theo* is going to break your heart. Alice Wein takes no prisoners in this vivid examination of a dysfunctional family and its effects on the boy at the center of it all. I couldn't stop thinking about it, long after I was done.

Goodreads
Carrie_loves_books rated it ***

I thought a lot of it was really well writen, but why did she have to kill the dad? I mean, I just don't think that's necessary.

Thank you to the publisher for sending me a free copy in exchange for an honest review.

Hadley Cooke@alltheboooks
OMG. This. Book.

11:47 P.M.-Jan 26, 2012

2.5k Retweets 28,762 ★ Favorites

III

Washington State

2012

The Artist

M iranda opened her mailbox and saw the cardboard package, neat and rectangular, the logo swooped on the side like a satisfied check mark. She grimaced. When it came to reading material, she preferred the used bookstore in her small island town. Sure, the old guy had been running it forever and his inventory tipped heavily in the direction of Louis L'Amour—but that wasn't the point.

Miranda's mother had a different attitude regarding the internet, embracing it like one of those fancy designer oxygen cannisters that tourists buy at high altitudes in Colorado. One puff and she was off and running. At the ripe age of sixty-three, she was the head of an advertising firm in New York and had been an early adopter of social media, evolving through its ever-changing iterations with an ease that would have made Darwin swoon. Her posts on *being your best self* had made her a minor celebrity.

"We could keep in touch better if you joined Twitter," she would say when she and Miranda talked. "Or Facebook."

"I don't want distractions when I'm working," Miranda said.

"How *is* your art going?" her mother asked, and Miranda's ears picked up the little vibration that was definitely not the cell phone connection. The undercurrent, Miranda called it—or, more accurately, the undertow: her mother's skepticism of Miranda's talent, her ability to take care of herself. Miranda was thirty-six and had managed to keep herself fed for almost two decades, thank you very much.

"It's going great," she told her mother. "A new store just picked me up."

She didn't say the store was the front desk of the ferry terminal—but hey, every passenger had to buy a ticket, so it was good traffic. And what better way to remember your trip than a bit of sea glass, perfectly suspended in curves of silver wire? Every day Miranda would walk the rock-strewn beach and forage for those glimpses of quiet color—pale green, blue, brown. She took them all. You weren't supposed to pick up the rocks, but sea glass wasn't natural. It was man-made, improved by nature, a reminder that anything can be broken. All rough edges made smooth.

"I'm just cleaning up," she would say if anyone asked. The locals never did; on the tiny island they all knew each other. Only about three hundred people lasted through the dark days of winter, mostly artists and organic farmers, along with a few hardy homeschooling families. It had been a quiet place, even in the summer, until the "secret" five-star restaurant moved in. Now they had tourists. The fishermen's shacks and old cabins were being torn down and replaced by behemoths, walls of glass facing a view the owners saw maybe two times a year. One of the biggest ones had made its way into a fancy architectural magazine. Miranda's mother clipped the article and sent it to her with a note: *Gorgeous.*

Miranda believed in small footprints. In feeding yourself. She'd left home at eighteen, driven across the country, waitressed her way through art school in Los Angeles. Four years of creations—photographs and oil and fabric and ink—reveling in all, focusing on none. Miranda loved the art that lay in the overlap, the mixing of metaphors and genres. Her senior project was a series of collages—images from old magazines and contemporary tabloids, mixed with traditional painting. A still life of a luminously painted bowl, filled with photographs of celebrity faces in place of fruit. A self-portrait with Botticelli's Venus as a coed, her scallop shell morphed into a tutu.

"Not exactly a way to make a living," her mother had said. She'd been obsessed with *making a living* ever since Miranda's father had taken off the year Miranda turned six.

After graduating from art school, Miranda had taken off herself, traveling the country in her old RAV4, sleeping in the back, gobsmacked by the glowing spires of Bryce Canyon, the giant skies of Montana. Her journal held no words, only colors, water-softened palettes that could bring back an entire world with a flick of a page.

She'd lived on peanut butter and white bread, gone vegetarian, then vegan, had affairs with men she should and shouldn't have stayed with. When funds ran low, she made more. When she was twenty-three, a boyfriend told her about seasonal work at a salmon cannery in Alaska. It paid enough to support her for the whole year, if she played her financial cards right and didn't mind the smell of fish and masculinity. Which she did and didn't, respectively, for years.

"But your degree?" her mother asked from across the country. "Wouldn't you prefer a real job? I know people."

Miranda let the money run out on the boardinghouse pay phone.

"Why do you even talk to your mother?" her latest lover asked when she returned to the room, hair on fire. "Not that I mind." He opened his long, tan arms. "The sex is great."

And she hurled herself into the bed, let the flames burn.

Miranda had been twenty-eight when she found the island. She was driving her truck down from Alaska to San Francisco at the end of the season when she saw the exit sign just south of the Canadian border. On a whim, she took the turn, then the ferry, and fell in love with the green. She'd found a cheap rental and fixed it up, settled in. Let the serenity slide into her.

It was only when the phone rang or a package arrived that everything rekindled.

Miranda had once met a guy who fought wildfires in the summer, and he told her they could travel underground for miles, along the roots. Come up again where you least expected them.

"But the person who lit it in the first place is always responsible," he explained. Miranda thought that sounded about right.

And now here was a new box.

Miranda's mother was the queen of unnecessary care packages, little missiles of love. Fancy face lotions. A flowing caftan or beaded T-shirt—aspirational hippie clothes, Miranda's friend Juniper called them, laughing. Miranda had started putting the items in her own version of a Little Free Library, only hers was painted in fifteen flamboyant colors with a sign that read: Little Free Stuff. The tourists were enchanted; it was her most photographed piece of art. And the bottles of lotion disappeared overnight.

Shaking her head, Miranda yanked up the box flaps to expose a hardback book, the cover in blues and yellows, the title a single word: *Theo.*

Of course, Miranda said to herself.

When Miranda was young, there had been two kids' bedrooms in their house, one painted pink, the other blue, and only one got filled. After Miranda started kindergarten, her mother had turned the blue bedroom into an office for her father, painting the walls a creamy white and bringing in sleek Danish furniture, as if disappointment could slide off those smooth surfaces and disappear. Then she'd gotten a part-time job at a local advertising company.

Now, almost thirty years later, Miranda started to put *Theo* into her foraging bag, intending to leave it with Roy at the used bookstore. Then she stopped. Her mother would want to *talk* about the book, and Miranda would have to have something intelligent to say. Besides, her mother's gifts always held some hidden message. Miranda searched the box, but all she found was the little note produced by the shipper: *Enjoy your gift!*

Miranda was used to coded meanings, though. She liked to say it was her mother's private communication system. Like sign language, only quieter.

Enough, she told herself. She could lose a whole day, a whole week, this way if she let herself. She had work to do. There was a big summer craft fair coming up, featuring a studio tour with regular hours—a new resident, one of those early-retired software guys, had decided the island needed to live up to its potential and he was the man for the job.

"People need something to do," he'd said from the podium at the island council meeting, and by *people* they all knew he meant tourists. She marveled at his unexamined confidence—but before anybody knew what was happening, a date in August had been selected, a schedule made. Giant banners were put up all over the island, alerting visitors. Studio tours! Gourmet foods!

There was a lot to do between now and then. Cut back the branches encroaching her driveway, clean her workspace. Build some shelves. Fill them, for that matter. She didn't have time to read a book.

"This is exciting," her mother said on the phone. "And you have such a darling studio. People will fall in love with it."

Miranda's mother had seen the studio on her visit to the island the summer before. She'd said she'd be happy to stay with Miranda—but Miranda's house only had the one bedroom, and the futon couch was old and lumpy. Miranda's mother had loved the island, however, and the little B&B with its bright-eyed owner who served her homemade scones and jam for breakfast. Miranda's mother had posted about the jam and now the B&B had a whole side business going.

"I could do the same for you," her mother said.

"I'm not a scalable enterprise," Miranda replied.

"Maybe it's time to think about that," her mother said. "You're almost the same age I was when your father left us. A woman needs to have a plan."

A couple weeks later, Miranda adopted a dog, an aged part shepherd, part who-knows-what. He'd been found on the beach, sopping wet, perhaps a case of dog-overboard from one of the visiting sailboats. No one else would take him, old and cantankerous as he was, but Miranda could tell on first sight that this dog had not fallen into the water. He'd jumped.

I would, too, she told him, letting her fingers dig into the thick ruff of his neck. *You're too big for a boat.*

She renamed him Herbert, because nothing could fit him less well, and they both seemed to like the joke of that. Herbert calmed in her presence, and she found she liked his company when she foraged on the beach or hacked at the wild black-berries that were constantly encroaching on her backyard.

Herbert tended to shed, however, and his age could make things tricky.

"Can't your neighbors feed him so you can come visit?" her mother asked. "I could get tickets to *Wicked*."

"Herbert's not good with other people," Miranda said. "It's a problem."

Now, Miranda put down the book and considered her options—foraging, art, or studio. The studio was not, in actuality, *darling*. It was a former gardening shed, barely changed in its new iteration, and, to be honest, Miranda hadn't cracked the door in months.

It had started early last fall—the balance between collecting and creating beginning to tip, and eventually falling right over. Before that, foraging for sea glass had been how she'd spent her afternoons after a morning in the studio. She'd head out, and the beach would clear her mind, get her ready for the next day. But somewhere along the line, after-lunch had turned into after-midmorning-tea had slipped into all-day, and it tended to make her mind less clear rather than more. By now she'd cleaned out the sea glass on every beach on the island, and there wouldn't be more until they had a big storm. There was no point in going, really.

Miranda looked at the shed, then at Herbert.

"I'll get your leash," she said.

When they returned in the late afternoon, Miranda's stomach was as empty as her collecting bag. She made a stir-fry with bok choy and garlic from her garden, and while she was eating, she glanced over and saw the book her mother had sent her. Just lying there. Waiting.

"Fine," she said in exasperation. At least she could get one thing off her to-do list.

She propped the book up against a heavy ceramic jug and opened it with her left hand. As her right raised a fork toward her mouth, her eyes caught on the first line.

Wandering is a gift given only to the lost.

Miranda put down her fork. *Are you kidding me?* she thought. So, her mother was telling her she was lost, was she? This book, a subtle-not-so-subtle nudge.

Miranda had gotten those nudges her whole life. *You could be so beautiful if . . . You'd be so successful if . . . I could help . . . Let me help.* When all her mother really meant was: *You'd be better if you were like me.*

This one was classic. *Wandering,* presented as something special, magical, a skill almost. *How clever you are.* Except that what you really were, in the end, was lost.

"The hell with that," Miranda said, and pitched the book onto the couch.

The phone rang. Without even looking, Miranda knew who it would be.

"Did you get the package?" her mother asked.

"I did," Miranda said.

"I hope you like it."

"I haven't had a chance to read. Remember that art tour? I'm really busy."

"That's great, honey. I can't wait until people see your studio. They're going to love it."

Not her art. Her studio.

They talked for a few minutes, Miranda's mother offering suggestions on paint colors for the shed walls. Then Miranda said goodbye, put down the phone, and saw Herbert watching her.

"Want to go hack some stuff?" she asked him, and she could have sworn he nodded.

Cutting back blackberries wasn't a battle you ever won, but the fight itself could be productive. When she was stuck or frustrated, sometimes the best thing Miranda could do was grab her machete and head to the backyard. She'd drive the bushes back, creating her own defensive line parallel to the house.

This time, though, she went straight in, creating a path through the stiff vines. Once in a while, she'd have to stop and drag out the cut ones so they didn't block her retreat entirely, but within an hour she'd managed to make it to the edge of her property.

She and Herbert stood there, Miranda catching her breath as she looked across the overgrown field in front of her to the old farmhouse on the far side. It had been slowly returning to the earth for decades, a slide as inexorable as a lamed horse crumpling to its knees. Once it had been beautiful, however, one of the few two-story houses on the island. The porch was long and deep, the windows framed by shutters, even though heat and hurricanes were two things you didn't have to worry about in the Pacific Northwest. Still, Miranda had always appreciated those extra touches. She liked imagining some early settler building this house for his wife, a thank-you after decades in a rude cabin. Or maybe they'd built it together, with their kids. There were times in the early evenings when Miranda thought she could hear those children calling as they ran across the fields, but it always ended up being coyotes.

Just a few days ago, as she drove to get groceries, she'd seen a big white sign in front of the house: Notice of Proposed Land Use Action. She'd slowed down, stopped. Saw the enlarged plan—what was left of the farm divided into neat rectangles, one of the lines going straight through the old house.

Now, the sun was coming in at a sideways angle that lit the windows into gold. Miranda looked at her watch; she had at least another hour before it got dark.

"What do you think?" she asked Herbert, who cocked his head in disapproval.

"Come on," she said. "Let's get lost."

She set off through the field, Herbert following close on her heels. A few minutes later, itchy but triumphant, she stood at the base of the porch stairs, looking up at the house. There was a grace about it, the paint weathered like sculpted sandstone, the glass in the old windows wavy as water.

"Shall we go in?" she asked Herbert. "They're going to tear it down anyway."

Miranda had once dated a guy at the cannery who was studying the psychology of criminal behavior, a subject fascinating enough that it kept Miranda monogamous for an entire summer. Well, except for once, with a guy from Montana, and only because her boyfriend had already strayed himself. Which had led to a discussion of the broken window theory. According to him, it meant that the appearance of a transgression on someone else's part was—while a temptation to transgress oneself—still not an excuse for criminal behavior. Or, in simpler terms: just because the window's already broken doesn't mean you can go in.

Except, maybe it did.

The steps creaked and shifted under Miranda's feet as she made her way up to the porch.

Most people wanted houses that were solid and well maintained, but Miranda liked a house with history, stories. After her father had left them for his suddenly pregnant admin, Miranda's mother had wiped his presence from their walls, their home.

We are our own family, she said.

And Miranda's mother had turned herself into the human equivalent of the perfect house—elegant, well appointed, and impervious to the elements.

Time had detached the mesh from the screen door, the metal fabric curling back like the spiral of a conch shell. The main door was secured, but one of the living room windows was not only broken but unlocked, and Miranda ducked her head and clambered over the sill, avoiding the pieces of glass on the floor. Herbert looked through the opening, puzzled and a bit concerned.

"I'll be right back," she said.

Teenagers had found their way into the house before her. Miranda saw an unrolled camping pad, a candle set on a metal plate. The silver foil of a condom wrapper. She remembered those stolen moments from her own adolescent years, when she'd slipped out of the confines of her ever-tightening home, grabbed a boy, and found an untended human burrow to nestle in. That feeling of playing grown-up and hooky at the same time.

Don't be like your father, her mother had said once when Miranda had come home, her lips puffed, her body lazy with sex. *Think of the consequences.*

I am, Miranda had thought. *I'll go crazy if I don't have this.*

There was no furniture left in the house, not even curtains on the windows. Miranda walked through a haze of side-lit dust to the kitchen, saw the original wooden cabinets exuberantly painted in alternating avocado and orange, some of the paint slopped onto the curved drawer pulls that hung down in a row of permanent, if ironic, smiles.

The burst of 1970s energy that had hit the kitchen had not extended to the upstairs. Every wall was covered with ancient wallpaper, even the closets. Stylized pagodas and peacocks, rows of violets. In the smallest room, the walls featured chubby-kneed children, fishing, gardening, handing each other flowers. On the back wall of the closet, across the image of a young boy standing at an easel, paintbrush aimed at the canvas almost like a gun, a child's hand had scrawled a word in crayon: *Mine.*

Miranda stood, gazing at the word, watching the letters morph into shapes and back into meaning, the way words could when you focused hard on them. *Mine* was a mercurial concept, anyway, if you thought about it. Susceptible to change, either internal or external. Back in the day, her art professor had said that her self-portraits didn't really take that idea into account.

But now, looking at the child's handwriting, the word, Miranda had an idea of her own.

She still had the machete she'd used to chop a path through the blackberries. She rested its tip on the wallpaper, about four inches above the word, and etched a square around it, going through what appeared to be several layers of paper. When the square was complete, she peeled back a corner, carefully removed the word from the wall, and slipped it into her shirt pocket.

Later, when she got home, she put the square on her kitchen window ledge. The next morning, the light shone through it and she saw the ghost designs underneath—a toy soldier, a portion of a blowzily blooming flower.

And for the first time in months, she was excited.

She had an idea, but she was less sure about the path to get there. This was how it always was with her art, a concept she had difficulty explaining to her mother, who always seemed to have both goal and path, charging into her post-divorce life like, if not a cow let out of the barn, at least a bull on a rampage.

"You have to know what you want, Miranda," she'd said. "You can't let anybody else tell you."

Which seemed kind of ironic, given her mother's circumstances at the time, but back then Miranda was more focused on her father's sudden absence and her mother's anger, which floated about the house like Casper the ghost's unfriendly alter ego.

Art became Miranda's hiding place. At first, she drew the highly stylized figures that were almost mandatory for eleven-year-old girls—cartoon fairies with big eyes, mermaids with hair that flowed forever. But soon she found herself falling into the greens and blues of the mermaid's tail, the curves of the hair, until even the last vestiges of realistic depiction slipped away, and everything became color and shape and movement.

She'd gone full Goth in high school, but the reality was she hated the limited palette, and her eyes always watered when she wore heavy liner. The armor of it all was a plus, however, as was the annoyance factor. When her mother—an account manager now at a bigger, better company—would comment that surely Miranda must have other things she could wear, Miranda would pointedly run her gaze over her mother's slim suits, her fuck-me-don't-fuck-with-me heels.

"Don't we all," she said, and turned before she could see her mother's expression.

She dropped the Goth look in art school. She didn't have the time. Finally, she felt as if she was somewhere that made sense, if only because nothing was supposed to. *Sense* now meant *senses,* the five of them, or six, if you were willing to go there. It meant the smell of paint, slipping out of a metal tube beneath the pressure of your fingers, the slide of it under a brush. The feel of fabric, the sound of a woodblock lifting away from paper. She loved it all, and maybe that was the problem, her inability to choose.

"All art comes from a center," her professor told her. "A place of knowing."

And yet, Miranda wondered sometimes, wasn't the wind of a hurricane what had the greatest impact?

Climbing in the window was easier the second time. The old house still held the cool of night as she opened the front door so Herbert could join her. He did, but tentatively, lingering like a conscience near the entrance.

"Mom always said you have to take what you want," Miranda said. Although she was pretty sure her mother didn't mean this. Wouldn't have set foot in this house, in any case.

Herbert just looked at her, eyes steady.

"Fine. Stay there," Miranda said, and headed downstairs.

The basement was dark, the smell thick, as the beam from her flashlight roamed over the shelves that lined the back wall. There weren't many objects: a few rusted cans of baked beans, a mason jar half-filled with black slime. An empty container of Yuban coffee, featuring a young woman, hair flipping just under her ear, a white cup raised coyly to her lips. *She probably wasn't expecting to find herself here either,* Miranda thought. Inside the can, she found rolls of thin wire, pieces of dusty red sandpaper, an assortment of bolts and nails and washers. Miranda took a plastic bag from her backpack and dumped the contents of the can inside.

At the end of the middle shelf, she found a rat trap, old and sprung, although luckily without an occupant. She smiled at the logo, and put the trap in the bag, too.

Back when Miranda lived in cities, she used to meander through stores this way. When the clerks, probably worried that she was shoplifting, asked her if she was looking for anything in particular, she would just answer, "Inspiration."

Because wasn't that what art was all about, in the end? Mentally shoplifting your way through the world around you, the thoughts inside you? Looking for the thing that makes it all click. Makes it all start. Makes it all worthwhile and whole and good again.

That could take a while. You might have to wander, but that didn't mean you were lost.

The rest of the room was empty, except for an old electrical panel in the back corner. Miranda opened its squeaking metal door and saw a row of three round glass fuses. She aimed the flashlight at them, peering closer. In the center of the first was two letters—OK—with a slim line through them. On the second, the word was partially obscured; on the third was a white cloud. A Goldilocks-worthy decision, she thought, but in the end, she took them all, unscrewing each one carefully, although the electricity was certainly disconnected. Into the bag they went. They clinked lightly against the other objects.

Back upstairs, she went into the kitchen, passing Herbert, who remained at the front door like a sentry.

"Or a gargoyle," she commented. He seemed unimpressed.

In the kitchen, she opened all the cabinets and drawers. Empty, every one. She stood back, considering, and then pulled out two of the rectangular drawers, a smaller orange one—what had probably been the junk drawer, she figured—and one a bit wider and avocado green. Then she and Herbert made their way back across the field, pack on her back, the drawers hanging down in her hands, brushing through the grass, the metal pulls tapping lightly against the wood as she walked.

Knock, knock.

Who's there?

Because wasn't that the question, really?

When Miranda opened the door to her studio, the spiders looked up in surprise. They, at least, had taken the space seriously, turning it into a gallery of webs. She looked through the shivering white threads to the jars on the worktable. The sea glass inside had gone dusty. Emerald turned gray. White to smoke, blue to ice. She thought of her necklaces. They had been her new career, the thing that would let her stay on the island in the summer. Give up the fish, the cannery, which was far less exciting by your midthirties—the young men no longer a distraction, being distracted themselves by younger things. Which left only the fish for her.

The necklaces had offered a sustainable simplicity, which had been appealing for this new chapter of her life. Besides, there was something deliciously ironic in selling tourists art made from something someone else had thrown away. But looking at the glass now, all she could see was the same thing, over and over. There were only so many ways you could twist a wire, make an old thing new.

Miranda's mother was a wizard at creating fantasy out of the ordinary. By the time she was forty-five, she was known as the woman who could turn a tampon into liberation. She could do it with anything—at least, anything that involved diet foods, cleaning supplies, face creams, or (on a lucky day) perfume. The products they gave her to market. *Caroline's niche,* her boss called it. *My own private ghetto,* she said at home, over a second glass of wine.

Then she left that company, started her own. Sold anything she wanted. She was good at it, too, always knew just what to say to make you feel as if your life was missing something.

Standing in her studio, Miranda remembered yelling at her mother in a twenty-one-year-old's rage. *Stop selling every-fucking-thing!* Her mother just shaking her head.

What job do you think kept a roof over your head?

I don't need your help, Miranda said.

Funny, her mother replied. *That's just what I said to your father. And thus, my job.*

Now in her studio, Miranda got a broom, sent the spiders flying, and carried the jars of sea glass to the bench outside. She cleaned off her worktable, spreading out her haul from the morning, along with the square of wallpaper she'd brought home the night before. The idea in her head was vague, but she allowed her hands to do the thinking. She spent the day moving the pieces here and there, the fuses eventually landing up toward the top, the orange drawer a bit farther down, the green one much farther yet.

She stood back, considered. *Too big,* she thought, looking at the orange drawer, and got out her saw. Cut it down to a depth of four inches. Then she switched to a hammer and knocked the front off the green drawer, discarding the rest. She put the reconfigured pieces back on the table, and, almost on a whim, laid the red sandpaper inside the orange drawer.

Better, she thought, nodding. She was getting somewhere.

She'd never done anything like this before. She'd always thought of herself as artistically eclectic, unconstrained by discipline, but now she realized she had never left two dimensions. This new piece was different. Its materials reached back into a past that wasn't hers, a history she could hold in her hands, solid and unmistakable—and then, through her imagination, the pieces changed meaning, becoming hers, becoming her.

Almost every day, she'd make a trip to the old house. Sometimes for ideas, sometimes for something she suddenly realized she needed. Strips of lath. Some one-by-ones. She could have gone to the local hardware store, but that wasn't the point. After she saw a group of three men walking the land one day, clipboards in hand, she redoubled her foraging efforts, although now she covered her tracks, sticking to the narrower and more circuitous deer trails through the field, just in case someone actually wanted those old shower faucets, and might try to track her down.

As the old house slowly lost its bits and pieces, the sculpture in Miranda's studio took shape. It was off the table now, standing, and she found that here, too, the process was different, working with a vertical surface, adjusting for balance and weight and height. Nothing like those

feather-light necklaces, barely detectable between her fingers. This art had heft, requiring the muscles she'd developed in the cannery and her garden, the skills with hammer
and saw and screwdriver she'd picked up keeping the rain
out of her house, the heat in. When she took a break, she'd
sit out in the sun with her back against her studio wall, and
feel the warmth on her face, her arms.

Time was an amazing thing, she thought one morning as
she woke up, ready to get back to work. The days had moved
like sludge just a few weeks before, but now all she wanted
was to be in her studio. In the house, the dishes stacked up.
The branches covered her driveway.

She was so close to finished. And yet, something was
still missing. She could feel it as she sat at her kitchen table,
drinking her morning tea, looking out toward the studio,
her sculpture.

She stood up and began to walk about the house, mug
in hand. *What what what what what do you want?* She was
muttering, she knew it, but sometimes that helped.

Then her foot tripped on the clogs she'd kicked off the
night before, and her tea sloshed over the rim of the mug to
land on the book lying on the table next to the couch. *Theo.*

She stared down at it.

Yes, she said.

She hadn't read another page since that first night over dinner. The book had moved from couch to table, where it re-

mained like a neglected houseplant. She'd told herself that she couldn't get rid of it until she confronted her mother and asked her why she'd sent it. Had an honest conversation, finally. Miranda was almost thirty-seven. It was about time.

Except she'd taken a walk with a machete instead, and now here was the book, having moved not an inch because of course it couldn't.

Unless she carried it. Which she did now, out to her studio.

It was a week later, an afternoon in the middle of August. The sun shone heavy in the studio, and Miranda had opened the door and windows for ventilation. Her creation stood in the center, taking up enough room that she'd had to move the worktable outside. She was hot and dirty, and she couldn't remember the last time she'd washed her hair. But the piece was done. Perfect.

"Miranda?" The voice came from outside, but it could have been in her head. That's where it lived most of the time, anyway.

But what would her mother be doing here, now? Without notice or invitation. She never went anywhere without both.

Expect a red carpet and you'll get one, she always said.

"Miranda?"

Miranda could hear Herbert, launching himself across the back field toward the intruder.

"Shit," she said under her breath, then yelled, "Herbert! Knock it off."

She emerged to see her mother crouched down, her right hand between Herbert's ears.

"You must be Herbert," she was saying. "What a good boy."

Miranda couldn't decide if she was more relieved that Herbert hadn't bitten her mother or jealous at the unexpected affection on her mother's face. Herbert was not even an attractive dog.

She took him by the collar, pulled him aside. "What're you doing here, Mom?" she asked.

"Well," her mother said, standing and brushing the dirt from her slim khaki pants. "It's the art studio tour this weekend; I thought I'd come and surprise you." She looked around, back toward the overgrown driveway, at the worktable sprawled upside down on the grass, the studio, which was obviously neither clean nor painted.

"What's going on?" she asked.

When Miranda was young, she'd brought home report cards for her mother's signature, a column of capital Bs, like a line of bisected snowmen marching down the page. Miranda was always tempted to fill in the other half of the circles, draw in a carrot nose, a pipe. A hat—maybe even a pointed witch's one, which would have been mixing metaphors but might have been mistaken for one of the As her mother wanted.

"School is not a Plan B," Miranda's mother would say.

Miranda didn't want As, however. Didn't want the life they offered. It hadn't made her mother happy, after all.

Then again, Miranda realized, she hadn't been happy either, at least not until the past few weeks. And now here was her mother, and the thought of her seeing, judging, the thing that had brought Miranda so much joy filled her with a sense of quick and brittle desperation.

But in that moment while Miranda had fallen headfirst down the rabbit hole of her thoughts, her mother had gone around her to the open door of the studio.

"Miranda," she said, and this time her tone was different. Soft.

The sculpture stood Miranda-height in the middle of the studio, the light through the still-dusty windows catching on the sturdy two-by-four legs, the one-by-one arms reaching up, fingers made from outstretched slats of lath. The hair, still longer slats, flying out like a spray of rocks behind a fast-moving motorcycle. All of it held together by nails and slim, spiraling strands of wire. Not a piece of sea glass to be seen.

Miranda watched her mother's eyes roving over the face: the glass fuse eyes—OK, not OK—the rat trap in the middle of the forehead, with its faded red logo, V for Victor. The orange drawer in place of a mouth.

"Open it," Miranda said. And her mother did, exposing a tongue of red sandpaper.

"Oh, Miranda," she said, and Miranda heard all the colors of the world in those words.

"It's extraordinary," her mother said. She reached out,

not quite touching the piece of wallpaper, placed where a heart would be, her mouth quirking increasingly upward as she looked at the round shower faucets on either side, then down at the green drawer front, stretched between pelvis bones created from parts of a curving banister.

"That one doesn't open," Miranda said, and her mother laughed. A full, hearty sound.

"You truly are my daughter," she said, and somehow Miranda didn't bristle.

And then—"Wait," her mother said, pointing to the wings that rose behind the figure's back, great arching things, the upper edges lined with blue and yellow, the feathers cut from paper covered with printed text. "Is that . . . ?"

"Yes," Miranda said.

"Well, I guess I don't have to ask you what you thought," her mother said with a wry smile.

Miranda, standing there in her studio, took a breath. Yes, she would do it. It was time.

"Why did you send me that book, Mom?"

Her mother looked at her, face puzzled.

"You asked me to," she said.

"What?"

"You said you wanted to read it. I thought it would be a nice surprise."

Miranda shook her head, her face an unwitting mirror of her mother's confusion. And then, slowly, she remembered. Her mother on the phone, going on about some new book, the one everyone was talking about on Twitter. Miranda saying she'd wait for the paperback. Meaning, *I don't need to buy something* Right Now *just because social media says it's good.* Meaning, *I am not you.*

It was like that fucking O. Henry story.

Except, not.

How long had she and her mother been doing this? Miranda wondered. Since her father left? Her whole life? Their communication like neon signs with most of the letters burnt out. What got filled in was only what made sense to you. What fit the story you already knew, the story you needed, whether or not it was any good for you.

Miranda looked at the sculpture in front of her. The piece born out of that evening—the thrown book, the stomp through the field, the weeks since. The purest artistic satisfaction she'd ever experienced. This, *this,* was who she was.

She stepped forward, touched the upper curve of a wing. All those words, turned into feathers.

"Well," she said, turning to her mother, "it did come in handy."

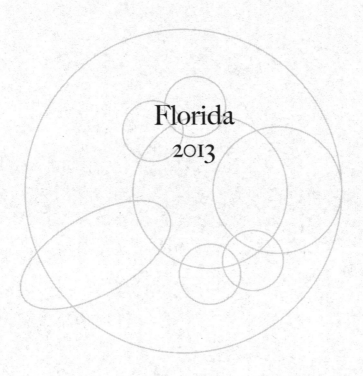

Florida
2013

The Diver

Tyler's girlfriend had left the book behind on his living room table, forgotten as she slipped quietly out the door that Sunday morning. Tyler could have told her she didn't need to worry about secrecy; his sense of hearing, honed from years of listening to his own heartbeat, his breath, was just fine. He, who could hear a dolphin breach the surface ten meters above his head, could surely detect the click of a door latch. But he thought he'd give her this one undisputed thing. Her own moment of escape.

Besides, he could never catch her on land now. Not in the water, either, if he was being honest.

He lay in bed, listening to the silence, trying to take himself down in his mind. Long, deep breaths, then sips of air, expanding his lungs, his ribs, imagining the sea around him, below him. Those first ten meters the water pushing back, his arms and legs working hard; the next ten a little easier, and then—the exhilaration as the depths accepted him with an almost audible sigh and he was pulled down, down. Down to where it was one body, one breath, all water. The blue of it, then the beautiful blackness below.

That was the trick, to know when deep was too deep, a seduction you couldn't give up, because now you were falling, and the fight must be reversed if you wish to find your way back up. Some days you don't know if you do. Down can feel so easy, as the oxygen leaves your brain and the dreams take over.

Tyler's girlfriend had never understood, not really, but he had to give her credit for trying. They'd met maybe three years before, on a beach, of course, Saylor one of many lithe blondes in bikinis, but somehow different, so that his eyes were drawn to her face, her gray eyes that searched his, the way his did the surface of the ocean. She'd seemed to intuit that his life was a solitary endeavor, but when they were in bed later, their breath chasing each other's, then finding, syncing, lifting them out of their bodies, he knew she thought she had him anyway. And he let her because she was the closest thing on earth to water.

Tyler's first memories were of a swimming pool, lit bright by a California sun. The warmth of his mother's hands holding him up as his toddler legs kicked, already swimming. Her laugh as she pulled him close, kissed his forehead.

"Not yet, little guy," she said.

But Tyler wanted the water the way other kids wanted candy or their favorite blanket. Any chance he had, he made a break for the nearest pool, whether at their house or someone else's. It was Southern California, after all; there were plenty of options: oval, rectangular, kidney-shape. When he was three, he even Houdinied his way out of an enclosed area set up for the children while the grown-ups had cocktails near the pool. That time he made it all the way in. He could still remember the fear on his mother's face as she swam toward him, her dress flowing behind her like wings, the way she grabbed him, heading for the surface.

"You can't do that," she sobbed, once they were on land again. She held on to him, tight. "I thought I'd lost you." But Tyler didn't understand—because he *had* done it, and he'd been the farthest thing from lost.

Later that night, he heard his parents arguing.

"It was embarrassing." Tyler's father's voice was sharp, like the prickly bits in between the blades of grass in their lawn. "There were people from my work there. You're his mother. Make him obey."

"But he's too young. He won't . . ."

The room went silent.

"I'm sorry," Tyler's mother said, quick as a sprint. "I'm sorry; it's my fault. I'll fix it."

Tyler's mother had a fence built close around their pool, got him toddler swimming lessons. Tyler learned how to keep his head above water, keep himself from going under. That never made sense to Tyler, though. Under was where the quiet was. Where you couldn't hear the glass hit the wall, couldn't hear your name being called.

Come here, Tyler. Now.

But some water was better than none, so he made the best of it, dog-paddling like a good boy near the steps, where his mother sat, her eyes never leaving him.

Then one day, when Tyler was four, their new neighbors accidentally left their side gate open, the wife returning home to discover Tyler facedown, floating in their pool. An ambulance had been called, although it turned out there was no need. Tyler's lungs still had plenty of air.

The wife was distraught. The husband was a lawyer. Tyler's father went over when he got home from work, and Tyler could hear the yelling. Then later, saw the lights flashing.

Soon after that, Tyler's family moved—inland, to a town with no swimming pools and a flat, arid geography that suited none of them.

"Our very own *Grapes of Wrath*," Tyler's father said. He had a different job, with longer hours. Tyler's mother had a job as well.

"Just until we're on our feet again," she told Tyler. But now there were babysitters, a series of old neighbor ladies who always smelled like they could use a good dunking themselves. And then later, school, full of kids who had never known anything but this dry town. There were times growing up when Tyler thought their life might simply desiccate into nothing. And he was the reason they were here, in this place they all hated. His father made that clear.

But I didn't need saving, Tyler would think, remembering the bliss of the neighbors' pool, his eyes open, looking down through the water below him.

For Tyler, the longing for submersion became visceral, and it only grew worse over the years. By the age of fourteen he'd discovered alcohol, the closest substitute he could find. When the vodka or rum or enough of the cheap-ass box wine hit his bloodstream, he could almost remember what it had felt like in that blue world where everything else disappeared.

It could have all gone very badly, but in a moment of divine capitalist intervention, the town, trying to lure tech companies to their part of the state, built a gleaming athletic facility, with a twenty-five-meter pool as its crown jewel. By this time, Tyler's mother had discovered the cache of bottles at the back of his closet, and the concept of drowning had taken on a whole new meaning. She signed him up for swimming lessons. Grown-up ones, this time.

"No lessons, no pool pass," she said.

"That's just perfect," his father said, his voice turning into gravel. "We had to move to this godforsaken place because he couldn't stay out of a damn pool, and now you're going to just give him what he wants?"

But this time, Tyler's mother held firm.

At the pool, Tyler learned, fast. He showed little interest in swimming laps, but at one point his teacher told him about a sport where people swam distances without breathing, then bet him he couldn't get to the other end of the pool without surfacing. Tyler succeeded on his first try. Soon it was two lengths. Then four. It was exciting, mesmerizing. At night he researched techniques, world records. Learned about people who dove deep, out in the wild—no tanks, just lungs. He doubled down on his training, swimming toward a place on the horizon, pushing off the walls of the pool, over and over and over. Small children would stop to watch him the way you would a seal, or maybe a lion pacing in the zoo. Back and forth. Back and forth. Month after month after year.

"He's a merman," one girl exclaimed. And he did look like one, because by now he had a monofin and could go so much farther, his body one long cascade of movement thrusting through the water. In the end, the pool managers had to give him his own dedicated swim time. Physically, it might have been possible to share a lane—he tended to stay toward the bottom, skimming along like a manta ray—but one look at the intensity on his face right before he went under, and you knew sharing wasn't really an option. Nobody wanted to work out next to him, either. It was a little creepy, to be sure, swimming beside someone who didn't need to breathe—but on a more practical level, who wanted to get backwashed out of their lane every fifteen seconds?

"He's like a human riptide," one elderly man had complained, and after that, the pool was Tyler's from 8–9 P.M. It meant they had to stay open a little longer, but the line of female lifeguards volunteering to take the chair during Tyler's sessions was more than sufficient to keep them staffed. It wasn't just his swimmer's body that had them all raising their hands; it was the angsty mystery of him. His feet, so sweetly human when they emerged from the monofin, his eyes that always seemed to be coming back from somewhere else when he removed his goggles. If you could catch him at just the right moment, they all thought, love him in the right way, you could keep him.

By now he was seventeen, and he slept with some of them. Having sex with Tyler was like making it with a dolphin, the girls said, especially as it often happened in the pool, after laps, after everyone else had gone. The trick was remembering to keep your head above water, but sometimes that was hard, when the rhythm was rolling and your body was liquifying and who the hell needed air when there was this. But after, when you were spent and happy, he would just put his goggles back on and swim and swim and swim, until finally you had to block his path and kick him out of the pool, even if you knew that betrayal meant your days with him were now numbered. The girls told each other this later, quietly, bitterly, after they understood that they were simply molecules of air to Tyler, something to be breathed in and expelled. Understood that there was no competition, at least among themselves. Within Tyler himself, competition was another thing entirely.

It was all about the lungs, and the ability to block out the rest of the world. When Tyler wasn't at the pool, he still trained, his face submerged in a filled sink, minute after minute, until his body screamed for air. Being motionless was actually harder, without the concentration on your own movement— arms, legs, flip, turn, swoosh—to distract you. It seemed the more your brain wanted new oxygen, the more it grasped onto old thoughts. *It's your fault.* Down the words would go into your muscles, your hands, your toes, replacing the air. *You're not good enough. Never good enough.*

But at the age of eighteen, when Tyler finally broke free of his dusty town, when he traveled to where the water was blue and deep, and back-and-forth became simply down, he found a place where he was good enough. At least, he could be if he just worked harder. Stayed under longer.

The girl on the beach had seemed to understand. He met her in the week leading up to his first big free diving record. The island was a white shoestring of land, floating in an ocean so clear and endless it made him feel like he'd mistaken the sky for water. The sand was soft and hot, his rented studio so tiny he could make coffee without leaving

the bed. He'd had to work three months at the movie theater in Florida to earn enough money for one week here,
living off as close to nothing as he could in both places.

But it didn't matter. The first time he saw the Blue Hole,
his life changed. A semicircle of white sand, a rim of tur-
quoise water, and then the infinite center, a blue so dark it
needed a name he knew he'd never find. They said the Blue
Hole had been a dry cave once, back when the world was
flipped on its head and oceans were deserts and deserts were
forests. Now it was a vase of quiet. Tyler swam out toward
the darkness, then dove down to the ledge and paused there.
The white sand slipped over the lip in sand-falls, cascading,
white and ethereal, through the water toward the bottom
some six hundred feet below. A millennium or two in the
future, the sand would fill up this hole, but that span of time
was no more comprehensible than the depth below him, the
immensity of it an endless invitation.

He slid over the edge, breaststroking his way down to
where the hole suddenly expanded, wide as forgiveness or
hell, depending. Dark, in any case. You could get lost, he
supposed, but that was a thought for the surface. Down
here, everything was the opposite.

He explored the intricacies of the rock walls, the fish, the
depths below. After a few glorious minutes, he floated back
up, the water lifting him, as if the air was eager to have him
back. He breached the surface, sucking in oxygen like the
mammal that he was, his feet still fluttering like a fish.

He stroked his way back to the beach, and there she was when he got out. Saylor.

When she came back to his room with him, the space, which had felt so small, opened like the underwater cavern. Saylor was laughter and confidence, the birthright of those who grow up loved. Leaning her warm arm against his, she showed him photos of her parents, and of a young woman who looked like a tired version of Saylor, standing in Central Park holding a baby in her arms.

"Who's that?" Tyler asked, pointing.

"That's Lara, my twin, and her son, Teddy." She looked over, grinned. "Don't worry," she said, seeing his expression, "he's a cutie, but I don't really see myself as a mother."

Saylor was a traveling nurse, determined to check the boxes of every state and continent. She pulled up pictures—urban, rural, cold, hot, dry, wet—her preferences eclectic, indiscriminate. For Tyler, who had only ever had two goals—water and down—her life felt like an unending kaleidoscope swirling around him.

"Why this one?" he asked, looking at a photo of a small town, its main-street stores half empty, three cars parked along its length.

She leaned forward to look at the tiny screen of her phone.

"Oh," she said. "They don't have any medical care generally. A group of us go there once a year for three days and just blast through everything—dental, medical, x-rays, blood tests, you name it." And she told him about the line of people that started before midnight, went around one block, two. About the six-year-old girl who had gotten her first pair of glasses and informed Saylor, awe splashed across her face, that grass was made of separate stalks.

"You're incredible," Tyler said.

"Don't put me up for sainthood yet," she said. "I wouldn't live there. I'm pickier about the places where I stay for a while." She showed him a cabin in the mountains. "Ski town." She grinned.

But Tyler could tell; she was different from him in this way. Her language was people. His was breath, and even that he held inside himself.

She hadn't come for the diving; perhaps the only nonresident on the island who could make that claim. She'd had a week between gigs; there was an extra seat on a plane; she had taken it.

"It was that or Juneau," she said, laughing. "Heat sounded good."

In some ways, it was a relief to be around someone who wasn't in the diving world, who didn't calculate her life in meters. Saylor was as happy on sand as in water.

"What's it like?" she asked him a few days later, as he was gathering his things for the competition. At first, he'd thought she meant the euphoria of it, the part he had no words for, but he was learning that Saylor always said what she meant as literally as possible—and so he explained the mechanics of filling your lungs, the weight placed around your neck, the flip and turn and dive, the going down.

"Is it dangerous?" she asked, watching his face.

"Not if you're smart," he said, and he told her about the wall you made inside your mind, the one that protected you, blocked the fear and kept you calm. But she was looking at him sideways now, so he shifted tack, explained about the lanyard that kept you tethered to the line; the plate, set at your pre-chosen depth, that let you know when to stop; the safety divers for backup. By the time he was done, it could have been a ride at Disneyland. He didn't mention the way the blood had foamed out of Larry's mouth at the last competition. The girl who had died.

But hell, you could be hit by a golf ball, just strolling around a course. Get knocked flat, crossing a street. You might as well do what you want, right? What calls to you. What you couldn't not do anyway.

He didn't tell her that part, either. He wanted her to still be there when he came back to the surface.

She was his lucky charm, he told her after the competition— although, like most free divers, he believed in mind over matter, the force of will, the absolute control of his body and its absolute communion with the water. All things that had little to do with chance if you did it right. But he had felt lucky that day. The air he'd drawn into his lungs felt cleaner, fuller; it seemed to last forever on the way down and buoy him back up on his return. When he broke the surface, he lifted his goggles, gave the okay sign, and said the mandatory three words that successfully completed a competitive dive—*I am okay*. And for the first time in his life, he thought they might be true.

He won that competition, and many others after that. Saylor got a job in Florida, where he was teaching free diving and working whatever flexible job he could find.

"A trial run," she said, but she stayed for more than a year, and traveled with him to competitions whenever she could.

She would snorkel, but she wouldn't dive, not deep anyway. She belonged to the church of air, she told him, laughing. He told her about going down into a school of fish so dense and sparkling it felt like swimming through the Milky Way. Of exploring shipwrecks, slipping through places the bulk of a scuba tank would never let you go. Of going down where the water held you tight, then tighter, until you became one with it.

"You're the only thing I need to hold me tight," she said. And he wished that he could say the same. Or rather, he wished that he could wish.

Because he loved her; that much he knew—stunned by her smile and how gracefully life rested upon her. There were times when he yearned to spoon his soul into the warmth of her belief that people were essentially good, and things would always turn out okay. But he couldn't, because he knew she was wrong. The world was not like that. In fact, sometimes it was the ease of her anecdotes about her family, her childhood, that drove him to dive on days when he was already tired. Defying the constraints of lungs, legs. Pushing the edge. Passing it.

People started to notice.

"How you doing, man?" asked Dave after a practice session one day. Dave had been free diving for decades, his skin tanned and tough as a tortoise shell, his flexibility of mind and body legendary. The guru of the deep, and Tyler's mentor for years, even if Tyler could never quite seem to achieve Dave's level of zen.

"I'm fine," Tyler said.

"You can't lie to the water," Dave said, looking into his eyes.

But Tyler always thought the water, the thing that knew him better than anyone, would know that he needed to be there.

"I am your lover. Me," Saylor would say, when his need to be in the water was submerging them, when his rough edges started to become hers.

She had taken the next job offered, in Utah. "You could come with," she said. Tyler looked at photographs—but the canyons, with their narrow rivers so far down in the bottom, just looked to him like so many drained swimming pools.

She heard what he didn't say. "I need a break," she said as she packed her things. That first time, she'd left a few behind, but whether that was for her or him, Tyler didn't know.

After that, Tyler changed to no-fins competitions. He couldn't go as deep, but in many ways it was harder. He set his sights on the next Blue Hole competition, and he pushed himself, down to where he could feel his thoughts expanding far beyond the reach of the lanyard that connected him to the line. Down deep, the mind was everything. The control of it, the ability to get beyond pain, beyond doubt.

Not good enough. Never good enough. His father's voice. And his.

Then back at the Blue Hole, on a practice dive two days before the competition, he proved those words right. As he passed sixty meters, the chemical balance in his blood tipped, nitrogen taking the lead, hallucinations tearing down the wall between discipline and panic. The blackness around him, so vast and welcoming a moment before, grew smaller and smaller as the pressure on his body tightened.

He changed direction, heading up, but as he battled his way back, the depth became his mind and he was gone, out, hauled to the surface by the safety divers, his lungs spewing forth a pink froth when he came to.

"What're you doing, Tyler?" Dave asked him that night at the bonfire on the beach.

"It's all good," Tyler said, but the words wobbled strangely in his head. Still, he went down on a practice dive the next day, even though his lungs felt like they'd been beaten with tire irons.

"How are you?" Saylor asked on the phone, from miles and miles away. They hadn't talked in weeks, and Tyler could tell that Dave had called her. The big competition was the following morning. Tyler had already lied his way through the doctor's evaluation, and they didn't have the kind of equipment here on the island that could verify your honesty. They assumed you wanted to live. People do that.

"I'm going to win," he said.

"Are you?" she asked, and her voice was like the sand in the Blue Hole, soft and falling into nothing.

"I'm fine," he said.

She told him then about her life in Utah, her patients, the trails she hiked, making the case for the normality of dirt and trees and sky. As she talked, he looked out at the water, planning his dive. He'd already chosen his depth, and the plate was set at the right spot, waiting. He'd told them five meters deeper than he'd ever gone, three more than anyone else was going for. He would win.

"Tyler," she said, and he swam back to the phone.

"Yes?"

"There's nobody down there."

He got her point, but he wondered if she knew that it was also his.

The weather was off the next day, the clouds and water slate gray. Nothing dangerous, but it made the other divers jumpy. There had been some bad dives already, and small globs of blood drifted on the water around the start point. But Tyler would never just scrub a dive. He lay on his back in the water, his concentration focused on releasing carbon dioxide and doubts. A harder proposition after his dark dive—but he knew how to rebuild the wall between then and now, and when the countdown began, he filled his lungs, big inhales, then sips, packing every nook and crevice, until it was time to go, and he turned his face to the water.

The first meters were easier than he anticipated, his arms and legs stronger than he had ever felt them, his bare feet propelling him through the resistance until the familiar pull began and he was falling through nothing into darkness again. Only this time it welcomed him. He was a dolphin, a merman, his energy infinite, liquid. He could have cried with the joy, the home of it. He closed his eyes and dove deeper, wanting only more. Down. Down.

Then, suddenly, he was yanked up short. Adrenaline spiked through his body. Grabbed the air from his lungs. He opened his eyes, disoriented, and saw the plate above him, his safety lanyard impossibly tangled below. He'd overshot.

Oh shit. Oh shit. Oh shit.

His fingers, clumsy with panic and the lack of oxygen, fumbled at the knots, getting nowhere. For five precious seconds he considered unclipping the lanyard, but he knew if he passed out before he reached the safety divers, still dozens of meters above him, he would be lost, drifting away. For a moment the idea was tempting, but then some animal part of him surged, deep in his mind, and he did want to come back, with the tag, but also to the surface. He wanted air.

But there wasn't enough. He freed his lanyard, but as he fought his way up, too fast, he knew.

It was a stroke, they told him later. A rogue bubble of air, finding its way to the right side of his brain. Taking away his win, along with control of his left hand and leg, and, apparently, the ability to read the face of the doctor giving him his prognosis. The doctor said something, then chuckled at what must have been a private joke, for Tyler understood only the words. Something about men needing the right hemisphere of the brain more, because women already had the advantage when it came to emotions.

The doctor was an asshole, Tyler thought, and then realized that while the doctor's emotions might be difficult to comprehend, his own were very much intact.

Saylor had come, first to the island, then on to Florida. She didn't say the things she could have, and for that he was grateful. And at first they were united, their goals common. Hand. Leg. Empathy.

If only the latter had come back first, he thought now.

She stayed for months. Through his recurring denials. His one-armed anger. His one-sided bargaining with fate, with science, with her. The questions that would not leave his mind. What would he do without diving? Where could he go? He felt like a fish beating its way around the bottom of a boat, hooked by his own stupidity.

"Find your focus," Saylor would say, holding his face, looking into his eyes. "Put everything you would put into a dive into getting better."

Sometimes, particularly in the beginning, he hated her. Not her, but her indecipherable facial expressions, her two capable hands, her lovely, graceful legs. He knew it wasn't right, the way he felt. Was desperately grateful that she was there. He tried to try, but he kept forgetting. The food on the left side of his plate. The fact that his left leg or hand didn't work the way it should. What the hell was going on in the novels she insisted on reading to him, telling him they would help him see a whole story, teach him compassion again.

She'd smiled when she said *again,* like it might be a joke. He got that much, although he couldn't comprehend what made it one.

"Do you want to call your parents?" Saylor would say sometimes, but Tyler shook his head. There was no way to call just one of them.

In the evenings—after they'd done a second round of physical therapy, after they'd stood together in the shower, her holding him, but not in the way she used to—she'd cue up inspirational movies of paraplegic former Olympic skiers, blind mountain bikers, one-handed rock climbers.

"What's next? *The Miracle Worker?*" he asked.

"How long?" she said.

"What?"

"How long are you going to stay under?"

"Three minutes and forty seconds."

She shook her head in the way that meant frustrated. He was learning that Saylor did not always speak as literally as he had thought.

"I mean," Saylor said, "when are you going to be *here*?"

"I was good, under," he said.

"Were you?" She stood up and went into the kitchen.

Later he heard her on the phone. "I don't know, Lara ..." she was saying. "I can't get in. I don't know how to get in."

Tyler had never heard Saylor like that, so hopeless. Asking for help. And she was wrong, Tyler thought, because she had two functioning legs and she could go anywhere, get in anywhere. Not like him.

Finally, after six months, she turned to him as they sat on the couch.

"I'm not the person for this job," she said.

"I'm not a job."

"Exactly," she replied. The next steps, she said, were up to him. His left hand was functional again; he could get around with a walker. His language skills were fine, if not exactly subtle. She had set up a service to check in on him. A neighbor lady to help with groceries.

She's probably old and smells funny, Tyler thought. *They always do.*

"Tyler." He looked over. "I love you," she said.

He could have said something in return, used the air in his lungs for words, but even now he held on to it. As if letting it go meant that he wouldn't, couldn't, need it for the water again.

She waited, eyes full. Then nodded, once.

"Healing is a choice, Tyler," she said.

The next morning she was gone, leaving only the book on the living room table, its blue-and-yellow cover catching his eye as he maneuvered his way through the empty room, after he'd finally stopped listening for the front door to reopen, finally stopped hoping that she'd just gone out for coffee.

In the kitchen, he made mac and cheese from a box, and brought the pot and a fork, carefully balanced on the seat of the walker, back to the couch. He pushed the book aside to make room for his feet on the coffee table, then turned on the TV and settled in. Scooped the food into his mouth, the cheese a bit gritty against his teeth. He was perfectly fine, he told himself. Sure, he had no idea what he'd do for work, or life, but he could feed himself, shit by himself, make it to the couch without falling down. He could even get into the bathtub, which he did later, filling it to the brim. But the water smelled of nothing—no life, no salt, not even the chlorine of a pool—and when he went under, lying faceup, nose barely covered, his lungs were screaming for air in less than a minute. As if every bit he'd held back from her was of no use at all. He broke the surface and stared at his traitorous body.

The book lay there during those first two weeks after Saylor had left, strange company as he watched sports he couldn't do, movies about people who ran, and wrote, and fell into each other's arms. It was on the day he was reduced to watching a documentary about the private gardens of England that he finally clicked the set off—and as he put down the remote, there was the book. *Theo.*

He'd heard from Saylor, every other day or so, check-ins quick as Ping-Pong. *How're you doing? / I'm okay / Eating? / Yes.* A quick volley—no slams, no spins. No zing to it, Tyler had to admit. But all he wanted was to keep it going, a few more rounds each time, turn it back into a game.

He'd never been into books, and since the stroke, reading had become a bone that he and Saylor tugged over. But sitting there, he remembered how in high school they always said if you wanted to get the girl, you should read the book she was carrying around. Or at least the SparkNotes. There was nothing as sexy as a guy who could talk meaningfully about mockingbirds as he reached for a bra hook. Tyler the merman hadn't needed any of that, but now he pondered Saylor's book, there on the table. A test, perhaps. Or maybe just a clue.

And really, what else did he have to do? The private gardens of England were flat-out boring.

He opened the cover, read the inscription:

For Saylor,
Maybe this will help.
Love, Lara

Help with what? Tyler wondered. He couldn't imagine;

Saylor was so supremely capable. He turned to the first page, curious now.

The book was about a boy. That surprised him at first, but hey, perhaps what Saylor had been looking for was insight into the testosterone side of the fence. So, he began to read, a story about a kid who didn't love water. Tyler almost put the book down at that point—why read about someone who hated the thing you loved? But he could tell from the wear on the pages that Saylor had spent real time with this book, so he kept going, and as he read, at first laboriously, then more rapidly, page after page, something started to happen. As the boy walked through his childhood, the sentences turned into rhythms, Tyler's breath mirroring their movement—take it in, let it out. Take it in, let it out. It felt—it didn't make any sense, but it was true—like swimming. His body calmed. He could feel the story, opening inside him.

He read for hours, going deeper, and the story took him into a garden, which, through the boy's eyes, wasn't a boring thing. It was life, joy coming from the ground, the sentences rolling one into another: the boy, his arms full of glowing red tomatoes, his face suffused with the bounty of what he had created.

Then, out of nowhere, the boy's father.

What you got there?

The words short, sharp, sparking like a lit fuse. Tyler's breath hitched.

The boy turned to his father and Tyler felt the smack of a hard, flat palm against the child's cheek. The flare of pain and shock. Felt the tomatoes spill from his arms, his body curling forward to protect itself, surely, but also, hands out, as if trying to capture all that was falling toward the floor. Felt the nothing in front of him.

He gasped and dropped the book, its opened pages still bearing the imprint of his sweating fingers. Instinctively, he closed his eyes and dove inside himself. *Please. No.* He wanted to go underwater, where it was safe, where he couldn't feel the boy's story.

But it was no good—and he could sense the wall between panic and control starting to break.

It's all about the mind, Tyler. Dave's voice, as they stood by the fire the night before Tyler's last dive.

It's always about the mind, Tyler thought.

Crack went the wall. *Crack.*

Please no, Tyler said. But his father was here now, in his head.

Come here, Tyler. Putting down his briefcase, his voice dry and hot, the day stuck to him like dust. *Now.*

Tyler could feel his father's need to swing his fists, create the wind that would make his day go away. Tyler was just the land the wind moved across. But it was his fault they were here, in this dry, awful place. Didn't he deserve what was coming?

Take it like a man.

All Tyler wanted was to stay in the deep—but there was no air down there. Sooner or later, you'd die. The surface had air, but also fear, and you didn't get one without the other. There was no choice for him, he thought now. Never had been.

You're mine, his father said.

No, Tyler said. And then once again, this time quieter, eyes still closed. *No.*

Deep in his mind, Tyler reached out. Unclipped. Let go.

For a moment there was nothing, just an endless floating; the first, imperceptible shiver of a current. But slowly the force of it began to rise, gathering speed. He could feel the crack in the wall growing and widening, the memories waiting, becoming huge. Suddenly, it all gave way—past and present slammed together and he was doubled over, anger and rage pouring through him.

I hate you. I hate you. I hate you.

And then.

It was not my fucking fault.

When Tyler finally opened his eyes, the living room had grown dark, the afternoon gone. He looked around, at the book on the floor, the blank, black screen of the television set. He was surprised to find himself there, not tossed up on some beach, half-drowned. But he had not drowned; he was here. He was alone, but in a way that meant perhaps he didn't have to be.

Tyler shook his head, reached his right hand across his chest and stretched his left arm, feeling the movement in his shoulder, his neck. Felt this body of his, both old and new. Broken and not. His, in any case.

He took a breath, rubbed his hands across his face, and tasted the sea.

Northern California
2014

The Teenager

The rain started around midnight, sneaking in through the roof of the gardener's shed, turning the Northern California air thick and cold. Nola pulled the blue plastic tarp out of the wheelbarrow and wrapped it around her body. She'd smell like mulch in the morning, but it was better than getting wet. Cotton took forever to dry.

"You should get some Gore-Tex," one of the girls said as Nola came into English class the next morning, her sweatshirt heavy with moisture. "I mean, if you're going to walk to school."

Nola didn't tell her that she had the shortest commute of all, the shed being at the edge of the school grounds.

It had been two months, and nobody had caught on. Hard to believe, Nola thought sometimes. But this was a *good* school, attended by *good* people, and some, like her, on scholarships. Scholarships, Nola had learned, were like a door to invisibility, or at least homogeneity. Once in, the good deed done, you were to be considered the same, right down to the casual, socially progressive sweatshirt and pants of your school uniform. The shiny kids had been told from the time they were toddlers that it was rude to point out differences. Not okay to beat up the gay kid. Or the fat one. Or tease the girl who came to first period with her hair wet. At least, not in a way that could get you caught.

"I think it's great that you can just let your hair air-dry," the girl, Tina, continued with a toss of her shimmering red curls. "Mine takes forever in the morning."

So polite. As their English teacher entered and the class settled into their seats, Nola wondered how much further Tina would take it if she knew about the towel in Nola's locker, the one that wouldn't really dry, would get that slightly moldy smell that made Nola's stolen morning showers in the school locker room even less appealing.

Strange, how it was the smells that got to her. Cold, she could take. Damp, even. But that hint of mildew, the whiff of pesticides or fertilizer following her wherever she went. The perfume of her now-life, an aromatic confession to the kids around her. Their noses knew something had changed. They shifted in their seats, moving away; they avoided her at lunch, but still they didn't seem to put it all together. Humans weren't good that way.

Animals were different. A polar bear, Nola had read, could smell a seal through three feet of ice. A male silk moth could recognize the scent of a female from six miles away, while elephants could track water across twelve. These were the facts Nola read at night, using the precious batteries in her flashlight. It beat thinking about the bottle of vodka the gardener kept stashed behind the bag of weed and feed. She couldn't touch the bottle, wouldn't touch it, although every part of her yearned to. She didn't want alcohol; that wasn't the point. What she wanted was sleep, and alcohol might have gotten her there.

Because, of all the things she missed from her old life—and there were many, although fewer at the end—what she missed most was the deep sleep of childhood. That sprawled-across-your-bed, arms-flung-wide-to-the-world sleep. The luxury of un-interruption, instead of listening all night to the noises outside, each of them maybe a human. Best-case scenario, she'd get ratted out. Worst case was what kept her pushed into the back corner of the shed like a child in a closet, staring at the lockless door, ears focused with an intensity that left them buzzing.

Pigeons, her book said, have a remarkable sense of hearing, able to detect even impending storms and earthquakes. They are also one of the few species, other than humans, that can recognize themselves in a mirror. That morning, as Nola had faced the image of her wet self over the locker room sink, she'd wondered about the scientists who devised that experiment. Why give a perfectly happy animal a mirror?

"Nola," the teacher said now, "did you hear my question?"

The story everybody told about Nola, the version she let them tell because it held a drama that was an armor all its own, was that she and her parents had been in a car accident when she was twelve. Her father tragically killed. Her mother injured, but she'd battled her way back, and managed, barely, to support her daughter, brilliant Nola, who had been unscathed in the accident but deserved some financial assistance, even though it was five years later and other mothers might, perhaps, have gotten their act together.

But that wasn't a nice thing to say, so it was only whispered.

What the story didn't say: the garden-variety carelessness of that accident. The myopically missed stop sign, the truck, the rip and shriek of metal, the heaving-in of their car, her father. The second truck, the metaphorical one that hit her mother, later.

"Nola, what does the albatross stand for in the poem?" the teacher, Ms. Hildegrand, asked her now. And Nola knew the answer, of course, because she *was* smart, but also because she knew what symbols and metaphors were. The things that helped you imagine the unimaginable.

Lunch was the high and low point of the day, although perhaps any high school student would tell you that, for as many different reasons as there are teenagers. For Nola, lunch meant food. Warm, real, subsidized—her little school credit card filled with charity, her currency as good as anyone else's, even if the color was different. But she could eat, and god, it tasted good.

"Can you believe how soggy this lettuce is?" Tina's voice carried from across the cafeteria as she poked at her salad like a seagull. Nola, by herself, ate her french fries and burger. She knew they'd probably make her face break out, but starches and protein lasted, and that's what she needed. It was going to be cold again tonight.

Nola watched as Tina laughed, twirling her fork. It was fascinating, in its own way. Nola had read that females dominate in less than 10 percent of the seventy-six mammalian species that have leaders. Humans, somehow, were not included in that list, perhaps because humans liked to think they were somehow different, or perhaps because male dominance was assumed. All Nola knew was that anyone who thought males ruled in a high school environment was not paying attention. Tina could wield that fork of hers like a queen's scepter bestowing knighthood, or the claws of a lioness. And if there was anything Tina loved, it was someone else's secret. Nola had watched her rip them open like packages wrapped especially for her, tossing the contents out to her adoring subjects.

The best way to survive, as any animal at the low end of the food chain understood, was to stay out of sight. Nola had experienced what happened when people found out, when they *helped*. That eight months in foster care when she was fourteen, after she'd found her mother unconscious on the floor and called the ambulance. When Nola got back to her mother, she'd sworn she'd never let any of those people get their hands on her again. Sworn she'd stay in this golden ticket of a school. All she needed now was to get to June and graduate. She'd been offered a scholarship at the local college, the last piece of mail she received before she had to make the decision between three weeks' rent or five months' food. It could still all work, she told herself, so long as no one found out that she didn't know where her mother was anymore.

It was not a small secret. But she'd been keeping secrets for a while now, and she knew how to stay low. Solo. Wood frogs can freeze for an entire winter and come back to life in the spring. Swifts can fly for six months without touching the ground.

Long ago, before the accident, Nola and her mother used to watch nature shows together. At night, if Nola had a bad dream, her mother would climb in bed with her, take her hand.

"Did you know, Nola, that otters sleep holding hands?" she would say. "All night long, so they don't lose each other."

A group of otters was a raft. A group of lions was called a pride. Sometimes in the shed, Nola would reach out and take the padded strap of her backpack into her hand. Hold it, all night long.

Nola's favorite hours of the day were between three in the afternoon—when school was over—and seven, when the public library closed. *She's such a diligent student,* the other parents said to their kids, which helped no one at all. But what did help Nola was the heat in the building. She'd burrow into the armchair near the radiator, bringing as much of the warmth as she could into her body. It wouldn't last outside; she knew that. But sometimes she felt like it was slipping into the book she was reading, and then, when she opened it later in the shed, she could pretend the light on the pages was the heat coming back out.

And in some ways, it was. When Nola was young, her mother used to tell her that books were like a giant neighborhood where every family was different, and every door was open.

"You can just go on in," she'd tell Nola. "Try on a new life. See how it fits."

After the accident, though, Nola's mother had decided that pills were a more efficient means of escape. There were so many kinds of pain, Nola learned. Some days, her mother would just sit at the kitchen table staring at her hands, although they were unscarred, having been on the wheel.

During this intermediate time, when the trajectory was bad but still, perhaps, alterable, books had taken on a different role for Nola. Cookbooks, so the world was not reduced to Cheerios. Home maintenance manuals, for the sparking outlet, the dripping faucet, and later, to help shore up the increasingly rugged apartments that took the place of their house. Novels, because novels were company that kept your secrets, would never look at you and your mother as if you were failing a test you couldn't study for. Novels, because of that time Nola had once, at the age of fifteen, opened her mother's pill bottle, thinking to take one herself, then stopped. Decided there had to be another neighborhood. A different door.

And there was, there were. The lives in the books not hers, but the pain and tangled love so often the same, creating a community of sorts. Books answered the questions she couldn't ask people. *Why can't I save my mother? Why can't she save herself? How can I love so much and be so angry at the same time?* The protagonist could be a thousand miles or two hundred years away; it didn't matter. In fact, in some ways the distance made it better. In some ways, reading about fictional people was like reading about animals, that little bit of distance making it all seem closer, more understandable.

A group of books is a raft, Nola had told her mother a few years ago, but her mother just shook her head, her eyes two-pills-in and fuzzy.

"What are you talking about, Nola?" she asked.

After 7 P.M., when the library closed, was harder. If Nola was lucky, she'd have had the library bathroom to herself long enough to get hot water in the faucet, add it to the Top Ramen in her mug, and slurp it all down, the noodles the wrong side of al dente, the flavor packet turned into little land mines of salt floating in the water. Still, better than cold, later.

Now she was heading back to the shed, via the grocery

store. Time for a restock on provisions. When your world has to fit in a backpack, you shop like a French matron: once every couple of days. After Tina's trip to Paris a couple years ago, she'd gone on and on about the tiny refrigerator in their apartment, the stylish women with their string shopping bags buying a slim baguette, two apples, an onion.

Ooh la la, Nola said, pushing open the door of the discount grocery store.

Sometimes, when she was stuck in a long checkout line with her three packs of Top Ramen and a box of granola bars or tampons, her gaze would wander over the magazines and land on a helpful headline about the aspirational beauty of owning less, and a fury would rise up in her so bright and hot she wondered that it didn't burn the place down.

According to the magazine, Nola should be the freest of them all, released of physical possessions as she was. What she had: a few packets of laundry soap, a comb, an extra T-shirt and pair of socks, a flashlight, a can of Mace, a spoon, a mug, and three pairs of underwear, stuffed at the bottom of her pack so they wouldn't fall out and expose a different story than the one Nola told: *My mother can't come to parent night; she's sick.*

Not a hard lie to tell, or even a new one. Nola's mother had been sick for years. Nola had been signing her own permission slips and school forms since she was thirteen. It was the address part that had gotten trickier, their domiciles like a series of Russian nesting dolls growing increasingly smaller until, finally, it was just Nola and the gardening shed. Her signature on a form was not a stealing of identity anymore, for if the person was no longer there, had simply left, leaving nothing behind, what was there to steal?

Now, as she waited in line behind a mother with a feisty toddler, Nola leafed through a magazine full of gorgeous actors with perfect lives and effortless smiles. Once upon a time, Nola had bought into that myth. She'd had a poster on her bedroom wall: one of those golden boys, base jumping off some building that reached up into the clouds. Back then, she'd believed in invincibility. In men running faster than bullets. In girls who could fly. In cars, flipping over and over down a ravine, their occupants emerging, hair barely mussed.

In front of her, the young mother's boxes of fruit leather and Oaty-O's beeped their way across the scanner and into a bag. As Nola waited, she made little rips in the pages of the magazine. One rip for each beep. Not big, but it felt good.

The upside of winter was that darkness came earlier, so Nola could retreat to the shed without worrying about people seeing her. That made for a long night, however, and this one was windy. She supposed that in some ways, she was lucky. She could be living in Montana or Vermont, somewhere it truly froze, and she did have the sleeping bag she'd hidden under a stack of burlap sacks near the lawn mower—but still, this was cold enough, thank you.

Nola crawled into her sleeping bag, opened her backpack, and took out the book that Ms. Hildegrand had assigned for English class, its cover blue and yellow, the title simple:

Theo. Normally, their syllabus would include *The Catcher in the Rye*, but Ms. Hildegrand said there was nothing wrong with expanding one's horizons. The change pleased Nola, who'd never been a fan of Holden's angst. It would have been nice if his replacement had been female, but a book in a shed was a port in a storm. She opened the cover, read the first line—and stopped on the last word. *Lost.*

Nola knew *lost.* Over the past five years, she'd watched her mother lose herself one piece at a time—love, compassion, imagination disappearing like paper maps flying out a speeding car window, replaced by guilt and grief and an overwhelming desire for oblivion. At first, Nola's mother had tried, worked the only jobs she was qualified for, read Nola's school assignments when she got home. But in the end, she couldn't hold on to that or anything else, and Nola had never known, not really, if her mother let go, went under, because she had loved Nola's father more, or because she knew Nola could never completely forgive her.

Not because Nola hadn't tried. More because, in a far back part of her mind, in some inexplicable but completely logical way, forgiving her mother felt like betraying her father. And loyalty was all she had left to give him.

The wind hit the side of the shed with a loud thump and Nola looked up, instinctively sending the beam of the flashlight across the wall, even though she knew it could alert someone that she was here. She snapped it off. Listened. Nothing.

You're okay. You're okay.

After a few minutes, she turned the flashlight back on, searching the corners of the shed the way she used to check the locks on every door in their house. There was no lock here, and not much space to check, but she did it anyway.

As the light roved across the rakes and shovels and bags, it illuminated a new object. A protein bar, lying on the rough boards of the potting bench next to a spade. The gardener must have left it behind by accident.

She knew she couldn't touch it. What if he noticed its absence? If she got caught, she'd have to leave, and there was nowhere smaller for her to live.

Crap, she thought. The vodka she could resist, but she was so hungry. The cold took it out of her, burning its way through that stupid cup of Top Ramen before she could even get into the sleeping bag. *Why did he have to leave a protein bar?* Nola wondered. And it was one of the good ones, too. Chocolate that didn't taste like sawdust. The kind where the flavor stayed in your mouth, rather than sticking to the roof of it.

Read, Nola, she told herself. *Don't think about food.*

Two hours later she reached out, took the crinkling plastic into her hand, ripped the wrapper open, and ate the thing in four bites.

Stupid, stupid, stupid, she told herself, even as she was chewing.

She overslept the next morning, the wind having stolen most of the night from her. Arriving in class groggy and disheveled, she managed to slip into her seat just as Ms. Hildegrand walked in the door. The kids around her were talking about plans for midwinter break, the places they'd go.

"So," Ms. Hildegrand said, breaking into the conversations, "how are we feeling about *Theo*?"

Nola wished she had an answer, but between the wind and lusting after the protein bar, she'd only read half the assignment. Even that she barely remembered. It wasn't like her, but not much was right now.

The class rustled like anxious chickens; clearly, she wasn't the only one who'd come unprepared. Ms. Hildegrand was unperturbed, however, and went to the whiteboard and wrote a sentence:

You get what they give you.

"What do you think?" she asked, then added helpfully, "He's talking about parents here."

"I wish my parents would give me the Caribbean," Gerard commented from the back of the room. "We just keep going to bloody Aspen."

Nola turned slightly to look at him. You couldn't not. Gerard was beautiful, his legs stretched out in front of him like freedom itself. He was famous for rerouting class discussions, but he always did it in a way that seemed more fun than confrontational, so he got away with it.

"You're lucky," Tina said. "The islands are getting so crowded these days. My mom had to reserve our house for spring break nine months in advance."

"I'm not sure that's what the author was going for," Ms. Hildegrand said.

The students turned reluctantly back toward the front of the class. That was the thing about Ms. Hildegrand. She wasn't cool, or scary. She was in her midthirties, Nola guessed, and probably could have pulled off the I'm-one-of-you fashion style so many teachers in progressive schools liked to adopt. But she didn't. She just *was*. And there was something about that that made the kids treat her with as much respect as they could give any teacher. She reminded Nola of a great blue heron, standing out on a sandbar, patient as the day was long.

Her watchful eyes slid over Nola, pausing for just a moment, then continued to the girl behind her.

"Kerry, what do you think?" Pointing at the whiteboard: *You get what they give you.*

Kerry put her hand on the book on her desk, as if to draw the answer out through its cover.

"Maybe it's like a present? Like a dog."

Christ, Nola thought. *There's literal, and then there's* literal.

"Perhaps," Ms. Hildegrand said, nodding her head. "But I'm wondering if we could push that a bit more."

Here it comes. Here it comes.

"Nola?" she asked.

Nola hadn't read that part of the book, but she had learned over time that most words, even those that weren't metaphors, have more than one meaning. *I love you. I'm sorry. It won't happen again.*

She looked at Ms. Hildegrand and could see by her teacher's reaction that she had let too much show in her face.

"I think," Nola said carefully, "it means that kids believe what they're told."

After class, Ms. Hildegrand called out to Nola as she was leaving the room.

"Got a second?" she said.

Nola gave a quick look at the clock over the door. "I'm late," she said. "Mr. Osterhout will kill me if I'm not to chemistry class on time. Tomorrow?" she added, to be polite. And slipped out.

One of the tricks of her situation, Nola had learned, was never falling for fiction. Letting your loneliness tempt you into the fantasy of the handsome football star who inexplicably falls for the unkempt outcast. The mean girl who ends up seeing the light. The big-hearted teacher who notices what no one else does and saves the day. Characters like that were what had made Nola stop reading YA. Even vampires were more realistic.

When Nola got home that night—*Funny, how quickly something becomes normal,* she thought, not for the first time—she checked the shed carefully, to see if the gardener had gotten suspicious and discovered her sleeping bag. But everything was where it should be, except now there was a dark blue scarf hanging on the hook near the door. That wasn't so unusual; it had warmed up a bit that afternoon, and the gardener must have forgotten it on his way out.

Everything is fine, Nola told herself.

She inhaled slowly, calming her breathing, and smelled something new, filtering through the scents of mulch and fertilizer—woodsmoke. Not new, old, faded like the far side of a dream.

She followed the scent to the scarf, put her face in the soft fabric, and breathed in. The scent surrounded her, and without even thinking, she was by a campfire, the redwoods tall around her, snuggling into her father while he told her stories until the last log burned out. He'd loved camping. Her mother hadn't, not so much, so it was always just the two of them.

We're pioneers, Nola, he'd say. *Braving the world.*

He'd taught her about staying dry and tying knots, how to sleep when the world felt big around you. It had felt like playing, at the time.

Don't go there, Nola, she told herself now. The nights were long enough already.

She pulled out her sleeping bag, took her book and flashlight from her pack, and put them on the bench nearby. She stood there for a moment, looking down at her camp. Then, before she could reconsider, she unhooked the scarf and wrapped it around her neck. She would put it near the mulch for a while later, she told herself, to cover up her smell. But morning was still a ways off.

The scarf seemed to cast its own spell. Tonight, the wind was quiet, the cold a bit less, the book in her hand a friend, company, the way she was used to. She'd been reading for an hour, hunkered down in her sleeping bag, when the boy in the book picked up the tomatoes and got ready to carry them into the house.

Something was coming. Nola could feel it. She wanted to stop reading, but she couldn't, because she could tell that this was the moment that would rip the boy's life into a before and after. Fiction and reality. She knew the lesson that moment taught you—that everything you believed was yours, all the cinnamon toast and hugs and campfires, was just something you'd visited, not something you were guaranteed as a generic human being, a special human child. No. You were the ant on the counter, heading for sugar. The mouse on the way to the cheese. Your time was short and real, and even if you survived, you would know now that there was always a hand, metaphorical or not, waiting above you.

But the boy in the book hadn't had time to contemplate such philosophical thoughts. Not yet. He was still standing there, stained with tomatoes. In the moment, as they say.

And Nola wouldn't stop reading because she couldn't leave him there alone.

Which meant another bleary-eyed morning in English class. Nola had, regretfully, left the scarf behind in the shed. She would have liked to have brought it. She'd worn it the whole night, its scent accompanying her as she followed the boy's story, watched him grow and fight both his father and himself. But she could only bring the boy with her to class, his thoughts mingled into hers until she wasn't sure where the division was.

It had always been that way for Nola, those days when she was caught deep in a book and the character lingered with her even when she wasn't reading, her dreams someone else's story, her vision that of someone else's eyes. Nola's mother used to joke that she was an *Octopus cynea,* a species that changed its colors to match its surroundings, its skill so subtle it could even mimic the passing shadows of clouds overhead.

"You go so deep," her mother said when ten-year-old Nola surfaced from her most recent book.

And Nola had imagined a sea of words, an ocean of possible colors.

In the years after the accident, reading had changed for Nola, the characters becoming lifelines. Karana of the Island. Meg Murry. Francie Nolan. Melba Beals. Beryl Markham. Katniss. Lisbeth. Escape hatches turning into flight plans. Their words, hers. Their lives, hers.

Her life, hers.

As long as nobody found out what that really meant.

"Oh my god, I explicitly told them soy milk," Tina announced as she entered the room, a white to-go cup raised in her hand like Lady Liberty's torch. "Idiots."

Nola considered Tina. In the spectrum of natural survival techniques, Tina was less *Octopus cyanea* and more *Arapaima gigas,* an Amazonian fish with scales so thick not even piranhas could chew through them. Tina's protection was made of iron-clad truths: hair products really did make a difference. Only losers ate gluten. Only unintelligent people were poor, or baristas. A simpler way of interacting with the world, although it did make the gray areas of literature and life a bit trickier.

Ms. Hildegrand had once floated the idea that Nola and Tina could study *To Kill a Mockingbird* together. *Trade some ideas,* she'd said hopefully. But that was last year, when Ms. Hildegrand was still new to the school.

"So," Ms. Hildegrand said now, holding up the copy of *Theo* to mark the official beginning of class, "anybody have some thoughts they want to share?"

Danielle—who had gotten into Yale but had heard the prize could be snatched away at the first sign of declining grades—was ready.

"I think the Christ imagery is fascinating," she said.

Nola settled in. Danielle was a big fan of Christ imagery, finding it, like Waldo, in every book they read.

"Really?" Ms. Hildegrand said. "Tell me more."

"Well, there's the whole question of Theo's paternity. It's unclear if he's actually his father's son."

Danielle did get points for close reading, Nola thought. The issue had been raised in a single sentence, an unproven insinuation that swam like a shark underneath the rest of the story. Subtle almost to the point of obscurity—and the knowledge that Danielle had seen it, too, gave Nola a feeling of communion. But the fact that the biblical Joseph was rather supportive of his wife and son, while Theo's father beat the shit out of both of them, seemed to render the comparison a bit shaky.

"You know what I don't get?" Tina interjected. Nola turned her face down toward her book so her smile wouldn't show. The possibilities were endless.

"I don't get the mother," Tina said. "She was just so passive. How could she stay?"

It wasn't the worst question, Nola thought. There had been times last night when she'd wanted to jump into the book and protect the boy herself. None of this was his fault. And his mother just stood there. In pain, sure, but not moving. Not saving him.

Do your damn job, Nola had wanted to yell at her.

"I mean," Tina continued, "you just can't let people treat you like that."

And there it is, Nola thought, her mind yanked back to the classroom. Tina's ubiquitous *you,* almost always partnered with its good friend *just.* Like her fork, the combo could be wielded in so many ways. *You can do anything if you just try hard enough.* Or: *You just have to get over it.* Or: *Just say no* (the *you* so obvious as to not even need inclusion). Its more obviously plural form—*you people*—had been carefully scrubbed from Tina's vocabulary by their progressive school, but it lingered, under the surface.

"It's not that simple," Nola said.

"But it is," Tina insisted, turning in her seat to draw the support of the rest of the class. "You just have to draw a line. I'd be out of there the first time someone hit me."

That, Nola thought, *is where the confusion lies.* In Tina's belief that the *you* and the *I* in those sentences, in any sentence, could ever be interchangeable. In her rock-solid certainty that lines could be drawn once and never move, never feel the wash of water over sand, shifting each grain to a new position. Day after wave after day.

God, I am sick of this girl, Nola thought. How many hours of her life had she spent studying Tina's opinions, habits, quirks, just to stay off her radar? Had Tina ever once had to do the same? Maybe it was the shed, or the cold, or the fact that she'd just found a piece of bark hidden in her hair, but Nola snapped.

"*You,*" Nola said. "*You* would. Not her."

Tina's eyes went wide, then narrowed.

Shit, Nola thought, her anger crashing into reality. *What have I done?* She could hear her mother's voice, in the years after the accident, when Nola was still asking for the things her old self wanted—a new book, the sweater everyone else had, heat on in the house. *We don't have the safety net for that,* her mother would say.

"What?" Tina asked. Throughout the classroom, chairs shifted in anticipation.

"Tell us what you see, Nola," Ms. Hildegrand interjected. "Tell us about the mother."

Nola took a breath. Tried to concentrate. How was she going to get through lunch if Tina was on the warpath? Nola needed to eat; the fatigue was making her even hungrier than usual.

And besides, she didn't know how to answer Ms. Hildegrand's question; she had, after all, been firmly team Theo until Tina started taking potshots at his mom.

"Well," Nola said, buying time, "I just think it's more complicated than that. I mean, where would his mother have gone? They lived in the back of beyond. There was no one to help her."

It was true, Nola realized.

Tina leaned forward, opened her mouth. Nola continued quickly, "And what if Danielle's right about Theo's parentage? How does that change things?"

Danielle looked both pleased and appalled to be thrust into the fray. "The guilt would be incredible," she said, nodding.

Yes, it would, Nola thought. She'd pitched the question to Danielle in the interest of diversion, but now she wondered: *How did the feeling of guilt change Theo's mother's life? Even if it was just a question, the shark underneath the water. If you think you deserve to be eaten, how do you leave the ocean?*

And in that moment, she saw her mother at the wheel of the car in the moment before everything changed, laughing at the joke Nola's father had just told them, looking over at him, her eyes lit the way they always were when he made her smile. A moment of inattention, or perhaps exactly the opposite. Too much attention, in what had always been the right direction until then. Death by adoration.

How do you live with that? Nola wondered. And she realized then that the answer was simple—you don't. Not in any way that your old self might recognize. Not in any way that does you any good.

"I don't care." Tina remained adamant. "A good mother would do anything for her child."

"Maybe she's not a good mother," Nola said slowly. "Maybe she's just human."

The words knocked around in her head, arranged themselves back into sentences, and then went quiet. Waiting.

Oh god, Nola thought.

All those fictional lives she had opened herself to, taking on their experiences, their emotions, like the good octopus she was—and the one story she had refused was her mother's.

Now here it was. The door open. And Nola understood that in this story, her father would not be her father, but her mother's husband. The love of her mother's life. The person she had killed. Unintentionally, yes, but that didn't matter, because you had done it and now all you wanted was to stay in the dark with him. But you couldn't—because here was your daughter, who had your husband's hands but her own eyes, eyes that watched you all the time, asking, needing. And you wanted to give, you did, but there was no one to give to you. No person, anyway. So you took whatever you needed to get through that moment, so you could stand the guilt, the pain, stay a bit longer. Except the equation kept shifting; you kept needing more and staying for less until the thing you needed was so much bigger than the reason. And then you were in the dark, for real.

It's so cold in there, Nola thought.

She looked up and saw Ms. Hildegrand watching her, eyes full of questions.

Nola was out of class before Ms. Hildegrand could call her back. She had to get somewhere quiet, alone. She went out the back of the school building; the trash bins were there, but also a beautiful view of the green and rolling grounds. And beyond those hills were places she'd never been.

It was so ironic, she thought, standing there, how her family always seemed to see things too late. Stop signs. Warning signals. The possibility of other worlds.

The last time she'd seen her mother, Nola had been heading off to school. It had been a bad month. They had six weeks' worth of rent in their bank account, if they didn't eat, so that was just funny math. Her mother had lost her last job, and *last* was now seeming more like *final* than *most recent*. The furnishings in their studio apartment had become a pure example of minimalism—a couch, a table, two chairs. Nola's bed was a sleeping bag her father had given her years before. A good one, soft with down. *Sleep is the most important thing when you're out in the wild,* he'd said, and he'd gotten her an adult size, even though she was only ten. *An investment in the future. Prescient,* Nola thought later.

That morning Nola had seen her mother do the scan— her eyes wandering over their remaining possessions, searching for value, landing on the sleeping bag.

"No fucking way," Nola had said. She'd grabbed the

sleeping bag and taken it with her, stashing it in the trees behind the gardening shed on campus.

When she got home, there was a note. *I'm sorry.* Her mother was gone, along with half their savings. Nola went to the bank, took out the rest. At the end of the month, when the landlord came for the rent, she gave him the key and left.

And now, here she was, standing by a bunch of trash cans.

She'd been so hopelessly angry, for so many years. Angry at the loss of something so unutterably dear to her. Then, later, angry that her mother couldn't be her father, couldn't hold down his job, their house, their life. Couldn't just get over it, get on with it, so Nola didn't have to. Her anger a precious bonfire, keeping her warm.

I don't need you. The last words Nola had said as she'd left for school that day. And her mother had looked at her and said, her voice oddly clear, *Did you know, Nola, that a human heart is the same size as a fist?*

"Oh, Mom," Nola whispered now. "I'm sorry."

The back door banged open, and she heard Kerry's voice. "Do we really have to be by the trash cans?"

Nola wiped her eyes and stepped carefully back. She was on the other side of the bins, but if they came farther out, they'd see her.

"It's so deliciously slummy back here." Tina. Again. The girl was like a zombie that wouldn't die.

Nola smelled a lit match, cigarette smoke.

"God, I needed that," Tina said.

"Yeah, what the hell got into crazy girl today?" Kerry said.

"Who knows," Tina said. "Did you see she had bark in her hair? It's like she sleeps in the woods or something." Their disbelieving laughter rolled down the hill.

"Hey." Nola heard a male voice and glanced up to see the gardener. He could easily see her, but he was looking at Tina and Kerry.

"Oooops," Tina said. "Sorry."

"Put it out," he said. "Get inside."

He stood there, his Carhartt coat stiff and worn, his work boots caked with mud, his hair brown and curly and just a bit too long. In his late thirties, maybe, but his expression looked older. Tired, almost angry, but in a free-floating way that Nola recognized, understood.

"Yes, sir," Tina said, and Nola could almost see her mock salute. There was the sound of her two-hundred-dollar boot grinding the cigarette into the pavement.

"Thanks," the gardener said, and started down the hill.

"You know he's a veteran?" Kerry's voice was low. "He's got PTSD. My mom says we should be nice."

"Thank you for your service!" Tina called out cheerily to his retreating form.

The gardener turned back. But when he nodded, once, crisply, he was looking straight at Nola. Then he turned again and headed down the hill.

"See what I mean?" Kerry said, her voice still low. "His eyes can't even focus right."

The door opened and the girls went back inside.

He knows, Nola thought.

Nola stayed at the back of the building through lunchtime. She'd be hungry later; she was hungry now, for that matter, but she had to figure out what she was going to do. If the gardener told the principal, she'd be sent to foster care again. Would they even let her stay in this school? And if by some miracle he kept her secret, she'd be putting his job at risk. She wasn't that selfish.

But she had to graduate; she was so close. It was what she had left.

Get a grip, Nola, she told herself. *Just act like everything's fine.*

She ate her last granola bar to keep her stomach quiet, and walked back into the building, got through calculus, history, the last bell. Her plan, developed while the rest of the students in her history class discussed the finer points of the New Deal, was to check out the gazebo in the park. She'd noticed a hole in the lattice underneath. Maybe there was a spot there, if somebody or something wasn't already using it.

"Nola." She heard Ms. Hildegrand's voice as she was opening the side door of the school, almost out. "Can I talk to you?"

Here it comes.

Ms. Hildegrand ushered her into an empty classroom. Nola took a seat, not knowing what else to do. Ms. Hildegrand leaned against the desk. On a different day, they might have been about to have an ordinary conversation. Ms. Hildegrand was one of the few teachers who really would stop you to ask about your day, how you were doing. More than once, Nola had been inclined to tell her. That was almost harder than not being asked in the first place, that desire to tell someone, to have someone hear. *I'm hungry. I'm scared. I love my mother. I hate my mother. I don't know where she is.*

Now she waited. Ms. Hildegrand met Nola's eyes, then looked off to the side. The principal must have picked her to deliver the news, hoping to lighten the impact. Like that trick ever worked. Nola's stomach started eating itself.

"I have two children ..." Ms. Hildegrand started off. "Eight and five."

Ahhh ... Nola thought. The old *I'm a mother so this is hard on me, too* approach. Ms. Hildegrand hated clichés, and that one was a whopper. Nola almost felt sorry for her.

"Anyway," Ms. Hildegrand continued, "the young woman who's been helping us, her mother is sick."

I get it. You understand about sick mothers. You're a good person. Really, why couldn't people just tell you the bad stuff quickly?

"So, she had to go back home ..."

How much does she know?

"And I could really use some help . . ." Ms. Hildegrand said.

What?

". . . after school—and for the summer, too, ideally . . ."

Please.

". . . I mean, I can only afford room and board and maybe a little more . . ."

Please.

"Would you consider doing it?" Ms. Hildegrand's gaze shifted back to Nola, reading her face. "Would your mother let you?" That last part casual, light as a dragonfly.

"Yes," Nola said. There was no other word in her vocabulary for this.

"The kids are great, really," Ms. Hildegrand added.

"Yes," Nola said. She didn't care if Ms. Hildegrand's children were aliens fallen to earth. In her imagination, she was at the park, kicking the gazebo to bits. *I will never never never sleep under you.*

A house, she thought. A bed. Food. A family. Not hers, never hers, but still a planet to orbit. Gravity to hold her down to earth.

"That's great," Ms. Hildegrand said, nodding. Then, almost as an afterthought, "I think it might be easier if we didn't tell a lot of people about this. Would that be okay with you?"

These things don't happen in real life. Nola's brain reminded her.

But the rest of her just said, *The hell with that.*

Nola had read that when a female bat gives birth, she does it hanging upside down, catching the baby in her wings as it falls. Reality has plenty of miracles.

"Yes," Nola said.

Ms. Hildegrand gave Nola her address, told her dinner was at six. Nola went to the shed to get her sleeping bag. She'd figure out a way to smuggle it into Ms. Hildegrand's house without anyone seeing. If they were going to pretend ignorance of Nola's situation, she needed to at least respect the pretense.

When she opened the shed door, she saw the sleeping bag, folded neatly on the bench.

So it was *him,* she thought. There had been a moment, when Ms. Hildegrand was talking, when Nola had wondered if her teacher had figured it out all on her own. But no. The gardener hadn't gone to the principal, though; that much was obvious.

Nola started forward to pick up the sleeping bag.

"You going to be okay?"

She turned fast. The gardener was standing a few feet away, off to her right.

It takes a lot of silence to be that quiet in such a small space, Nola thought.

She nodded. "You told her?"

He nodded back. "I hope that's okay."

"Yeah," she said.

"She helped me get this job," he said, then added, "We were in foster care together for a couple years when we were kids."

Nola nodded, seeing now. They stood, not saying anything.

"Do you know," he said after a while, "when the Allies bombed Berlin, what the first thing was they hit?"

She shook her head, imagining buildings, platoons, tanks. He was far too young to have been in that war. Where was he going with this?

"An elephant," he said.

"What the hell?" Nola said.

"Life," he said, shrugging his shoulders. "Sometimes it just lands on you."

Nola couldn't help it. She looked to the corner where the vodka bottle was hidden.

"And sometimes you need a little help," he said. "Take the good kind, Nola." He collected his gardening gloves and walked past her to the door. "Good luck," he said, and headed off.

After he was gone, Nola took the two steps to the bench. As she picked up her sleeping bag, she saw the blue scarf, carefully tucked in the top.

It stopped her, the small grace of the gesture. She stood there for a moment, and then raised the scarf to her nose. Smelled the scent of herself. The shed. Campfires. She held it all close, and then unzipped her backpack and put the scarf inside. It slid down next to the book, the blue wool meeting the blue-and-yellow cover. She thought of the gardener, and the boy inside the pages, fighting, finding a way out of a life he had not made.

She pulled the book out and left it on the bench. She'd find another copy. She'd get in trouble for losing this one, but she didn't care.

Maybe I'll just say it's wandering, she thought.

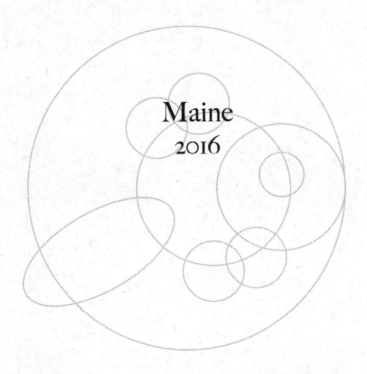

Maine
2016

The Bookseller

In Kit's experience, most authors who came into a bookstore would introduce themselves, preening in the presence of their works like unfurling peacocks. But the young woman had simply picked up a book, paid for it, and exited.

"Do you know who that was?" The bookstore manager had come out from the back and was watching the woman walk by the store's plate-glass window, off into the rest of her life. "That was Alice Wein."

Kit knew the name. Her book, *Theo*, had come out about four years earlier and was a steady seller in their Local Maine Writers display. Not Stephen King numbers, but a respectable amount. Kit had yet to read the book—faced with the weekly Tuesday tsunami of new titles, he'd let word of mouth and the little paper shelf talker do the selling. But while *Theo*'s author was known to be reclusive, she lived about ten miles outside of town, so a visit to their store was not out of the realm of possibility. If Kit had been paying attention, he might have put two and two together.

The manager shot Kit a look. Kit knew it—that *get your head in the game* glare he'd received throughout his life when his mind had wandered off to more interesting realms.

"We could've gotten her to sign stock," the manager said, shaking his head. Then he took over the front desk and sent Kit to the back room to unpack the UPS boxes.

If the back room was supposed to be a punishment, it never worked that way. In all the steps needed to take a story from writer to reader, the unpacking of a box in a bookstore was a ridiculously small one, and yet to Kit it always felt like being at a party where the books were the guests of honor. He liked to take each one from the box, raising it slightly in the air.

May I present the honorable Great Gatsby/Snow Child/ Olive Kitteridge . . .

In the third box he found three copies of *Theo. Yes*, Kit thought, *signing stock would have come in handy*. Customers loved that special touch—the author meeting up with the finished product, writing on its title page, sending the book off into the world for a second time. *This was mine; now it's yours*. A kind of literary communion.

Kit turned the book over and looked at the photo on the back. There was nothing remarkable about the author: a pale young woman with dark hair. But he'd heard customers rave about *Theo*, and he felt guilty for not recognizing her, so he took one of the copies and set it aside. Maybe it was time to change that.

Time. He checked his watch. 5:10 P.M. Twenty more minutes before his shift was done and he went home to Annalise.

He heard a customer enter the store and returned to the front, *Theo* forgotten on the shelf.

Kit and Annalise had encountered each other some six months before in a meet-cute that would have been clichéd in a book but in real life just felt lucky. The blind date, so carefully crafted by their friends, had in fact been orchestrated for them to meet other people, who were waiting inside the warm coffee shop. Annalise and Kit never entered, having arrived simultaneously at the door, and looked at each other once, then again, recognizing in the other the expression of someone searching for something they might not want to find. Seeing it change to something more like fascination. Or relief, depending.

"Are you here for a . . . ?"Annalise had said, and Kit nodded.

"Do you like coffee?" Annalise said, shooting a glance at the shop in front of them. "I'll be honest; I hate it. I'm more of a tea person."

And Kit, captivated by her directness, said he liked tea just fine, so off they went to another place, a different life.

A split-second event, friends said later. *How appropriate.*

It was her precision that drew him in. Annalise was like cut glass, all her surfaces smooth and clean and clear, her eyes like thinking itself. She lived in a world of glittering nanoseconds, and he, coming from a life that was far more ambiguous, was fascinated by her immaculate foundation. Her absolute certainty.

She'd been participating in a conference on Coordinated Universal Time, the blind date slipped in between debates over leap seconds.

"Over what?" Kit said, pushing aside his tea. It turned out he didn't like tea after all, certainly not this stiff black stuff, which was already giving him the jitters. Or maybe it was the sheer electricity of being near her that was making him vibrate. He wanted to reach out, touch the short, fine hair on her head.

"A leap second," she said, as if she was used to being asked to repeat things. As if she'd do it once, but not more.

Row or get out of the boat, Kit's family used to joke when one of them was not following the subject at hand. It was a frequent occurrence. Kit's father was a historian, his mother a psychologist, his younger sister, Ruby, off on one deep research dive after another—celestial navigation, the invention of buttons, music cryptography. Their dinner-table conversations were free range, oxygen rich, generously competitive. When Kit was in college, he used to joke with his friends that he was lucky if he was even *in* the boat. Usually he was swimming behind, trying to keep his head above water.

But that wasn't true, either. The truth was, he was just easily distracted.

Did you know that the eye actually sees things upside down, and then the brain flips it back? His mother had mentioned this once when he was six, and Kit lost himself for weeks in a fictional universe where things were, in fact, the opposite of what they seemed. Where beauty was hidden and ceilings were floors, and people dreamed while they were awake and did dishes while they slept.

ADHD, the school psychologist had said, but Kit's mother shook her head.

Active imagination, she said, smiling benignly. *Don't you wish you had one?*

But while Kit appreciated the warmth of his mother's support, hers was an opinion not widely shared in the scholastic environment—and Kit's wandering mind could occasionally get in the way. Like now.

"Leap second," he said, focusing, finally. "Tell me."

In the end, Annalise did not go back to the conference that day. They talked instead, as the afternoon drifted toward evening.

"A day, measured by an atomic clock, has 86,400.002 seconds," Annalise said. "People think those couple milliseconds don't matter, but they do."

"It's kind of like commas," he said. "There was a lawsuit once because someone left one out. It put the meaning of an entire contract into dispute."

"Exactly," she said.

"I think you're the first woman I've ever met who could keep up with my family," he said, marveling.

"Thank you?" she said, and he realized that *keeping up* was probably a port she'd sailed past in kindergarten.

"It's a compliment, trust me," he said, toasting her with his now-cold tea. "What about your family?" he asked. "Tell me about them."

She shook her head. "No need."

And he leaned into the way the sadness softened her face, her voice.

"I'd like to hear," he said, but her face closed back up, like a sea anemone touched with the tip of a finger. Still, he'd seen that bit of her. Great books often started that way— the glimpse of a character opening to astonishing stories. How could you resist?

She looked down at the watch on her wrist.

"Do you have to go?" he said. "We could have dinner."

She tilted her head, watching him. "I *did* already give my talk."

"Stay," Kit said.

Annalise's finger reached out to his wrist and touched his pulse, which doubled at the contact.

"Look at that," she said.

"Leap pulse," he said, and put his finger on hers, which was slow and steady. He wanted to make it race.

Which—not too many hours later—he did. The experience, he thought afterward, was like unleashing time. Annalise, unbound. Like sex was air, and she was a bird, all wings and speed.

And stamina. My god. He'd had to spell words backward in his head just to last as long as she did.

"Holy shit," he said afterward.

"Look at you," she said, "keeping up." A sly smile tugged at the corner of her mouth.

"Thank you?" he said, and grinned.

"Food?" she asked.

For someone who probably weighed a hundred pounds, Annalise could eat like a wolf, Kit thought, watching her wield her chopsticks through a gigantic mound of yakisoba. He'd presumed, looking at the lean line of her, that she'd be a salads-only kind of gal, but that was clearly not the case.

"Tell me about your work," she said, chewing.

Here it was, Kit thought, the break point. That moment in every first date when the woman realized he worked a job that could barely support a single person, let alone give him the wherewithal to be a husband, a father, an equal provider of any sort. It would have been easier if he'd been an aspiring author, selling other people's books on the side. There was something romantic about that scenario—plus its potential of future success, no matter how improbable. It's what women went to first, in any case.

So, are you a writer, too?

It reminded Kit of a *New Yorker* cartoon, two men standing on a sidewalk, one of them with a hand over his mouth in embarrassment. A book, lying on the pavement in front of him, as if he'd just horked it up like a hairball. The caption: *Everyone has a book inside them.*

Kit did not. Or rather, he did—he had thousands—but they were written by other people and that made him supremely happy. He loved knowing a store's worth of stories, matching them to his customers, changing their lives, one book at a time. He was a book yenta, he'd say to those women whose interest hadn't already shut down.

If the date did get past that first awkward moment, women generally went into fix-it mode, declaring in the most supportive of fashions that he was so smart—he could be a teacher, a professor. The underlying message: *You could do so much more with your life.*

When in fact, he was doing exactly what he wanted.

What he didn't tell these women, because by that point he didn't want to, was that he was doing just fine financially. The bookstore where he worked was in an affluent-enough neighborhood that people didn't wait for a special occasion to purchase a hardback. When he first started working there, straight out of college, he paid attention to his customers' book choices, but his ever-wandering mind also made note of the fancy to-go cups of coffee, the sleek yoga pants taking the place of jeans. The year Lululemon went public, he bought stock in the company. It went up. A lot. He bought Starbucks on a day in 2009 when the economy was still shuddering back, but he'd had to ask ten customers to take care with their venti mochas. Last year, he'd made a quick profit when Fitbit went public, then dumped the stock when he saw an Apple Watch on the wrist of a stay-at-home mom. He hadn't bought a house yet, but he didn't have to have a roommate in his apartment, either.

"I work in a bookstore," he told Annalise now. A challenge.

"Cool," she said.

And so, while Annalise finished off her dinner and a third of his, he told her about the excitement of a new release, and how, when he put the right book in the right hands, everything fell into place for one beautiful second.

"Yes," Annalise said. "Exactly."

They moved in together after three weeks. A new place. A new life.

"When will we meet her?" Kit's mother asked over the phone. "This seems fast."

"But inevitable," he said, riding the feeling of it all, the way Annalise's precision provided a framework to his world. He'd spent his life in the spin cycle. Being with Annalise felt like the perfect combination of structure and exhilaration.

And if that meant that the mugs always went into the cabinet in a line of alternating blue and yellow, that was fine with him. It was kind of pretty, actually. He'd never thought of making art out of the arrangement of plates, of placing the jars of flour and white or brown sugar so that they stair-stepped down in height. Never loaded a dishwasher so that it could be emptied in eight simple steps.

"Do you think about these things?" he asked her.

She stopped, pondered. "Not really," she said, "it just feels right."

And Kit, who had always judged books in a similarly instinctive way, marveled at how two people who could be so different, could be so fundamentally the same.

The only two disciplines where anything is possible are science and fiction, Kit's mother used to say. And while Kit's father liked to disagree, at good-natured length, it seemed to Kit that his relationship with Annalise was living proof of the theory.

Six weeks. Nine. Two lives folding into one another, a neutron and proton creating their own nucleus. (*See?* he thought. *Even her images are becoming mine.*) Their atom-world was a little isolated, perhaps, but there were so many parts of each other to discover. Then there was the sex, which was phenomenal. He quickly learned that meals were better afterward, which made sense in a way, because Annalise was the opposite of other women he'd dated, who always thought dinner should come before the rest.

"I never saw the point in wrapping paper," Annalise said when he mentioned it. He marveled, both at her answer and her lack of jealousy regarding past lovers and partners.

"Why would I care?" she said. "Time moves forward."

He'd lie in bed in the mornings, watching as she dressed. His own private Clark Kent getting ready for the day, he alone knowing what happened when the clothes came off at the end of it. He was so caught up in the image, he forgot that he loved wrapping paper, the way opening a package revealed one layer at a time until you finally reached what mattered.

"Italian tonight?" she asked.

"After?" he said. It was like a secret handshake, a recognition of the twosomeness of them. The way they fit.

He told himself he wasn't hiding her from his family. It was more like those days when you're reading a great book, before you hear what anyone else thinks. He'd worked in a bookstore long enough to know that no matter how good a book is, someone will hate it, and they're likely to tell you. But as long as that book is only in your head, it is still perfect.

On a Saturday in early April, the end of their third month, The Big Event, as Annalise had begun to call it, finally arrived. She spent an hour figuring out what she was going to wear, an unusual event in itself; she normally just threw on jeans and a button-down shirt. She wasn't nervous, Kit thought, so much as very alert. He made sure her morning tea was in the blue mug, his coffee in the yellow—although honestly, as neither one of them was likely to mistake one drink for the other, color coding really wasn't necessary. Still, wasn't that what relationships were? Knowing someone well enough to smooth out the edges, hers or yours?

In any case, now they'd made the forty-five-minute drive and were at the family dinner table, the ritual interview process well underway. In Kit's childhood, weekend dinners almost always included guests, from ceramicists to diplomats to a street musician Kit and Ruby passed every day on their way to school. Kit's mother steadfastly refused to start by asking any guest about their work—that was too easy. Besides, the best stuff resided elsewhere, she always said, and generally this was true, although sometimes a bit more than expected (a discussion of polyamory, started by an innocuous-looking professor of physics when Kit was seven years old, remained a standout). Still and all, it did tend to be exciting, and when Kit had eaten at his friends' houses, he was often stunned by the vapidity of the conversation. *How was school? How* did *you make this meatloaf?*

The older he got, the more he'd realized that what made those family dinners lift into something vibrant and revelatory, if sometimes messy, was the unusual nature of them. What he couldn't say, even after all those weeks in their little sequestered world, was how Annalise would respond.

"Go easy on her, Mom," Kit had said on the phone the night before.

"I thought you said this one could keep up?" his mother replied, merriment in her voice.

If you can't stand the heat, get out of the kitchen was another of his family's sayings, and while there was genuine affection in the words, what they didn't seem to understand was that not everyone liked to cook.

By this point in their dinner, Kit's mother had already pitched a series of elementary questions to Annalise. Perhaps his mother had taken his request to heart, Kit thought, although he had to admit it was making for one of the duller evenings on record. The problem was that while most people would take an opening to talk about themselves and run with it, Annalise's answers were to the point, no more or less information than asked for. Family: *one brother* (parents not mentioned). Place of childhood: *Arizona*. Favorite climate: *not that*.

Kit watched as both questions and answers became shorter, quicker, Annalise and his mother like two tennis players coming to the net. Both of them tiring of the game, in different ways.

"Mom, it's not an interrogation," he interjected.

"All right, all right," she said, laughing. She turned back to Annalise. "So, tell us about your work."

It wasn't a defeat, Kit thought. Annalise's work *was* fascinating—or, if not always the work itself (the complexities of it mounted up fairly quickly), at least her love of it.

Kit watched Annalise reaching for her mental file entitled *Time for Dummies*. He'd seen her do this before, including with him. He often thought it must be exhausting to always have to simplify your life's fascination for others. And tonight—maybe it was all the questions that had come before—Annalise's tank seemed less full than usual.

"I work with leap seconds," she began.

"With what?" Ruby said. Kit felt a wave of sibling camaraderie at the sight of her befuddlement, followed by the embarrassed realization that he was probably seeing a reenactment of his own expression that first time over tea.

"Well," Annalise said, "you know about leap years."

Kit's father lifted his wineglass. "Started by Julius Caesar in 45 BC."

"Exactly," Annalise said, turning to him, tilting her head in surprise.

"History geek," Kit's mother said, winking at her husband.

"Except," Annalise said, "that system was based on a solar day. Now we have atomic clocks, which measure with far more precision. The problem is that the rotation of the earth has an extra point zero zero two seconds per day, on average."

"Two one-thousandths of a second," Kit's mother said. "Who'd have thought?"

Annalise looked pleased, but Kit remembered his mother standing in the kitchen, saying, *Precision is best reserved for baking, Kit. Humans are messy creatures.*

"And thus," Ruby broke in triumphantly, "leap seconds."

"Yes, but," Annalise said, raising an index finger, "it's not as simple as adding one every five hundred days. The earth's rotation isn't predictable. There are earthquakes and volcanoes. The northern hemisphere is sometimes heavier than the south, which throws it off."

Ruby's mouth opened in question. "Snow," Kit said quickly. Ruby closed her mouth again.

Annalise nodded, while looking at the rest of the table. "So, a group of us scientists determine if we need to adjust. When we do, on June 30 or December 31, the official clock changes from 23:59:59 to 23:59:60."

"Wow," Ruby said. "You change time."

"No," Annalise said. "I correct it."

"Oh," Ruby said. "Of course."

The table was quiet.

"Time ..." Kit's mother mused, turning to Annalise. "Such an interesting concept."

Here we go, thought Kit. On a normal night, this might be when the second or third glasses of wine got poured and conversation started flying around the table like a murmuration of starlings. But this dinner hadn't felt normal for a while now.

Kit's father held out the bottle of red toward Annalise, then noticed she was only drinking water.

"Oh," he said. "Whoops." Annalise flushed.

"For example," Kit's mother continued, nodding thoughtfully, "in humans, our understanding of any one moment is made up of all the messages sent by our nerves and muscles and eyes and ears. It takes a while to get them all to the brain, so in the end our *now* is actually always about a half second after the fact."

"*We live in hindsight,*" Ruby intoned, looking more like herself again.

Annalise turned to Kit, confused.

"Mom used to say it all the time," he explained. "Obviously, she still does."

"Oh, oh, oh!" Ruby said, eyes lit now, almost laughing. "So that means one of Annalise's leaps would actually give us a half-second head start on something!"

Kit could feel Annalise shift next to him. He knew that

shift, as if her slim hips were releasing a frustration that she'd learned not to say in words.

Those hips don't lie, he'd joked to her once, but she'd only looked at him with the same expression he saw now. That falcon-on-a-wrist look, as if she couldn't wait to get back to the air, where flying was effortless, and the wind currents made sense.

"All I'm saying is that when it comes to reality, I think it's good to have an open mind," Kit's mother said, smoothly corralling the conversation again.

"An atomic clock loses only one second over one point four million years," Annalise said. "What's more real than that?"

"Such a good question," Kit's mother replied, looking at Kit.

"Anyway, who's up for dessert?" she said to the table at large. "And afterward, there's a walk I think Annalise will love." She got up and headed to the kitchen.

"Welcome to priming," Kit said to Annalise with a rueful smile.

"To what?" Annalise said.

"This is what happens when your mother is a psychologist," he said, putting his hand on the tight muscles of her thigh. "You don't have a chance. You might think that what you really want to do after dinner is lie around with your stuffed belly in the air, but in fact, you're going to take a walk. She'll insist. But you'll end up loving it, because she's already put the idea in your head that you will."

"Ahh, my smart boy," Kit's mother said as she returned with a chocolate cake.

"I like to think we make our own decisions, based on the available evidence," Annalise said.

"Yes," Kit's mother said, cutting a slice and handing it to her. "And yet the other happens all the time. You two, for example, were primed to love each other. You walked into that coffee shop with the belief that friends of yours thought you were meant for each other."

"Technically, we didn't get inside," Annalise said.

"Which rather proves my point," Kit's mother said, smiling gently. "Don't you think?"

"You could have been nicer," Kit said to his mother as they walked along the rocky beach. "She's new to this."

"To what?"

"Family—and especially ours. We aren't easy, Mom."

"Well, honey, I don't think *easy* is what's for dinner here." She looked ahead at Annalise, striding along the path, three steps ahead of Ruby and Kit's father. "That's a pretty tight spring you've got your hands on there."

"Mom. Be nice."

"Kit, honey, my job is to love you. Nice may or may not be appropriate." And then she kissed his cheek and set off to catch up with Kit's father and Ruby.

"She hates me," Annalise said when Kit finally reached her.

"No . . ." he said, pulling her into his shoulder.

"You think I don't see these things?" she said.

"No . . ." Although come to think of it, maybe.

"I just generally prefer to stick to what's real," she said, and Kit started to ask her what that meant, but then they were back at the house and suddenly it was all about keys and cars and heading home because it was getting late and the roads would be dark but it had been a marvelous time, everyone agreed, and they should do it again soon.

And they would, too, except for the *soon* part.

When it was just the two of them, however, it was easy to put any concerns aside. With Annalise, the days, then months flowed by in a crisp, constructive order. Kit's mind had always been a messy place, a swirl of *what ifs* and *maybes*. Laundry and grocery shopping were things he did only when it became obvious that he was flat out of everything. Now there was a task chart, clean clothes in the closet, food in the refrigerator, a plan for Friday night (a movie, watched from their couch; a glass of red for him and white for her). The fact that sex had been relegated to Tuesday, Thursday, and Saturday nights did not diminish its wildness when it occurred.

"Let's get married," he said one night in late July, as they lay panting next to one another.

"Okay," she said.

"How can you marry someone whose family you've never met?" Ruby asked Kit as they ate lunch at their favorite restaurant. Kit hadn't been there in a while; Annalise said the food wasn't good. She was right, but the place was a perfect hole-in-the-wall, with outdoor tables set in a vine-covered back patio that you'd never know existed from the street.

"Not every family is like ours," Kit said.

"My point exactly," she said. "Besides, what do you really know about her? She could be a serial killer." She widened her eyes dramatically, fork in the air, slightly overcooked spaghetti dangling from its prongs.

"But a very clean one," Kit said with a smile, leaning over with his napkin to catch a drop of red sauce before it hit the table.

"What are you doing?" Ruby said, staring at him as he folded his napkin back onto his lap. "Where is my brother?" But the joke lost momentum in its delivery.

"I'm serious," she said. "Is this who you'll be if you marry Annalise? Somebody who cares more about a clean table-cloth than a conversation? I mean, being around you before could be like talking to someone on the moon, but at least it was interesting."

"I'm interesting," he said.

Increasingly, however, he wondered.

Still, Kit and Annalise went forward. There was an end point—a wedding—to aim for, and they took the steps to get there. They agreed it would be a civil service rather than a church ceremony and decided on a date in early September. It would be just them and Kit's parents and sister; Annalise's brother was in Europe, and it appeared her parents were not an option.

"Are you sure?" Kit said.

"As I am about anything," she said—which for most people indicated a general insecurity about all things, but for Annalise meant *yes.*

Annalise found a dress, insisting it be something she could use again, which seemed utilitarian—but when Kit saw her, standing in the store's dressing room (Annalise caring not at all for the traditional secrecy angle), he was stunned at how the simple lines of the dress became grace itself as they fell over her slim body.

"You look like a selkie," he said.

"That's just another cautionary tale about women want-ing to be themselves," she said. "Here, unzip me." And she shed the dress and stood there, strong and sure.

"My mother always said *be yourself,*" she remarked as she bent over to pick up her shirt.

Kit's ears perked up. He'd never even seen a photo of Annalise's mother. "Did she follow her own advice?" he asked carefully, not looking at Annalise.

"Sure," she said, fingers moving rapidly over buttons. "Right out the front door."

"How old were . . . ?"

But Annalise was out the door herself, the dress over her arm, heading for the cash register.

If he'd thought that moment meant Annalise might open up about her family, he was wrong. In fact, if anything, she seemed to become less interested in being part of his. When they were invited to Sunday dinners at his parents' house, she always said she had to work.

"Those seconds must really be slipping away," his mother said with a smile as she passed Kit the platter of moussaka. Her new obsession was Greek cooking. Kit's father said if he had to eat any more grape leaves, he'd start growing vines out of his fingertips.

"It's a tricky time at work," Kit said.

"Ha ha," Ruby said. "*Time.*"

"I mean, the ice caps are melting . . . That affects the rotation of the earth."

"At least something is thawing," Ruby said, delighted with a second joke in as many seconds.

"Behave," Kit's mother said. But her eyes were on Kit, full of questions.

"Everything's fine," he said to her.

"It doesn't have to be," she said. "Sometimes *fine* gets in the way."

He didn't go for family dinner as often after that.

Then, two weeks before the wedding, Alice Wein walked into the bookstore again. This time, Kit recognized her, although honestly, it helped that she was standing in front of the Local Authors display, staring at the handwritten shelf talker for *Theo*.

Kit walked up next to her. The shelf talker was one of

Doris's, he noticed. Doris worked two days a week, which was probably just as well. She loved books, but tended to view customers as an encumbrance.

> THEO BY ALICE WEIN.
> A hate story. A love story. It posits the question:
> Can you survive your childhood?

Doris did tend toward the cryptic, Kit thought. It was a wonder they'd sold as many copies as they had.

It was hard to imagine the young woman standing next to him writing the book Doris described. Alice was quiet and still, her eyes riveted on the words in front of her. She smelled of woodsmoke, soft and earthy, and Kit found himself wondering if it was on her coat or in her hair.

She looked over then, seeming surprised to see him there, but maybe it was just that thing that happened when you'd been inside written words and had to switch back to the real world.

"Is it weird?" he asked, going for the icebreaker.

She cocked her head, confused.

"Reading your own press," he said.

She paused, as if assessing something so deep inside him that he hadn't even seen it yet. Then she nodded. "It just doesn't feel like my book they're talking about."

He'd heard other authors say much the same thing, usually with a kind of false modesty, but this time the words felt simple, vulnerable.

"Is that hard?" he found himself asking. "Your book turning into other people's?"

"Sometimes, yeah. I mean, I want it to be other people's story, and I don't need him to stay with me, but . . ."

She'd said *him*, not *it*. Theo, he guessed. Which told him a whole lot more about her relationship with this book than anything else.

"It's weird," she said, "when one thing can be so many things at once, you know?"

He opened his mouth, wanting to tell her that he knew what she meant. Not about the book, per se—he wasn't a writer. But he understood the feeling of living in a world where few questions had a single, solid answer. Understood, too, that in that world, creativity often dwelt next to confusion.

But then the manager came over and sent Kit off to help another customer. The manager asked Alice to sign her stock, and by the time Kit was done, Alice was gone.

This time, however, Kit took *Theo* home with him. Annalise was working late; Kit poured a glass of red and sat in the big chair, opening to the first page, feeling the words draw him into their world. When Annalise came home a few hours later, he barely looked up. He gave her a kiss, and said he'd be to bed later. She looked surprised, but this was not the first Tuesday they'd missed recently. She went down the hall and he heard the shower running, then the sound of her getting into bed.

Kit had the next day off, and he spent it immersed in the

book. His life had no particular parallels to Theo's; there was no *someone else sees what I've gone through* moment, and yet he couldn't stop reading. He cared about this boy. He wanted him to get free.

Kit was usually a quick reader, but on that day he was not. He let each word roll about in his mind, each moment open in its own time. It was five o'clock before he got to the scene that broke his heart, his eyes filling with tears as Annalise walked in the door.

"Have you even moved?" she asked, kicking off her boots, lining them up on the shoe rack.

Kit looked up. Pondered her question.

"Should we do takeout?" she asked.

What he wanted was to be alone in the kitchen—chopping, washing, cooking. Letting time turn the scene he'd just read into something he could hold without feeling like it would burn him.

"I've got stuff in the fridge," he said. "Why don't you go take your shower now? I'll make dinner."

They sat at the table. Kit was on his second glass of wine, having made his way through the first one while cooking. It wasn't how he thought of himself, a two-glasses-on-a-weeknight kind of guy, and yet, these days he kinda was. It helped smooth out the complexities of Annalise's work—tonight, a controversy about optical versus cesium measurements of time. Except that right now, it was just making his mind wander back to the book.

"Anyway," Annalise said, "it's a problem."

"That must be frustrating," he said. He had no idea what she'd said, but he'd realized early in life that you could use that sentence as an effective response to 90 percent of what most people talked about.

Annalise nodded, ate another bite. It was one of her favorite dinners—pasta with tomatoes and basil, a salad, lots of bread.

"So," she said eventually, "how are things at the store?"

And then—maybe it was that second glass of wine, maybe it was because the story was still so alive in his head—Kit told her about the book. About the boy, Theo, who was beaten by his father. How the boy became a young man and made a plan to escape, learned to swim in the cold, open water that he hated. How he tricked his father into taking him out in a rowboat at night, handed his father the bottle, watched him drink until he passed out. And then Theo slipped over the side, swam for shore through the dark water, so his father would think he was dead, and he could be free. But his father had woken up, seen his son missing from the boat, and screamed his name, not in anger, but in agony. Dived into the water to try and find him. And drowned. Leaving Theo on the shore, where escape was no longer possible.

"Imagine," he said. "How would you ever get over that guilt?"

Annalise was looking at him, puzzled.

"What?" he asked.

"It's just . . ." She paused. "I mean, these aren't real people, right?"

As if he was a child, playing in a sandbox with imaginary friends.

"Says the woman who measures seconds with an invisible atom," he said, trying to inject humor into his voice. Because honestly, the options were to make this a joke, or acknowledge that she didn't understand him at all.

Or they could ignore the whole thing, he supposed. Plenty of marriages went forward on that principle.

"An atom which exists," she said firmly. Pretty much obliterating options one and three.

He stopped, regrouped. "I'm not saying it doesn't exist. I'm just saying that a character can be as real as a person. Or teach you as much, anyway."

She shrugged, just the slightest movement, as if she couldn't not. As if his reading was an eccentric if not always charming habit, like signing your text messages or eating cold pizza for breakfast. Something about your partner that you got past because that's how relationships worked.

"Then how can you love me?" he asked.

She shrugged again, bigger this time. "It's hard finding someone who can keep up."

He looked at her, waiting—for the smile, the memory. But she was just waiting for the next sentence. The next second. He wondered if she could hear them ticking by in her head. Maybe she even heard that extra .002, every day.

And that, perhaps, was the difference between the two

of them, he thought. Science heard that fragment of a second and wondered how to make it fit into a whole. Fiction wondered what hearing it felt like.

"It's okay," she said gently. "People need books."

Like they were sugar.

Which she didn't eat, anyway.

How long has it been like this? he wondered. *Since the beginning?* He'd been no better than one of those characters that drove him crazy, the ones blinded by love while he sat above the page yelling, *You idiot! Don't do that!* Had he really just not seen?

Well . . . he could almost hear his mother saying. See her left eyebrow raising.

Shit. What was he going to do?

Annalise had given him a coffee mug once: *Books are my drugs.* They'd laughed. He'd taken it as supportive, empowering.

Oh god, he thought.

And then, a second thought—what do you do when everything you thought you understood means something different now?

You go forward, his mother would say. *Or sideways. Take your pick. Your. Pick.*

"It's okay," Annalise said again. She was so calm.

"No," he said, shaking his head. "It's not." He paused, looking around the room, which suddenly seemed like somewhere he'd never been before.

"Look," he said, taking a breath, because it was very

important to get this right. "I'm sure it's easy to think you're in charge of the world if you're the one measuring it. But Annalise, you're just the one holding the clock—the thing that's being measured is what matters. The beautiful, complicated *everything* that happens during that moment."

"Which is what books are about, I suppose?" The chill in her voice would have helped the melting ice caps significantly.

Kit stopped. "Yeah," he said slowly. "I suppose so."

"Which makes you right, then?"

"Jesus, Annalise," he said. "It's not about *right*. Don't you see? That's my whole point." He thought he might explode. Suddenly all that fascinating precision of hers just felt like so many paper cuts.

"We're coming at the same thing from different angles," he said. "You have a clock; I have words. One isn't necessarily better than the other."

"Well," Annalise said, "technically . . ."

"What?"

"They aren't your words." She sounded almost apologetic, as if she was sorry to have to educate him.

He stared at her.

"Oh my god," he said, and went for the door. Wondered if she could hear this as well, the sound of everything breaking.

"Well," his mother said, "at least there aren't a lot of people to uninvite."

Kit sat at the breakfast table in his parents' house, staring down at his coffee.

"How could I have been so stupid?" he asked his mother.

"You saw something you needed to see," she said, and handed him a piece of toast. "We all do it—which is why writers will never run out of stories, and I will never run out of clients. Speaking of, I need to get going. You're welcome to stay as long as you want."

She kissed the top of his head, and headed for the door.

He waited until he knew Annalise was at work, and then he went to their apartment and collected his things. He left her a note on the kitchen table—*I can't do this. Let's talk*—although he knew they probably wouldn't.

When he was done, he stood there for a moment, looking about the immaculate kitchen. Then he went to the center cabinet and opened the door, digging around behind the row of alternating blue and yellow mugs. He found the *Books are my drugs* mug at the back and pulled it out. Then he lined the rest of the mugs back in their row, leaving two yellow ones at the end.

He knew he was being petty, predictable. But anger was a propulsive form of energy; that's what made it so attractive. It was easier to use it to blast off, fly away, rather than stay and pick up the necessary weight of another's point of view. Would he even want to listen now if Annalise was willing to open up? Let him see through her eyes?

But these were moot questions, he knew, because she was

never going to let him in. She hadn't ever, not really. And he'd made that easier all along. He'd been fascinated by the mystery of her, eager to fill in the gaps with narratives of his own making. Turn her into a character in a story he'd always wanted to read.

"Oh hell," he said quietly.

He went back to the note on the table and picked up the pen. Added *I'm sorry*. But he left the mugs the way they were.

The next two months were chaotic, but the normality of that was welcome. He took long walks and thought whatever he wanted. At the bookstore, he recommended titles with a fervor and a sensitivity to the needs of their customers that made sales skyrocket.

"What's gotten into you?" the manager asked.

Me, Kit thought, but that was a weird answer, so he just shrugged and smiled and handed a copy of *Harold and the Purple Crayon* to the little kid whose big brother kept telling him what to do.

It was nice, being at home for a bit. It was like old times, throwing topics around the table. Nobody brought up Annalise, although there were moments when Kit felt sorry that she couldn't be there, part of a family, although it wasn't clear that would ever have made her happy.

After a couple months, he rented his own place. As he unpacked his things, he spotted the copy of *Theo* at the bottom of a box. When he'd moved out of the apartment he shared with Annalise, he wasn't sure he'd ever want to see the book again, this catalyst that had blown everything up. But he was coming to see that he'd used the book, walked into that conversation with Annalise with a reasonable suspicion of what might happen. Maybe not consciously, but that was the beauty of books, wasn't it? They took you places you didn't know you needed to go.

Now Kit took *Theo* out of the box.

"You have a thing or two to answer for, Alice Wein," he said, but he smiled.

And then, because it was starting to snow, the air outside perfectly cold, Kit left the rest of the unpacked boxes where they were and sat down in his big chair with the book. There were a hundred and twenty pages left. Anything could happen.

Northeastern California
2017

The Caretaker

As William was getting ready to close the trunk of his already stuffed car, his daughter, Clara, slipped in a box.

"Yes," she said when he started to protest, "you have room." And her voice sounded so much like her mother's that William just nodded and pushed the box a little farther in, its sharp corner shoving into a banana that would—although he didn't know it yet—dominate the olfactory atmosphere for the rest of his journey.

"Okay," he said. "It'll be a surprise to look forward to."

Although he was pretty sure he knew what was in it, knew it wasn't really for him.

Clara reached out and they hugged each other, hard. William could feel her lanky frame against his, her arms tight around his neck. *She'll be okay*, he told himself. Then he got in his car and headed west like any good pioneer, pretending that he was moving toward adventure when really, he was running from everything.

If you had asked William eighteen months ago what he thought he would be doing that day, his answer would have been just this side of stultifying: *Get up. Go to work. Come home.*

We need something to shake us up, his wife, Abigail, had said, and the idea started something fizzing in him. The last truly new thing they'd thrown into the mix was Clara, twenty-five years before, when Abigail was thirty-four and they'd pretty much given up trying for a baby. But Clara was fledged, and they needed a new focus, Abigail said.

Yes, he'd said. *Let's shake things up.*

Life, hearing the wish, had granted it, if not in a way they had anticipated. More expected might have been a puppy, discovered along the side of the road. A newfound passion for ballroom dancing. A class in Indian cooking.

It's not a story without the unexpected, Abigail always said. But even she had to admit that some plot twists were better than others.

So now William, at the age of sixty-two, after Abigail's death to what everyone else called a *battle* with cancer but Abigail had dubbed, far more accurately, a *rout,* was in the car, on his way from Denver to his new position as a caretaker for a ghost town in Northeast California.

The job made no more sense than anything else; he knew that. Up to that point, William had been a civil engineer, a man with a solid job still a few years from retirement. But he'd seen a story about the ghost town in one of those weird clickbait articles that had littered his internet searches after Abigail's death.

That's what you get, he could almost hear her saying, *when you Google "how to get a death certificate" at midnight.* And he'd listened for her laugh.

But the room had been quiet—of course it was quiet—so he'd clicked and read. Apparently, the man who owned the ghost town, a former tech guy with too much money, had extravagant plans to turn it into "the ideal self-actualization center, the perfect blend of luxury and authenticity." In the meantime, he needed someone to keep an eye on his investment. Maybe do a little fixing up here or there, nothing major.

William had found a late-night irony in the idea of a widower being the caretaker of a ghost town. He applied, not telling Clara, because what was the chance? But the owner, faced with hundreds of applications from wandering millennials, had appreciated William's maturity and engineering degree (overlooking the fact that William designed roads, not buildings). He offered him the job. Which was the last thing William had expected, but perhaps, he thought, he should be getting used to that, too.

Just for a while, he'd told Clara as he packed his things in the car. She nodded, looking away. She was grown up now. Had a fiancé, even. She'd be okay, he told himself, and he needed to be somewhere else. Somewhere so completely else that the grief wouldn't find him. Ignoring the fact that grief is not a stalker but a stowaway, always there and up for any journey.

Although it would take some real persistence to stick with him, he thought two days later, as his new-used four-wheel-drive Subaru took the turn off the highway and began lurching its way up the rutted dirt road to his destination. The potholes were legion, the switchbacks too sharp by half. He slowed his speed to five miles per hour, trying to ignore the increasingly precipitous drop to his left. The whole road needed an overhaul.

Well, he said to himself, *at least some of my knowledge could be put to good use.*

By mile fifteen, he was second-guessing every decision he'd ever made, while trying hard to ignore the fact that the closest civilization—a blink-and-you'll-miss-it town near Mono Lake—was now a good three hours behind him. He was beginning to wonder if he'd make it to his destination before nightfall when he went around yet another curve and there it was in front of him—a once-town named Fortune.

It was an aspirational name for a collection of pieces of wood, some stuck together better than others. Maybe seven buildings in all. The owner had sent him photographs, the PR kind, taken at sunset, the light glowing and sentimental. A view of the valley below, framed by a rough-hewn window. A wall of intriguingly small drawers in a general store. The front of the former hotel—a grand rectangle which was, he now realized, a false front for a far less imposing building, trailing behind like a mutt chasing a train.

Next to the hotel was the general store, its windows tall and welcoming, but also missing a fair amount of glass. Farther down, a bleached-out box of a building that might have been a boardinghouse. A few cabins crumbled their way up the hill, most with their roofs caved in.

As a place to stumble upon, it might have been exciting. A discovery. But now William stood in the midst of the silence, discarded lives permeating the air around him. He'd done some research and learned that Fortune had only existed for two years before the luck ran out and everyone left. At its peak, three thousand people had lived here. Instant city—just add gold. There were saloons, churches, two banks, and three brothels. Even a post office inside the general store.

This was what was left. Behind the vestiges of the buildings, the hills continued up, roadless, their time measured in entirely different increments, waiting for this new intruder to move along.

What the hell am I doing here? William thought.

Whenever he and Abigail had gotten lost on a road trip, or over-ordered at their favorite Chinese restaurant, or found themselves faced with the noise and angst of Clara's teenage years, Abigail would lean over to him and whisper in her best Oliver Hardy voice, *Here's another fine mess we've gotten ourselves into.* William never corrected her wording, or her terrible impersonation, because all he really cared about was the laughter in her eyes. The way *you* and *me* turned into *we* in her version. Even Clara picked it up eventually, although none of them had used it during that last year.

Oh, Ollie, William thought, looking at the decrepitude before him.

One of the wandering millennials might have spent the last hour of late-April daylight exploring the town, but after a second five-hundred-mile day, his mind pounding with doubts and the thin air at seven thousand feet, the only thing William wanted was sleep. From the glove compartment, he dug out the heavy, ornate key the owner had sent him. Then he grabbed his sleeping bag and the cardboard box of his more perishable food and let himself into the hotel.

The key, it turned out, was purely decorative, the lock loose in its hole. The door opened to a shadowy space, the windows covered with cobwebs, the smell a mixture of dry sage and time. On one side of the room was a bar with open shelves; on the other, two tables and a half-dozen chairs in various states of disrepair, tipped about as if they'd given up on a vertical position three drinks back. Abigail would have populated the tables with characters, feet up, backstories in hand, but William just put down the box of food on the bar and made his way across the room, avoiding the most obvious sags in the floor, and up the creaking stairs.

He'd been promised *a room with a view of the valley.* The owner told him to bring his own pillow and linens, but the rest would be ready and waiting. What hadn't been wait-ing, however—what had, in fact, been quite busy—were the mice. The mattress had been efficiently subdivided into nests, scattered about the room like some small animal Easter egg hunt. What was left of the bed was damp to the touch. William looked up to see the sky staring back at him through a hole of missing shingles, and he knew what his first project would have to be.

An old man like you shouldn't be climbing around on a roof, Abigail had teased when he put up the Christmas lights.

There are a lot of things an old man shouldn't be doing, Wil-liam said when he got back in the house, as his hands slid up the front of her shirt.

Stop it, William told himself now, and went and slept in the car.

The next morning, his back cricked, William reentered the hotel to discover that the mice had, once again, been busy. The box he'd brought in was chewed open, the damn banana smooshed across the floor; granola, dried apricots, rice, macaroni, and the bright orange contents of dehy-drated cheese packets scattered around it like dinner a la Jackson Pollock.

Before he'd left, Clara had warned him about the white-bellied field mice that might, or might not, carry hantavirus.

Don't touch anything they've touched, Clara told him.

Swearing under his breath, William got a pair of gloves and scooped up the ripped bag of rice, the nibbled boxes, the boxes next to the nibbled boxes, and shoved it all inside a large plastic bag. A third of his food, ruined or gone. His plan had been to bring enough supplies for three weeks, during which time he'd assess the situation. After that, he'd go to town and restock, or if things were truly untenable, quit.

I'm not completely out of my mind, he'd told Clara.

Just promise me you won't make this a martyr thing, okay? Clara had said, although it was clear she thought the cow was already out the barn door on that one.

The thing was, he knew better than to leave food out—he was the one who'd taught Clara how to hang food from trees to protect it from bears, after all, and the evidence of mice had been all around him. He'd just been too tired the night before. Absent-minded—an excuse that was covering all sorts of atypical behavior these days.

When Abigail had been pregnant with Clara, her thoughts always wandering toward this new and arriving being, she used to call it *baby-mind.* After Abigail was gone, William decided there should be such a thing as widower-mind, that endless, internal search for someone who was no longer there, no longer, never, on her way to you.

He should go, he thought. Go home. Call it a day, and a bad one at that. Problem was, he had no home to go to. After the unrelenting speed of Abigail's death, selling their house in Denver had seemed like the only way to get off the train. Put a period on that awful sentence. He couldn't change the story, but he could stop it, he'd thought.

Except, of course, he'd had that exactly backward.

If you ever read fiction, Abigail said in his head, *you'd know that.*

Abigail had loved stories, reading every night in bed, listening to audiobooks while she cleaned or walked or gardened, so caught up in the narrative that sometimes he had to tap her shoulder twice to get her attention. The two of them had met in a literature class their sophomore year in college—a core requirement for him, and nothing he'd been excited about. But then, as he'd sat two rows behind her in the huge auditorium, Abigail raised her hand and asked a question that made the assigned story open into everything. Later, he asked if he could walk her home—a line from a bad novel if there ever was one—and she said yes. What should have taken fifteen minutes turned into four hours. They walked across the campus of their sprawling California university, then through town, and ended up on the beach, talking. William had never been much of a conversationalist, but with Abigail it was different, the smoothest of back-and-forths, like navigating a series of perfectly banked curves, the feeling more like flying than driving.

Always start with words, Abigail would say to Clara later, when Clara was a teenager and falling for one beautiful boy after another. *Words last.*

And they had, until they hadn't.

Tell me a secret from your day, Abigail used to say to William every night before they fell asleep. And he would dig around in the minutia of his life and find something.

I saw a crocus on the way to the bus stop. I added salt to the soup when you weren't looking.

What he didn't say those last months—*I went into the closet and smelled the clothes you haven't worn this year.* The ones that still smelled like the woman he had married.

I'm not a quitter, William told himself now. He had enough food for a couple weeks. But if he was staying, he'd better get to work. There was the bed to shore up, the windows to fix.

And that roof. There was no repairing it from the outside—not without a thirty-foot ladder (which he didn't have) and rope to secure himself to a sturdy chimney (ditto, and also ditto). It was a relief, honestly. He was no novice when it came to home repair, but the thought of falling and breaking a leg with no one else there was a scenario he hadn't imagined. He was the caretaker, not the patient. But things can change in a moment.

Instead, he dug about in the shed off the back of the hotel and discovered a ten-foot ladder, its bright aluminum an odd flash of modernity amid the pieces of rusted iron. On his way out, he found a faded metal No Trespassing sign and stuck it under his arm.

Back in his room, ladder in position, he wedged the sign under the rafters, between the shingles, hammering the whole thing into place.

Stop-gap, for certain, but he was pleased with his inge-nuity. Only later, when he got off the ladder and looked up, did he realize he'd attached it with the writing facing down.

Back when they were in college, neither William nor Abigail had much money, but he did have a ratty car, and they spent every weekend they could exploring the deserts and mountains, camping out under the stars. One day they'd gone for a hike, well beyond a No Trespassing sign that Abigail had declared past its expiration date. They'd been about to turn around when they came upon the remains of a town—a series of square depressions in the earth, with some blackened logs still attempting some form of connection. The only thing still standing was one empty doorway, looking out to the valley below.

Abigail had stepped inside the frame, taking in the view. "Who do you think stood here before me?" she asked. She spent the rest of the hike back spinning out scenarios— a lonely miner, a strong-minded woman, a one-armed gunslinger—each one more extravagant and detailed than the last.

It had struck him, the way he could look at that doorframe and see structural integrity, and she would see a life. "But isn't that the point?" Abigail had said. "Otherwise, it's just like looking at yourself all the time. Wouldn't that be boring?"

It is, he wanted to tell her now. *It's excruciating.*

In addition to the bed, the owner had promised water from a hand pump, an outhouse, a woodstove, and oil lamps. *A true pioneer experience,* he'd said. Before he arrived, William had imagined something a step up from camping; not glamping exactly, but at least safe. That belief had gone by the wayside the first time he grabbed the stair railing and felt it sway like the rigging of a ship.

1. Banister

He wrote now on his list of things that needed fixing. Followed by *windows, floors, stairs, walls, roof* until finally he simply wrote *Everything.*

Given the grandiosity of the owner's vision, there was every chance the hotel would be torn down, swept away on a glorious wave of high–thread count sheets and shiny new slipper tubs, with a bit of original wallpaper framed and hung by the new front door like the first dollar bill above the cash register of a diner. Really, there was no need for a list.

On the other hand, William thought, if he was going to stay here, things could not remain as they were. He had two weeks to see if crazy could be turned into tenable. He needed a plan.

Begin with a thing you know you can do, Abigail always told Clara when she would be overwhelmed by homework or life.

So William got a box of mousetraps from the car, and seeded them throughout the hotel. Then, dust mask and gloves on, he bagged the nests and hauled out the sodden mattress, opening the windows to clear out the smells of mold and mice. He closed off the other bedrooms and took a broom to the main room, yanking down cobwebs and sending drifts of dust out the front door. He washed the windowpanes that were still intact and covered the others with cardboard from the boxes he'd brought. He worked with a kind of raw, physical energy he hadn't employed in years, his lungs working overtime in the altitude, sweat adding weight to his shirt. It felt good, not thinking.

By the end of the second day, he had achieved a rough semblance of order. The bedroom now contained the blow-up mattress he'd brought, thank god, as backup. On the main floor he had a table and a functional chair, a desk in the corner, his canned goods and a couple pots and pans arranged along the open shelves of the kitchen. His other food he'd stored in snap-locked plastic tubs that had previously held his tools and cleaning supplies. Hardly 1890s accoutrement, but William figured there was no one else to see it.

The more important point was that he was doing this. Making, if not a life, something livable. And the mice, according to the abundant evidence in the traps, did not, in fact, have white bellies.

To celebrate, he sat in his chair, opened a can of warm beer, and drank it down. Then he went out to the car and brought in the rest of his things. He put his clothes in the chest of drawers. On top he put a framed photo of Abigail and Clara at the Grand Canyon, the land opening into air behind them.

When everything else had been brought in and unpacked, he turned to the box Clara had snuck into his car
when he left Denver. When he opened the flaps, he encountered four books—novels, he saw upon looking closer,
each with a note taped to the cover, written in his wife's
smooth cursive. *Yosemite, 1999. San Francisco, 2004. Victoria, 2010.* Then, in Clara's handwriting: *Home, 2016.*

William picked up the last one. *Theo.*

When he read, William gravitated toward history and
biographies—big, fat tomes that could take you through
a winter or a year. He found something dependable in the
reality of their contents. Of course, he understood that even
nonfiction wasn't truly objective, but the effort was there,
wasn't it? The quest for Truth?

Fiction, though—that was something else. A leap into
the blue. A disregard of boundaries. Nothing like the com-
forting solidity of names and dates.

"That's what drives me crazy about history, though,"
Abigail had said on their first walk. "Historians say a war
started on such and such a day, but that war really started
years before—when a man got on the wrong train and met a
stranger, or a boy wasn't loved by his mother, or a girl said no.
And that war didn't stop on its end date, either. Its effects
kept going, down through the children and grandchildren,
but they didn't understand where it all was coming from
because historians care more about the rocks than the river."

She stopped for breath. "You see?" she asked.

"Okay," William said, although he didn't, not completely, not yet. "Say for the sake of argument that's true. Where do novels fit in?"

She had looked at him, serious, but then grinned. "They're the boats, of course."

After their daughter was born, the household scales tipped hard in favor of fiction. When William would pass by Clara's door as Abigail was putting her to bed, he heard his wife's voice filling the room with elves and brave girls and magic. On every road trip, their first stop would be a bookstore in a new town, where Abigail and Clara would choose their books—reading them aloud in the car, around a campfire. Later, when Clara was older and home on college breaks, mother and daughter would sit at the kitchen table and talk about heroes' journeys and character arcs and points of view like they were landmarks on their next adventure.

"Join us," they would say as he passed through the room, and he'd make some comment about *girl time*, as if his absence was a gift he was giving them, and they'd look up and smile at him and then fold themselves into a little world of two.

Now, standing in the bedroom of the ghost town hotel, William put the copy of *Theo* back in the box. He closed the flaps and pulled the tape tight across the gap. The mice would get into it otherwise, he told himself.

He could feel it before he opened his eyes and saw the No Trespassing sign on the ceiling. The tightness in his lungs, the weight on his chest, the buzzing in his head that meant the loop was about to start playing.

No, he said to himself. *Don't.*

But that never worked.

You'll drop your glasses down the outhouse hole. The roof will fall in while you sleep. You'll cut your hand and get lockjaw. You'll come across a bear/cougar/rattlesnake/survivalist. You'll get two flat tires going for provisions. You'll light the wood-stove and burn the whole town down. It will snow in May, and you'll be stuck here forever.

The *whirling,* as he called it, had started soon after Abigail's diagnosis. A couple times a week, then increasingly more, he'd half wake into a liminal state that shimmered with danger. A million things that could all go wrong. As if the protective mental barrier between himself and the actual dangers of the world had slipped, leaving him exposed. As if anything could happen now.

He'd heard people wax on about how they lived in *a world full of possibilities.* Why the hell would you want that? he'd wondered. And he would lie there, feeling his body race without moving, willing his breath to even out. To not wake Abigail. Sometimes it worked; sometimes it didn't. In any case, after a while, he would force himself to get out of bed and go to work, and no one there knew otherwise.

After Abigail's death, he'd woken in the mornings to a haze of nothing. No whirling. Just nothing. It was like the deafness after a bomb. He'd thought that, perhaps, having gone through the worst, there was nothing left to fear. But he'd mistaken the fog for success, and now he was whirling again.

Ollie, he thought. *You're screwed.*

When Clara was an active toddler and Abigail was at the end of her maternal rope, she would call him at work and William would say, in his calmest voice: *Go outside.*

And she would, and when he got home, she would hug him and say he was magic, and he'd feel as if he could solve anything. Which wasn't true, of course, and would only become stunningly less so, but at the time it was everything.

Go outside, you chickenshit, he told himself now.

There was a difference between cleaning and actual renovation—a fact the morning light made abundantly clear. When William stepped out of the hotel and saw the ragged town in front of him, the amount of work needed was stunning. How had the owner ever thought this town could become something functional while still retaining even a portion of what it had been?

He pulled open the creaking door of the general store and went inside. There were the high ceilings and the wall of many drawers the photographs had promised—although it all lost a good bit of the glamour in the translation back to reality. He opened the drawers, one after another, feeling the stick of their sides, inhaling the scents of old dust and tobacco. Most were empty, but one held a tiny clay pipe. He put it on a shelf in the sunlight, next to an old oil lamp and a rusty tin can. Peering closer, he read the label—*Wedding Breakfast Coffee, Denver, CO.*

When William had decided to propose to Abigail, he took her for a weekend to a ghost town that had been turned into a living museum. A scenic three-hour drive, a night in a restored nineteenth-century hotel with a bed he hoped wouldn't squeak too much. In the end, it was cheesy as hell, the tour guide's patter sprinkled with *like*s, the boardwalks crowded with tourists. Their own dinner, while incredible and expensive, was the farthest thing from authentic.

"You wanted hardtack?" Abigail asked as she licked the last of the chocolate mousse from her spoon. "Because *this* part I'm okay with."

He had a whole speech ready, about the difference between fool's gold (which glittered) and real gold (which shone). He was going to lean across the table, or maybe go down on one knee, and present her with the small black box from his pocket. He thought the whole thing rather Jane Austen-esque, but in the end, he did none of that. They'd gone back to the room and made the bed squeak and she joked that that was probably the most authentic part of the whole place, given that they were sleeping in what had once been a brothel.

And he'd leaned across her naked body and grabbed the box from his jacket pocket and handed it to her, as simply as you would a glass of water. And she said, smiling,

"Of course, William. Of course."

He was tempted to give up, go outside. But there was still the post office part of the store—just a corner, really, but with its own set of drawers. *Finish the job,* he told himself.

The drawers were empty save for the occasional dried spider, legs brittled into sharp angles, but he methodically kept at it, and in the middle of the bottom row, he found a sketch the size of a postcard, done on heavy paper. It looked like a view of the town from the top of the hill.

Before he arrived in Fortune, William had wondered if he would find any hidden old photographs or letters. But this sketch was no historic artifact, he realized as he looked closer—the paper was barely beginning to yellow. William turned it over and saw a message:

Allie girl, wish you were here.

A postcard then, but no address, no signature. Left behind in a post office that hadn't functioned for more than a century. William flipped the card over, looking at the drawing again. It was not refined, but there was a feeling to it, a sense of—what? Isolation? Compassion? He put the postcard in his pocket, and later, when he got back to the hotel, he set it on top of the dresser, propped up against the photo of Abigail and Clara.

The next morning, when William felt the whirling start, he forced himself out of bed, rolled up his sleeping bag, and put it in a plastic bin away from the mice. Then he made coffee on the two-burner stove, each action a moment of control. Afterward, he went outside and walked the length of the town. The general store and the boardinghouse might be salvageable, even beautiful, he decided, although the owner might well feel otherwise. The cabins were another matter. Single rooms, the darkness alleviated only by a doorway. Shelters in the most denotative sense, gradually returning to the dirt that had probably been surprised by their appearance in the first place.

His evaluation done if not detailed, he headed up the hill behind the town. The thin air made his heart pound, and his feet slipped on the loose rock and dirt of the slope, but the postcard had made him curious about the view. When he got to the top, breathing hard, he looked around him at the hills and the valley below. Deep, wide spaces.

He spent the rest of the day hiking, and then the day after, and the one after that. There was a certain kind of silence up that high, a relief that only vast expanses of uninhabited land could offer. After Abigail died, he'd become *a widower*, a remarkably public label for such an intimate situation. Everyone had their own ideas of how he should be—heartbroken, saintly, bravely moving forward (but not too fast), mourning (but not too much). His grief, which sat in his bones like a troll guarding its gold, fit none of those visions. Up in the hills, however, it could be whatever it needed, and the relief he felt was immense.

On the morning of day twelve, he realized it was time to restock his supplies. He'd been an Eagle Scout; he knew you never let your food get down to zero. It hadn't been on his radar, though—at first, because he thought there was no way he'd even make it a week. After that, time had lost its boundaries. But now he needed to address the situation.

The prospect of being around other people, however, even if it was just a clerk in a small store, gave him pause. He thought about the flood of emails and texts that would hit his phone the moment he got reception again.

Call me the first chance you get, Clara had said, and while he wanted to hear her voice, he also didn't. Because when he did, he would be Clara's father again, and thus Abigail's widower. And while he wanted the first, he didn't know if he could stand to pick up that second mantle again.

Tomorrow, he told himself. He'd go tomorrow. First, he'd give himself one more day in the hills.

He'd hiked for hours, and now he stood on the rise above Fortune. The town looked so different from this perspective—the whole enterprise more fragile, but also held in the arms of the hills. He could understand the desire to sketch, to make meaning.

Abigail would have looked down and seen a town that started billions of years ago, when stars collided, and their energy produced gold. She would have seen a town on its way to a new iteration, either through decomposition or renovation—but something different in any case.

The river never stops, she'd always said.

And it was then, looking down at the town, that William truly understood that he would never hear a new story, a new secret, from Abigail. He'd known the physical reality of that, of course. But this was a different understanding, more complicated and subtle. *More literary,* Abigail said in his head.

Which only proved the point—that Abigail's words now could only ever be things she had said, not things a future Abigail, altered by events that had not yet happened, would say. There would be no more surprises.

After Abigail died, people said, *But you have your memories.* And yes, he did, he practically lived in them, but one of the things he'd treasured most in his life was watching Abigail change and grow, her imagination expanding to meet the challenges of a job, a child, the death of a friend, the possibility of a new trip. A constantly evolving Abigail, with new ideas and things to say. But that river had stopped with her death, even as her death itself had carried him forward, changed him.

Obituaries often referred to the people the deceased had *left behind,* but that wasn't accurate, William thought. He was the one who had gone ahead, no matter how hard he'd tried not to. She was the one held in place. Her words in his head now reminders, not explorations. Memories, not true conversations. And the difference between the two could break you.

Just one more, he said to the universe. But standing on the top of that hill, he knew—he'd already had his chance, months ago, and he'd been too scared to take it.

William spent the next day in bed, staring at the No Trespassing sign above him. He just couldn't muster the energy to get in the car. He'd go tomorrow. The book about grief that the helpful neighbor had given him—the one he'd read the first chapter of before pitching it in the trash—had talked about *giving yourself time*. So he would.

Day turned into evening, and William made no move to get up. A body could last longer without food than you might think; he knew that. The clouds moved across the sky, changing the light in the room. He watched. Not thinking. Thinking.

He woke the next morning shivering, certain he must be sick. But when he got up, he saw a cold, flat whiteness outside his window. It took him a moment to understand. Snow. In mid-May. If he'd had cell reception, he might have known what was coming, but now he was surrounded by the stuff, piling up on the ground, on the roofs, still falling from the sky with determined intensity.

You idiot, he said aloud. *You damn idiot.*

He ran downstairs to the front door. The snow was already six inches deep. The four-wheel drive on his Subaru might have been able to handle that in the city, but the dirt road out was unmarked, its edges precipitous. Even he, who had designed roads, could not predict the ruts and holes beneath the snow.

He looked behind him at the kitchen. There was enough food for one more day at his regular caloric intake. And no firewood. The owner had told William that he'd have a supply brought in before the winter, perhaps wanting to avoid the expense until he knew William would stick around. There had been a small pile out back, but William had used it up test-driving the woodstove on some of the cooler evenings. Summer had been coming; no need to be miserly.

Don't do anything stupid, Clara had said. But really, had he done anything else since Abigail died?

He looked outside again—at the unending whiteness of the sky, the snow drifting up against the buildings. *Think, William,* he said to himself. *Think.* Because even if the day before he might have said he wanted to die, the irony of expiring through simple stupidity after all that had happened was intolerable. And he would not do this to Clara twice.

The first thing he did was go through the shed and all the bedrooms, collecting any old building supplies or pieces of unpainted furniture that were no longer usable, busting them into pieces that could fit in the woodstove. By the time he was done, he had enough fuel for a day or two. The exertion made him hungry, however, and while he knew there was plenty of town left to burn, food was another matter.

Calm down, he told himself. *It's a freak storm. It'll be gone by tomorrow.*

Except it wasn't. The snow wasn't gone the next day, or the day after. To minimize the heat he would need, William had put on every piece of clothing he could and brought his bedding down near the woodstove. He'd rationed himself to minimal calories, but even so, his food disappeared quickly, and while by now his body had stopped being hungry, exactly, it wanted fuel. He had to be careful when he went out to get snow to melt or lumber to burn, because the light-headedness would catch him when he straightened up. After two more days, he could feel his heart rate speed up, his breathing slow and go shallow.

So this is what it feels like, he thought.

On the afternoon of day six, he carefully made his way up the stairs and got the box, the photo, and the postcard. Brought them down and set them by the chair next to the woodstove. Then he pulled the tape off the box and took out the top book. *Theo.*

He opened to the first page and saw the note Clara had written inside.

> I asked Mom why this book. Other people might have wanted something easier toward the end, but she said she wanted to look life in the eyes.

He stared at the words until they blurred into shapes. "Oh, Abigail," he said.

When they'd received Abigail's diagnosis, thirty-seven years to the day after he'd proposed to her, it had broken time in two. Broken them in two, as well—although they didn't see that coming either; wouldn't have believed it, anyway. They, who had always talked about everything.

You can do this, he said to her in those first months, as if she were Clara learning to ride a bike for the first time. *We can fight this.* As if gravity hadn't just changed its rules. She'd looked at him, at first in belief, but soon as if he had betrayed the very essence of her. Of them.

He knew he was saying the wrong things, not asking the question that sat there, obvious, between them. Not just an elephant, but a whole damn zoo in the room.

He wanted to ask. No, that wasn't true; he didn't want to. Because if he didn't ask, none of what was coming could happen—a reasoning as impossible as the diagnosis had been, but far more reassuring, and thus, plausible.

Ask me, her eyes said, but he just changed the sheets, called the doctors to find out about more options that didn't exist. After that, she'd picked up the book, *Theo.* Raised it like a shield.

When Clara had come home for that last month, he'd gratefully removed himself to the kitchen. Made soups, then broths. Poured his love into them. Brought them with shaking hands into the room where his daughter sat by the bed, reading aloud, hour after hour.

"Do you remember that time we were camping in the Hoh Rain Forest, Mom?" he overheard her saying. "The water was dripping on the tent. I didn't want to go outside, and you said *One more chapter and then we'll go exploring.*"

From the doorway, he'd watched his wife's body, the body he'd touched so thoroughly, knew too well, tighten its way through the pain without letting their daughter see. He'd thought, angrily, *Don't ask your mother for more than she can do.* But then he saw Abigail's eyes open, saw her love pour into their daughter, and he realized that it was not Clara who was asking for too much.

Even then, however, he couldn't let the question leave his mouth.

What do you want, Abigail?

Then one day he'd walked into the bedroom and seen his daughter eating Abigail's bowl of soup, and he saw their eyes meet, then drop. He teased Clara gently, told her he'd bring her a bowl of her own, but he understood then. Understood that his wife's rapidly diminishing body was now a choice. One they had not shared. Because she couldn't or he wouldn't, or because the edges of those words would cut their life into pieces. And yet, as he had looked at the spoon in his daughter's hand, William realized that this was a secret Abigail had been able to share with Clara.

He wanted to scream. To cry. To argue. But all he'd done was take the empty bowl back to the kitchen. Make more soup that his wife would pretend to eat. And he told himself that this, too, was the loving thing to do.

At her memorial service, people had talked about William and Abigail's relationship, their bond. They made her death sound like *Love Story*, Ali MacGraw going so gently, so beautifully into that good night. No pain, just sadness, and perfect makeup.

You don't want to know, William thought as he listened to them talk. *You don't want to know how many ways we fail.*

William was starting to put the book down again when he saw the exclamation mark, written toward the bottom of the first page, next to a metaphor about the movement of wind through grass. He could imagine her starting the book, experiencing that little moment of pleasure. She was always an active participant in the act of reading, smiling or frowning along with the characters on the page. More than once, he'd seen a fellow passenger on a plane stop what they were doing just to watch her face.

He riffled through the pages and saw they were scattered with underlines and the occasional note—generally just a word, Abigail-code. But it was her, on the page. Not a photograph he'd seen a hundred times. Not a phone message he'd listened to so often that now he breathed along with her as she spoke. No. This was something new—Abigail after they'd stopped talking. Scattered bits, yes, but more than he thought he'd ever have again.

What did you want, Abigail?

It was like watching her read, except that instead of her facial expressions, he got the intensity of an underlining, a *yes!* in the margins. He could feel the pen in her hand, her happiness when the mother taught her son how to grow a garden.

Peaches, Abigail had written in the margin. And William remembered the summer they'd planted the tree, when Clara was small. How Clara had wanted fruit immediately, and Abigail had explained about delayed gratification, then taken Clara to the produce stand and bought a bushel.

Mostly, William read Theo's story as a backdrop to his wife's thoughts, a necessary context. But when he got to the scene where the father hit his son, he simply read, forgetting everything but the boy on the page. It was only at the chapter break that he looked back and realized that Abigail had not made a single notation on those pages. It felt like the times they used to drive through tunnels on their road trips, holding their breath together until they got to the other end.

Is this what you had with Clara, he wondered, *when you talked about books?*

He kept going, stopping only to add more wood to the fire, placing the postcard in between the pages to hold his place. Reading *Theo* was a slow process, he found, not only because of the brain fog, which was slipping in more often now, but because each word Abigail had written in the margins was an opening, a trail to follow, and he wanted every one of them.

He read through the night, using up the last of the oil in his lamp, but that didn't really matter anymore. By early afternoon the next day, he was most of the way through the book. Theo had accidentally killed his father, fled to the city, and was in danger of losing himself in that place, in his past.

In the margin, Abigail had written the word *mules*.

It took a moment, but then he had it—the only real low point of the weekend he'd proposed.

They'd hiked up to the mine itself, partly to get away from the crowds, partly because he'd thought maybe it would be a good place to pop the question—up there, looking out over the valley. But when she'd started to read the sign at the entrance to the boarded-up mine, he'd heard her startled exclamation, half moral indignation, half pure sadness, and he'd known the proposal would have to wait.

He'd leaned in next to her as she read aloud about the mules. How they were lowered into the shaft, blindfolded, their hooves bound so they wouldn't batter themselves on the walls if they panicked.

"If?" Abigail had said. "If?" She continued reading. When she stopped, her eyes were full.

"They stayed down there for life," she said. "They went blind."

Now William looked at the page, at the description of the boy, caught in a life he had not asked for. He could feel Abigail's yearning to set him free as strongly as if she had been standing next to him.

And then he saw the sentence, a bit farther down the page, underlined in Abigail's firm hand:

Guilt is easier to drown in than any ocean.

In the margin she'd written a *W.*

It was a small thing, but wasn't that what marriages were, in the end? The ability to hear love in an exhalation, to see frustration in the twitch of a finger, forgiveness in a single letter of the alphabet.

Oh, Abigail, he thought.

He sat there for a long while, eyes closed, and when he finally returned to the book, he discovered there were no more marks, the last fifty pages filled only with the words of the author.

Why did you stop, Abigail? he asked. But then he realized—that must have been when Clara arrived and began reading the book aloud.

A blaze of jealousy filled him—for their time together, their secrets. But then he stopped. He was too hungry, too tired, too alone, for that kind of bullshit. He knew as well as they had that no one had ever asked him to leave them alone. It had always been his choice. He'd been scared of the lush ease of their early intimacy, then, later, scared he'd appear ignorant. At the end, scared of what he'd hear.

And now it was his choice again. Abigail was handing it to him. There was someone who knew what she'd been thinking. Someone who might have her own thoughts to add to the equation. Someone who was still trying to live a life, without either of her parents—because he was a mule, and he'd put himself down the mine.

You see this girl? Abigail had said to him the day Clara was born. *This is the best conversation we'll ever have.*

He'd told her he would forget nothing, and yet he'd forgotten this.

William put the book down and went to the door of the hotel. His legs were shaking from hunger, but when he walked outside, he saw that while he was reading, the clouds had disappeared, and a bright sun was melting the snow into slush. It would likely turn to ice when the sun went down in a few hours. A small window of time, but a smart man—a man who understood roads—just might get out.

Southern California
2018

The Coordinator

It was only natural that Juliet became an intimacy co-ordinator for movies—one of those ironic/not ironic instances of name-job convergence, like their local orthopedist, Dr. Bohn, or the weatherman, Fred Rayne. When Juliet's mother learned that her daughter was choreographing sex scenes, she was shocked, but really, what could you expect? Juliet's life had been one long series of joking wherefore-art-thous, and roses by any other name, and requests for satisfaction. The job was just a logical extension.

Juliet could still remember the first time she saw the play. She was only twelve, but she had argued that it was *her* play, after all, so her parents relented and brought her with them. She'd sat in the audience in that large, dark space, the dialogue rushing past her in an incomprehensible flood, but it didn't matter because she was captivated by the swordplay in the opening scene, the intricate patterns of moving bodies, the way the actors could bring the swords so close to an arm or heart that you could swear they touched—and yet she knew they couldn't. There would be blood, there would be problems. But there was magic in the lack of contact, the lie-not-lie of it.

Then, not so much later, Romeo and Juliet's eyes met. The moment was built for a kiss (even young audience Juliet could tell that) but first everything slowed to two hands touching, palm to palm. And there was something about that small, quiet gesture, the way it both invited and delayed what was to come, that made Juliet fizz in parts of her she suspected shouldn't be fizzing while she sat in a fancy theater with her parents. But she didn't care, because it felt good even if it wasn't real.

After that, Juliet went on a fizz-hunt, as she thought of it. She'd always been a reader, but now she haunted the library, searching for books with the pages worn in certain corners. Adding her own warm touch as she read about long glances; fingers meeting while passing saltshakers, bottles of wine, letters; slim arms encircling a strong male back while riding horses or motorcycles; strong arms encircling a slim waist while teaching how to shoot a bow, hit a golf ball, fire a gun, row or steer or sail a boat. So many ways to get to the same destination.

She knew, in a way, that it was a destination not really meant for her. Those heroines were beautiful, or vastly intelligent and beautiful enough. Or morally pure. Or secret heiresses. In any case, things she was not. Her brown hair was unremarkable, and it did not appear as if her incoming hormones would give her the curvaceous body that would mean a ticket to the big show. But still she read, because what did it matter if it was words, not hands making you feel this way? You still got there.

Once, when Juliet was fourteen, a friend had shown her porn she'd discovered on her brother's computer. Juliet watched as flesh smacked against flesh in metronomic tempo. Her friend's eyes were lit with guilty excitement, but the whole experience reminded Juliet more of the time she had stolen a piece of See's candy off a counter, slipping it into her pocket only to find it later, half melted and covered in lint. Still recognizable as chocolate, sugar, but it felt as if that was no longer the point.

And so, Juliet went back to books.

It was at about this time that her high school, after almost a decade of lapsed attention due to budget cuts, reinstituted a physical education requirement. Juliet had never been interested in volleyball, and the idea of running around a track or climbing a rope to a ceiling did nothing for her. But there was another option. The history teacher had been enlisted to teach fencing, and Juliet remembered sitting in the theater and watching the swords moving in sweeping arcs through the air. The magic of it. She signed up.

In an odd way, there was something that felt familiar about fencing. The initial stance, looking sideways, measuring up your opponent. The feinting and parrying. The way you controlled the speed with purpose—moving in slowly,

slowly, only to lunge *now*. The pleasure of a hit, which was only a touch.

They used foils that were blunt on the end, and wore masks. The latter to protect the face and eyes but which also made the whole thing mysterious, impersonal, and yet (you were, after all, attempting the sports equivalent of murder) intimate. That's why the uniforms were white, the teacher informed them, so that back when fencing was done with sharper implements, the blood would show. Nowadays, it only made it more difficult when you had your period, Juliet thought.

But blood flow issues aside, she loved fencing. She thrilled to the speed of it, the way each movement of your opponent meant something—a flick of a wrist, the slight turn of a head, the tensing of a knee. When Juliet was in a match, her concentration was complete, every molecule, every thought focused. And when she won, tore off her mask in jubilation, the release was immense. By the time she was sixteen, she was a state champion. By the time she was eighteen, she had a scholarship to college, where along with fencing she planned to study politics, which, if you thought about it, shared many of her sport's essential qualities.

She went off to college and perhaps everything would have gone as planned, except that one day in her junior year, an extraordinarily beautiful young man came by fencing practice. He was in the acting department and was going to be in a play with a sword fight. He needed help. *A coach,* he said hopefully.

Of course, he picked the girl in the room. Honed in on her like a proverbial honeybee. Beautiful straight men always went for the woman, knowing the reception would be positive, having been cooed over by females since birth.

Don't coo, she told herself. But then, *Of course,* she said to him, looking at the blond hair, the lean muscles. *I'd love to help you.*

They slept together, once. More like a thank-you note on his part, Juliet thought later—but of the email variety, quick and not handwritten. Still, it wasn't the worst way to lose your virginity. Her own namesake had only gotten one night, after all.

And in the end, it wasn't the sex or even the beautiful young man she fell in love with. It was being in a theater, part of the movement of it all. Making the movement happen.

"Start in your head," she said to the beautiful actor as he rushed across the stage, holding the fake sword in a decidedly fake grip. "Think of it like seduction. You can't just blast in there." Although she realized he probably often did, with a high likelihood of success.

To be fair, he was no slouch when it came to acting—which is why he eventually got it. Wielded that fake sword like it really could cut an artery or take off a head. The other actors started coming to watch their practice sessions and asking for help themselves. The director happened by and solicited her advice on staging—which led to her choreographing a whole scene, then learning about boxing and martial arts, and eventually ending up with a career in how to make all that punching and stabbing look real to an audience that was fifteen or forty feet away. Yes, it was strange to have a woman telling (mostly) men how to fight, but there was something about her scenes that felt different, real.

You make it part of the story, one director said. And she thought, *Duh,* but didn't say it.

Because really, fighting wasn't that dissimilar from those scenes she'd read in the books in the library. How much difference was there between a slow-slow-lunge and a young woman, standing quietly at the edge of a ballroom, and then gently, casually, dropping her handkerchief?

Which was, perhaps, why a director asked for her help with a sex scene. Or maybe it was because she was the only female not actually on the stage, she wasn't sure, but in any case, when she saw the wide eyes of the actress, half-undressed for no particular reason, the clumsy paws of the actor reaching for whatever body parts he could get away with, she stepped forward.

How does this scene serve the story? she'd asked, careful to make her voice curious, not accusatory. The actress sent her a grateful glance. Then Juliet repurposed those big paws to their best advantage, as weakness as well as strength. And she put the nakedness back on the actress's face, where it belonged. The scene was a success, and sexy as hell.

After that, Juliet had two careers. An apartment in New York City, small, but hers. A group of friends, mostly actors, mostly acting, but always good for a drink in the evening. If sometimes she wondered what it would feel like to be in a love scene herself, to have someone else's fingers brush her cheek, she would shake her head and file the fantasy away as fodder for a future job. She turned twenty-five, twenty-eight, twenty-nine.

She met Richard on her thirtieth birthday. It was August, ridiculously hot, and she'd gone to the bar straight from rehearsal, her hair clipped up in a tousled mess, her tank top still more clothes than she wished she had to wear. Like a bad movie, the others had drunkenly paired off, leaving her alone. And there he was, all suit and loosened blue tie, a Manhattan in his hand, which seemed a bit on the nose, but his smile was open, not acting, and that was a relief.

He was—the irony of it—in politics. A consultant, not a candidate, he said.

"We're in the same business then," she said, and he cocked his head. "We make other people look better," she clarified.

And they toasted to that.

Life with Richard was fingertips slipping along skin, flowers on their first-month anniversary (him), coffee waiting in the pot in the morning (her), a wedding at two years. A life, if not exactly like the ones in the books, certainly better than Shakespeare gave his heroine. And then there was Josie, the year Juliet turned thirty-three, a seven-pound firework blowing up Juliet's world, leaving her in a new one made only of smells, textures, sounds. Being a mother felt like that moment when you won a fencing match, exhausted but every part of you alive.

Four months after Josie was born, Richard had come home from work, excitement pulsing off him. There was a senate campaign in Southern California, he said. Richard had been dying to get back to the West Coast where he'd grown up, and the candidate was everything you'd hope for—tall and idealistic, with a perfect hard-luck-hard-work backstory. Juliet was on maternity leave, anyway, he said. She could stay home with Josie, if she wanted.

Just imagine, he said. *A backyard.*

So they moved, because honestly, a fourth-floor walk-up was less enchanting with a stroller. Juliet and Josie spent their days in the Santa Monica sun and went to parks and made sandcastles at the beach. Three times a week, in the evenings, Juliet taught acting classes on fighting and kissing.

"Think of touch in levels," she told her students. "You can make contact as if you are reaching for skin, or muscle, or bone. Each choice tells a different story. Think of Madame Olenska in *The Age of Innocence,* barely touching Archer's knee with her fan. Or Jimmy Stewart's character in *It's a Wonderful Life,* finally giving in and kissing Mary with everything he's got."

After class she'd return home and crawl into bed with Josie for a few minutes. Feel the warmth of her daughter's body fill her soul. Life was good, as the T-shirt said. Josie turned three, then five. Started kindergarten. Juliet expanded her teaching schedule. Richard got a job with a consulting firm in LA—less travel, if more hours.

But just when everything seemed to be heading for endless normality, a presidential candidate got caught on tape and managed to blow up everything but his own career. Then, a year later, a story everybody already knew broke in *The New York Times,* and there was no pretending that Hollywood wasn't just as bad as politics. After decades of movie actors being told to *just go for it* when filming a sex scene, there was a call for "intimacy coordinators," who were sometimes the human equivalent of pasties, but sometimes a full-on choreographer. And there was Juliet, in the right place at the right time, with all the right moves.

Suddenly, she found herself on movie sets, negotiating boundaries, wardrobe, hand placement. Changing a monotonous *unh, unh, unh* into something more unexpected, musical, so sound could carry some of the weight of the scene. Angling bodies so they appeared closer than they were. Still, there was only so much you could do to create some distance for the actors.

"Think about it," she said to Richard one night, as they stood next to each other at the bathroom sink. "When you do a fight scene, no one expects you to literally stab or hit someone. But a kiss *is* a kiss."

"The sex isn't actually sex, though," he said.

She wondered for a moment if he was talking about movies or the two of them. Life was good, but some parts of it could certainly be better.

"No," she said, figuring the answer would work for either. "But even if you aren't having sex, there's a lot of contact going on. And it's amazing how hard it can be to say what you want. Or don't."

Richard looked at her for a beat longer than usual, but then he passed her the toothpaste and they continued toward bed, and sleep. They both had early mornings coming up.

Two years passed, full and complicated. And then one day, Juliet was flying home from Paris to LA, having completed a period drama involving the slow removing of corsets, preparing for an action flick set in a dystopian future where women had, apparently, developed an allergy to any clothing not made of spandex. In a world that seemed to be changing by the hour, Juliet thought, some things did not.

Generally, she liked the long flights. The time-travel feeling of entering a small space, turning off the lights, letting go of the last project and readying herself for the next. Intimacy coordinators did not rate business or first class, but she'd learned to give herself a drink allowance and use it early, put on her noise-canceling headphones, and pull up the next script on her computer screen. She'd do a full read-through, feeling the narrative build, the characters intertwine. Some coordinators might go straight to their scenes, but for Juliet, those moments could only truly grow in context, and as she read, coming to see the subplots and themes, words turned into gestures and movements in her head. There was such power in the small choices. She could raise the tension before a first kiss by slowing down the hero's crossing of the room to eight counts instead of four—or speeding it up to two. She could change the meaning of a scene by choosing to have the actress put her free hand on her partner's face, or hip, or chest. *Micromanaging,* one director called it, but Juliet had been a fencer, and she knew that humans were hardwired to read the smallest cues, even if it was subconsciously. Lives depended on it.

Sitting in her seat on those long flights, she would test out potential choreography using her hands, feeling the energy, the balance, the power shift. Together, apart. Slow, quick. Half the time she did it without even thinking. She knew it was an odd thing to do in public, but she had learned to tell curious seatmates that she was learning sign language. Those long uninterrupted hours on a plane were too precious to give up just because of a funny look or two.

Except this time, nothing worked as it should.

The new script was not attached to the email from the director's assistant. And when the plane reached altitude, it became clear that the Wi-Fi was out, as were the movie selections, and there was no reason to believe any of it would be reinstated for the duration of the twelve-hour flight. Grumbling rose and fell along the rows of seats. The only people not upset appeared to be the parents who came preloaded with episodes of *Clifford the Big Red Dog* on their iPads, and the few readers who had already pulled out paperbacks or e-books and settled in.

Damn, Juliet thought. Not having that script meant

she'd have to read it on a weekend she'd already planned to spend exclusively with Josie and Richard. She'd been gone five days and Josie, now eight, was full of plans for their time together. All Juliet wanted to do was to dive into that world of real bodies and fingers sticky from peanut butter. She wanted to lie in a bed in a ratty T-shirt and not think about how high the sheet would need to be to protect the augmented breasts of an underpaid actress. She wanted to be pounced on with all the knobby knees and elbows her daughter possessed, feel those wiry curls on her face as Josie snuggled in.

She could try to sleep now, hoard up the hours to be spent later, even though that would destroy any hope of getting back on the right time zone. But even there she was stymied, having used her last Ambien the night before to mellow out the adrenaline that always came with the end of a shoot. She had no books; she'd bypassed the airport bookstore, certain she had more reading material than she had hours for.

With a sigh she took out the in-flight magazine and read about places she could have gone in the city she was now leaving. Places she could go in Los Angeles that would never allow children. For the first time in her life, she found herself wishing for a book on her phone, even though she honest-to-god did not understand how you could feel the momentum of a story when you could only read twenty words at a time.

But then she remembered. She did have a book. A couple years back, her friend Terry had sent her an audiobook as a gift, one of those try-it-and-you'll-get-hooked marketing promotions.

I loved this! I bet you will, too.

Juliet had downloaded the book, not wanting to appear ungrateful, then promptly forgotten its existence. But there it was, using up space in her phone's memory, if not her own. Maybe it would help her fall asleep. It couldn't hurt. The couple behind her were running out of fuel in their bitch session about the Wi-Fi, which likely meant they would turn on each other soon. She put on her headphones and then clicked the book icon on her screen.

Theo, *by Alice Wein, read for you by* . . .

The man behind her pushed a sharp shoulder into the back of her seat as he dug around in his carry-on. Juliet readjusted her headphones, shifted position toward the window, and closed her eyes with intent.

It took her a full chapter to recognize the voice of the reader. The beautiful actor. The one she'd taught to fence. She remembered, vaguely, seeing a magazine headline while standing in a grocery store years ago, something about his flaming out, disappearing. She'd felt a momentary pang, but she'd been pregnant at the time, and a wave of morning sickness, brought on by a whiff of sauerkraut from the deli counter, had sent the whole thing sideways.

Now she listened to his voice, which had always been as golden and flexible as the rest of him. The actor she'd slept with could get anyone to do anything, believe anything—and if the voice, the muscles, didn't work, there was the smile. But this voice was different, somehow, vulnerable in a way she didn't remember, inhabiting the life of the boy, Theo, as if its broken places were a geography he knew well. And while that might have been acting, she wasn't sure it was. Maybe there had been something real behind that story in the magazine. *What changed you?* she wondered.

Or maybe she was reading things into it. Long plane rides could do that, disrupt your usual modes of behavior. Before she'd learned the trick with the headphones, she'd found herself in more than one confessional conversation with a seatmate, spurred on by a cone of light in an otherwise darkened cabin, the feeling that you were two human beings who would walk away at the end of the flight, carrying each other's secrets, to be known but not used.

Her prior experience with the actor had been rather the opposite—used, but not known. This voice in her ear felt different, however. Intimate. Although that might have had something to do with the headphones, she reminded herself.

Still, she kept listening, the voice of the actor and the voice of the book weaving together, becoming one. Sometimes the experience felt so dreamlike she almost fell asleep, but the words floated along with her until she came back and found them again.

It was probably six hours later when Theo met the love of his life. There were no fireworks, no steamy glances across a room. Just two human beings, falling together like puzzle pieces, which made sense because both of them were broken, their edges not the smooth arcs or straight lines of others, which fit easily into so many situations. No, there was only one place each of them belonged, and that was with the other. It sounded dramatic, but wasn't. More like an animal finding its natural habitat.

Their eventual love scene came about ten hours in. Pivotal, but described in only the briefest of sentences. *How would you choreograph that?* Juliet wondered, pausing the audio to think.

The trick, she decided as she took a sip of her second vodka tonic, would be making the scene feel entirely equal. Not just a trading back and forth of power (the old flipping-positions-from-top-to-bottom-and-back-again), but a complete and total sharing of it. Here were two people who'd had to learn to read between the lines of those around them—and for the first time in their lives, they were with someone who saw them with the same perceptivity they saw others.

It would be tempting to choreograph the scene so that the lovers' actions mirrored each other, but that wasn't the point, either. Even if their skill level was the same, these two characters were different. He had grown up interpreting the movements of his father the way fishermen read the sea, always looking for what lay beneath. She'd lost her parents far too early, had to make her own way through a world of strangers. Same skill, different origins. Same noun, different verbs. Anyone can love their mirror image; it's the easiest thing in the world to love what you already know. But how do you love difference as if it's a part of you? And how would you show that on-screen?

Romeo and Juliet, she thought now. *With a twist.* Two palms coming together, but the camera's focus would be on the characters' faces rather than their hands, each of their expressions breaking open—one into healing, the other into joy. The allusion to the original play adding its own layer of meaning—*You could live, this time.*

It was an old-school love scene, for sure, but there were days—or nights, on a plane that was quiet and dark—when Juliet yearned for a long, slow look across a room, a hand on a cheek for a count of four. So much of her work involved fighting against the tide of the scripted quick-and-efficient love scene (*characters kiss and fall into bed*). Or, just as bad, the emerging-couple montage (*musical interlude while new couple walks on the beach/eats at a restaurant/laughs in a park*)—which was occasionally cute but usually just felt like the screenwriter couldn't be bothered to develop a relationship.

When did we give all that up? she wondered.

And then, *Why do I want it so?*

She turned the book back on, and there was the beautiful actor's voice, turning her yearning into sound.

But why yearning? she found herself wondering. She was happily married. She'd loved Richard from that first loosened tie. Her hands knew every muscle of his body, her memories held his every gasp of pleasure or pain or frustration.

And yet, she realized, these days she felt rather more like a filing cabinet for that information than an active participant. It had been that way for a while. Having a child changed a marriage, of course; she knew that. There had been the rapid onset of more responsibilities than she and Richard had ever imagined, fewer hours, no sleep. The shift into *mom* and *dad*, which provided its own form of distancing. When Juliet worked with actors, she taught them the concept of *de-roling*, a way of stepping out of a character at the end of the day so you could return unencumbered to your other life. But the parenting role, once assumed, tended to stay put.

It was more than that, however—because the thing the experts didn't talk about when giving you advice on breast-feeding or bottle-cleaning or sleep-training was how fundamentally motherhood changed your vision of human relationships. A child could make you love bone-deep, make you try to see further into another person than you ever thought possible, to understand who they were, what they needed, wanted. But with that astonishing depth of love came the realization that no one was doing the same for you. And that could make you lonely.

It was easy to say (and many had) that that kind of love was simply maternal, a product of hormones and circumstance not feasible in relationships between adults in a busy world—and that sex was the ultimate grown-up alternative.

Her own industry contributed to that mindset. There was catharsis in those hot sex scenes, and back in the beginning of her relationship with Richard, she'd seen the effortlessness, the adventure of their sex life as a sign of their perfect communion.

And yet, now she thought about those long looks, that palm-to-palm kiss. What made them sexy was not the tease of it. No, what created the fizz was the hearts, the minds, behind those eyes and hands, reaching bone-deep.

The voice of the beautiful actor seemed to understand. She could hear him searching his way into the words, trying to reach inside them. Carving, curving, leaning into every choice, paying attention to every comma, every consonant. The book was rounding a corner, getting ready for the end; she could feel the change in his voice as if it was the weight of the last fifty pages themselves shifting in her hands.

Not yet, Juliet thought. *Just a bit more.*

Suddenly, the cabin lights switched on. "We are now starting our descent into Los Angeles International Airport," announced the flight attendant.

Classic, Juliet thought. But that didn't make taking off her headphones any easier. Ninety minutes left, she saw as she clicked Stop. All she wanted was to finish.

It was 1:30 in the afternoon when Juliet exited the airport, eyes squinting against the Southern California sun. She'd taken off at 10:15 A.M., Paris time. The plan had been to read the script and zombie her way through a movie, maybe two, not really falling asleep but giving her body enough of a break that she could stay awake until Josie went to sleep. A plan which might, with the help of a couple Advil PM and some melatonin, get her back on track the next day. But instead, she had dived into a voice, left her body behind somewhere over the Atlantic. Now she had to drag it back into her real life—along with her mind, which was, it could be argued, still a bit waterlogged as well. Still not here.

She had an hour drive in front of her. She got her car from long-term parking, plugged her phone into the jack, and turned on the book. Let the voice flow around her like warm fingers on the sore muscles of her neck.

Traffic was oddly nonexistent, and when Juliet drove her car into the driveway exactly sixty minutes later, Josie blasted out the front door, a rainbow sparkler of plaids and flowers, hair flying six ways to Saturday.

"Mommy!" she yelled, pulling open the car door, throwing herself inside. She smelled like sugar and chlorine and dirt, and without thinking, Juliet pieced together her day— doughnuts, pool, backyard—before she even looked up to see Richard smiling at her.

"I swear she chose her own clothes," he said, as if she might have thought it happened any other way.

"Who's that talking?" Josie asked, pointing at the dashboard. "He sounds sleepy."

"Just a story," Juliet said, turning it off. "It's almost done."

"Can I listen?" Josie asked.

"It's not for kids," Juliet said.

"Can *I* listen, then?" Richard said. He had that *it's been five days since I've seen you naked* tone in his voice. Usually, Juliet thought it was attractive, or at least cute. Now, she put on the face that would normally greet this kind of repartee. *I've missed you, too.*

But no, he would not listen to the book, because something told Juliet that he wouldn't get what she was getting out of it, and his not getting it would absolutely wreck hers.

It wasn't like she was having an affair. It was just a voice. A book. A book that had another thirty minutes left, and all she wanted was to take it to the goal line.

"Daddy said you'd make cookies with me when you got home," Josie declared.

Daddy was going for a run because Daddy had been on deck for five days. And that was true and right, but as Juliet put in twice the amount of vanilla and almost lost the rubber spatula into the moving blade of the mixer, she thought that perhaps a bit more adult supervision might have come in handy. Or maybe a nap. Why did children stop taking naps?

When Juliet was young and declared that she no longer needed to sleep in the afternoons, her mother had instituted a tradition that she called a "reading rest," which meant that who the hell cared if you slept but you still had to go to your room for an hour and be quiet. What her mother did during that time Juliet never knew. She also didn't think about it because she actually *was* reading, and it was magical, leaving her life for an hour in the middle of everything, going someplace else. Even before the fizz-hunt started, those hours felt secret, stolen. Different from sleeping, where you had no choice where you went. Picking up a book was a decision: *I'm going to go away.* The exciting possibility: *I may not come back the same.*

Which was pretty much the problem now, Juliet thought as she watched her daughter dropping blobs of cookie dough onto a baking sheet. She wasn't quite back, and she wasn't quite the same.

"Don't lick your fingers," she said to Josie. "Remember?"

"Yup yup yup," Josie said, but Juliet saw her index finger make a quick dip into the bowl and then her mouth before she dragged the step stool over to the sink to wash her hands.

Juliet made it through the afternoon, and dinner. After Josie was finally in bed, Richard and Juliet had sex, because Richard *was* a good father and he *had* been on deck and maybe it would help her sleep anyway. Except she was too tired to stick with it long enough to do any good for herself.

"Are you sure you're okay?" he asked. "I can . . ."

"No," she said, "we're good."

Which left her lying in bed next to Richard, who had rapidly fallen into oblivion. Her own body thrummed like an airplane, refusing to sleep.

But wasn't that what she'd been wanting since she got

home, after all? A little peace and quiet so she could get back to the book?

The idea of listening to the beautiful actor's voice with Richard right there next to her felt strange, but he was knocked out, and the bed felt too good to switch to the couch downstairs, so she put on her headphones one more time and clicked Play.

It was a quiet ending. No villains to conquer, no fight scenes to choreograph. Just two people, finding their way out of the thorns that were their lives. Seeing a path before them. It was a beginning more than an ending, and likely to be a complicated one—but that, the book told her, was okay.

All that matters is that we try, the beautiful actor's voice said in her ears.

Then he went away, leaving Juliet in the darkened bedroom, not wanting it to be over, wondering what to do next.

She thought of doing a Google search for the beautiful actor—*Rowan,* she remembered now, although she couldn't retrieve a last name. She guessed that wouldn't matter. A scandal (and she figured it had to have been to get the magazines so excited) left you with first-name fame: *Mel. Brad. Britney.* She wondered where Rowan was living these days, what he was doing.

But each of these thoughts, the sheer reality of them, was intruding on the experience. All she wanted was to be in that story, with that voice, and never leave. Maybe she should go back to the beginning, start again.

Get off the plane, Juliet, she heard a voice saying in her head, and this time she realized it was her own.

At first, she honestly wasn't sure what she was telling herself, but after a few moments, sitting there in her own bed, next to the man she'd been married to for over ten years, the words made a weird kind of sense. Because really, this whole experience had felt less like reading and more like one of those late-night conversations on a plane. The kind where you didn't have to worry about who was going to wash the dishes or figure out how to make a relationship feel new when it absolutely wasn't. The kind that took you back to who you used to be. De-roled you, as it were.

But eventually you got off the plane and went your own way. Because even when she was single, Juliet had always known those conversations were special precisely because they were separate from real life, and that the connection would never withstand the transition. In the same way, she knew that she didn't want Rowan. She'd already had him, for that matter, and she could bet he didn't remember, no matter how sensitive his voice sounded through the headphones. She didn't want a man who didn't know the crazy of her days, or the exact pitch of her daughter's giggles.

Sitting there in bed, Juliet remembered giving birth to Josie, the mind-blowing pain of it, the relief and euphoria when it was done. Richard afterward, holding her face in his hands, looking into her eyes.

You are extraordinary, he'd said, and she'd known then that he didn't mean just what she'd done in the last ten hours, or nine months, or three years. He meant her, all of her, right down to the bone. The memory of that moment had gotten lost somewhere in the middle of potty training and peanut butter sandwiches and calendar scheduling, but now it came back. A gift from the man lying next to her, his breathing just loud enough to let her know he was there even when she wasn't looking.

Juliet turned off her phone and placed it on the nightstand. She lay down next to Richard, feeling the warmth of his back against her chest and stomach, her curves and angles finding their place in his. Then she put an arm around him and let her hand slide down the front of his body for a count of one, two, three, four. He stirred, waking.

"Let's try that again," she said into his ear.

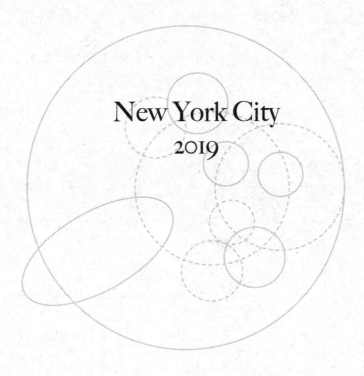

New York City
2019

The Agent

They called her the Empress of Deals, the Queen-Maker of Literature. She was the Doyen. The Dragon Lady. The Fixer. She liked to say she'd had more titles tested out on her than any novel she'd represented. All of them, like every book title, more or less accurate, more or less trite. Designed for marketing purposes, in any case, as no title could ever really capture a story.

Fleet little things, stories were. For more than fifty years, Madeline Armstrong had been their net. They'd been her children, her collection, lining the walls of her office and home.

Good insulation, one lover had said, looking around her living room. He was a carpenter, originally brought in to build more bookshelves, so the comment made sense. And he was right, although maybe not in the way he intended.

* * *

There was a feeling when a new story fireworked off the page, made its power and beauty known. She loved that moment, always had. Her sudden clarity that this book would affect not just her, but others. Lots of others. Because while people liked to think that literature was about words, publishing was about numbers. And someone who could take words and translate them into numbers gave royalty a whole new meaning.

Madeline had that. She could see the gold among the gloss, could turn a bit of glitter into something substantial, viable, a career.

It had all started with a voice in the slush pile. Strong and female—*which was probably why it was overlooked*, she would say in her acceptance speeches for the lifetime achievement awards that were, in her seventy-sixth year, coming all too often now. Tiny brooms, sweeping her off the stage.

Before she'd found *that voice*, she'd been working as an assistant in a literary agency, barely out of college, her hair straightened and flipped at the ends, her dress short-but-not-too-short-but-it-didn't-matter-because-they-were-going-to-pat-your-ass-anyway. Still, she'd believed that if she could find the next big thing, they would look at her differently. It took five years of handing off promising manuscripts to male agents who took the credit (and the 15 percent), but finally she found the extraordinary one they didn't think could sell. And she made the deal that made all their jaws drop.

By the age of thirty-five, she had her own agency—small but mighty, she liked to say. By the time she was fifty, it was big and mighty, and she liked that even more. Because she had quickly learned that getting a book sold and published had everything to do with who and what she knew. Yes, the voice, the story, was critical, but perhaps even more so was knowing which editor was secretly pregnant and would be susceptible to a memoir about a mother's hunt for her missing child, or which one had recently divorced and might relish a snarky female serial killer. Books spoke to specific people for specific reasons, and it had everything to do with where they were in their lives. Madeline's knowledge of these crucial details had gotten the big sales, and that was why for decades when she had put out the whisper that she had *something special,* editors would drop their Friday-night plans and read until dawn so they wouldn't get scooped by the other ten they knew she'd told.

Sometimes she'd done it on Saturdays, just for fun.

Lately and increasingly things had changed, however. Literature was being clear-cut down to flashes and tweets. New authors were heading for her younger agents—a bit farther down the ladder, yes, but perhaps with more athletic climbing abilities.

There were times, too, when she woke up in the morning feeling foggier than she preferred. Her mind would have to search too long for the day of the week, or even month. Her right hand strangely weak. It generally cleared up in a few hours, or days. But she'd been late to work twice, and she'd had to start double-checking her emails before sending, after an embarrassing switch of *witch* to *bitch*. "It wouldn't have happened if vampires were still de rigueur," she muttered, and then wondered when muttering had become something she did.

How old is she? she'd heard the new receptionist asking one of the assistants. A murmur of laughter.

Laughter. Seriously. She could pay all their salaries off her authors alone.

Do you know Queen Elizabeth is the longest-living British monarch in history? she wanted to say to them. *And before her, Victoria? Women stay in power as long as they damn well please.*

"But do you want to?" her friend Savannah asked over lunch one day. Savannah was a good twenty years younger and an editor at one of the big houses, but she had never, not once, acted like Madeline was a conduit for income—or her mother. Originally there had been some mild flirtation, but both had come down on the side of friendship, and it had lasted.

"What a question," Madeline said.

But it was exactly that—an interrogative. An interruption in the rhythmic flow of her narrative. A flow she had no intention of breaking, thank you.

She decided to walk back to the office after lunch. It was a beautiful September day, the city bustling just the way she liked it; she a big cog in its machinery.

It could tempt one to hum the theme from *The Mary Tyler Moore Show*. Throw a blue beret in the air.

And it was at that moment that the right toe of her elegant high heel caught in a crack in the pavement. *Christ, I hate unsubtle irony,* she thought, even as she was falling.

A FOOSH, the brisk emergency room doctor called it when he examined her wrist. Fall on outstretched hand. FOOSH sounded like a title for the kind of book her newest agent was always excited about. But her wrist, if not exactly broken, was definitely cracked. And of course it was her right one, so there went signing contracts, or writing notes or . . . hell, just about anything.

"Although how you didn't do an ankle or a hip, I have no idea," the doctor was saying.

Hip. The old-lady bone.

"Strong legs," she said. She held up a shapely calf like a challenge and saw to her embarrassment that her knees had not come out of the experience unscathed. She hadn't banged one up since she was seven and had really gotten into books.

"Did you hit your head?" he asked, pulling back her hair, examining her scalp. His fingers were impersonal and efficient. Madeline thought of the carpenter, mornings in bed. A different kind of touch. Too long ago now.

"I don't think so," she said, forcing her mind back to the exam room. "It happened pretty quickly. The wrist took the bullet."

"I want to do a CAT scan just in case," the doctor said, "given your age."

The man could use a little sensitivity training, Madeline thought, and then remembered Savannah had recommended the same thing for her once, joking but also not.

"They're writers," Savannah had said. "This is their life they just handed you. You could be kinder."

"They're in a profession, not a preschool. That's the first lesson."

She'd had to learn some toughness herself, back in the day. But now, sitting on the crackling white paper of an exam table, Madeline thought perhaps Savannah had been right: a little kindness wouldn't go amiss.

The CAT scan led to an MRI. Madeline was about to get on her high horse about health insurance scams, but something in the technician's face stopped her, and when the doctor returned, maybe sooner than he should have, she sat up, ready to listen—if a little floaty from the hydrocodone they'd given her for the pain.

"Do you know what CAA is?" he asked.

Really? "Creative Arts Agency," she said. He must have figured out who she was. Oh lord, was he one of those doctors who had secret writing aspirations? A screenplay in his back pocket?

"Cerebral amyloid angiopathy," he clarified. "It's a buildup on the walls of the arteries in the brain."

"And?" Part of her was still hoping they were talking about a questionable movie plot.

"When the pressure builds up enough," he said, "the wall gives. You have a stroke."

When—a good writer could turn a plot on the choice of one word, she'd always said.

"It appears it's already occurred a few times," the doctor continued, "on a smaller scale."

Madeline thought of those slow mornings, the games of vocabulary hide-and-seek. The headaches she'd attributed to her new assistant's incompetence. The eight hours she didn't talk about—when her vision had gone blurry and she'd had to cover her absence at work with a story about a secret meeting with a reclusive author.

You've been busy, she said to her brain now.

The doctor was still speaking. "The impact on your life depends on the severity and the side of the brain. Left looks most probable in this case."

"Which means?" she asked, cutting in.

"Language, processing, organization."

Everything, then.

It was like tripping on the crack in the pavement a second time, fate smacking you in the face when all you were doing was walking. *Doesn't he know,* she thought, *the reader needs time to absorb the big reveal—a chapter break. A paragraph of description.*

But the questions had already started. *Did she smoke? Drink?*

Are you kidding? she wanted to say. She'd been a literary agent since the 1960s. Every lunch had been a miasma of smoke. Even after she'd quit cigarettes in the '80s, she'd known better than to ask an author or an editor to stop. Alcohol wasn't even worth talking about. *Occupational hazard,* she'd always called it.

"How soon?" she asked.

He looked at her as if she'd missed a major plot point.

"Any time," he said.

In the meantime, he continued, eat healthy, don't drink alcohol, blah blah blah—and did she live with anyone? Were there stairs in her home?

Ha. Ha. Ha.

Madeline's new assistant, Owen, arrived as she was getting ready to leave. He was a nice enough boy, but originally from Ohio and had no idea how to snag a taxi. No wonder it had taken him so long to get to the hospital—but at least it had given her a chance to frame the narrative in a truthful, if highly edited, form. *I tripped. Cracked a bone in my wrist. Everything's fine.*

The rest was her business, and only hers. She'd worked with enough authors to know you never gave away a whole story until you knew what you were going to do with it.

Out on the street, she launched her black-casted wrist into the air. A Yellow Cab stopped with a deeply satisfying screech. Owen looked at her, eyes big.

"You're amazing," he said. "Why am I even here?"

A question worth asking.

Owen filled the ride back to her house with platitudes and a debriefing of the afternoon at the office. At some point, Madeline stopped listening, her thoughts jostling along with the wheels, pondering the doctor's pronouncement. A death sentence. Or worse—a dangling participle of an existence.

She remembered a *Modern Love* essay she'd read a few years back, written by a young woman whose mother had died of cancer. Technically, the mother had died of starvation, her choice of the least painful exit. The daughter had written beautifully about how her mother had hidden the plan from her husband in order not to hurt him. About how—in their fear? Their love?—her parents had never talked about what was so obviously coming. It ended on a soapbox about the injustice of a system that left only the slow road to starvation when there were simpler alternatives. Soapbox aside, the writing had so impressed Madeline that she'd actually contacted the young woman—what was her name? Christa? Something starting with a C—to see if there was a book in it. But it hadn't worked out.

Now, though, Madeline thought about the mother, and that last part of the essay. What would it be like, being stuck in a body that no one would let you leave?

Never, she said to herself.

When they got to her address, the taxi stopped, and Owen's eyes got even bigger.

"You live here?" he said. "It's like the old woman who lived in the shoe." And then he clamped his mouth shut.

"Indeed," she said.

"Should I . . . ?" he said, looking between her and the house. "Do you need . . . ?"

"I'll be fine," she said firmly. "It's just a wrist. You should get back to the office. I'll call a service first thing." Although honestly, she had no intention. She didn't need flutterers.

The cab drove off, taking Owen back to the beehive. She could imagine the scene going on there. There would be jostling for position. It might be just a cracked bone, but the symbolism was glaring. *She who wields the pen*—or can't, and all that. Two agents wanted the top slot. Lara would be the calm third, not quite ready for that much power, but better suited temperamentally than either of the others.

None of them taking over yet, she told herself as she entered her front door and started climbing the stairs.

She'd lived in the same home for thirty years now, an architectural oddity, only twelve feet wide (less, once she added all the bookshelves), slivered between two of New York City's now-finer brownstones—although none of them had been particularly fine when she'd bought hers. But she loved the neighborhood, near a small park, and she relished the Swiss Family Robinson feeling of constantly climbing upward from one room to the next, kitchen to miniscule living-and-dining room, to bedroom, to office. A home for one, although at times two had made the brick walls rock.

Her novella, she called it, and even though people had been telling her for more than a decade that it no longer made sense, she swore the exercise kept her in shape. And she'd fallen on the sidewalk, for Christ's sake, not the stairs.

Besides, this place was hers. After thirty years, remarkably so. The antique faucets that had been her first splurge, the honey-colored walls of the bedroom and the deep blue fainting couch with its view out to the street; the tiny patio with its ancient wisteria and a pair of slingback chairs. She'd read manuscripts in every corner, every chair, in the bed, the tub. A Memory Palace made real—*here is where I found the Pulitzer Prize winner; there is where I discovered the novel that took five years to go into paperback. That's where I read the first memoir that made me sob.* Stories seeped into the walls like paint. People asked her sometimes if she was lonely living on her own, and she wanted to laugh. She was the least solitary person she knew.

But there was solitary, and there was *solitary,* she thought now as she entered her silent kitchen. She texted Savannah, who was there in half an hour (now that woman could hail a cab), bringing six perfect little meals from the local deli. Soups and custards and salads. No casseroles, thank heavens. She packed Madeline's tiny fridge and promised to bring more.

"Any time," she said.

Any time. Funny how those two words could be reassuring—or terrifying. Madeline opened her mouth to tell Savannah about the doctor's pronouncement, but just then

Savannah closed the refrigerator door, saying "Do you want me to stay here tonight? Or call a nurse?"

And Madeline thought, *I will not be an invalid.*

"It's only a wrist," she said. "Let's just sit for a bit." So they settled into the chairs in the living room, Madeline's forearm propped appropriately above heart level, and talked about rude doctors and scuffed shoes and Savannah's new girlfriend who was tattooed and wonderful and only read Twitter.

An hour or so later, Madeline sent her on her way—but first Savannah insisted on bringing everything Madeline might need up to the bedroom and helping her change into more comfortable clothes. There was a time when she might have worried about Savannah seeing her less-than-perfect body, but not now. Now it was just nice to feel hands upon her. Unbuttoning, buttoning. Lifting covers, slipping her in.

There should have been more of this, Madeline thought. *There could have been more of this.*

"Are you sure?" Savannah asked. It took Madeline a moment to understand the question.

"I'm fine," she said. "Down to Tylenol already. Off you go."

Because while the comfort had been nice, some small animal part of her knew what she needed was time alone in her head. To figure this out. Not the wrist—that was stupid and would heal—but the other.

A reader should never know the ending too far in advance, she always told her authors. In real life, however, Madeline had liked knowing where she was heading. She'd been the girl taking the advanced classes in school, getting the internships, climbing every ladder at work, using those sharp high heels to keep the rungs free below her. She'd loved the clarity of it, the same single-mindedness that had allowed her to enter the chaos of an author's work and emerge with something clean and marketable. The proof was all around her on her bookshelves. The walls of a most beautiful ivory tower. Her monument.

She'd built an incredible life, aiming for the known goal. But now, her casted right arm like a small, useless log on the top of the comforter, her brain ticking its way out of existence, she found herself thinking that this time she could have done without the foreshadowing. Preferred a plot twist that cut short her story without a moment's notice. Wrecking the narrative tension, of course, but what would she care? She wouldn't be here.

Unless, of course, she *was* still here after.

She hadn't really considered that possibility before today. Should have, certainly; she was seventy-six, after all. But humans tended toward myopia when it came to their own mortality, a necessary suspension of disbelief that—and here was irony, raising its head once again—only seemed to get stronger with age.

But the reality was that if she survived whatever was coming, she would almost certainly be carted off to some euphemistically named *home*—while this real home, this life she'd created would become . . . what? Someone else's to deal with. The most inelegant of epilogues.

Lying in bed, Madeline cast her mind through the four stories of her house, her imagination moving across the objects she'd collected over the decades. The Matisse sketches. The plates she'd brought back from Turkey. The furniture she'd carefully chosen, piece by piece. Things that had kept her company, things that had felt like family. But now, viewing them through her new perspective on life (or not-life), she realized that most of these possessions did not, as the bestseller said, *spark joy*.

Her books, though—they were different. Each one held that zing she'd felt when its story opened her mind in a new direction. That moment of satisfaction when all the pieces—writer, editor, cover art, layout, and, finally, the paper itself—came together into the object she held in her hands. These books, both containers and uncontainable. Who would take care of them?

The sorting alone could take weeks, she thought. Or not— maybe someone would come in and box them up, dump them on some poor, unsuspecting used bookstore. Never noticing the inscriptions, never knowing the history. The thought of her books being touched by uncaring hands made her own shake with frustration.

Not on my watch, she said, right before the Tylenol PM pulled her down into sleep.

When she woke the next morning, it was already 9 A.M. Madeline called in to the office, encountering a flurry of *how are you*s, a fluttering of concern. She could almost smell the talcum powder.

"I'm fine," she said, "and I've decided to take a week off." Savannah had told her once that saying *and* instead of *but* made people feel more positive about your statements. She thought it sounded ridiculously awkward, but she was willing to give it a go.

"Of course," Owen said quickly. "There's nothing that can't wait." A phrase that absolutely had never been uttered in her agency before.

Crack. Crack. She could hear it happening, even over the phone. The rungs of the ladder going out beneath her.

But oddly—perhaps it was her Jacob Marley-esque experience of the previous evening—she found she didn't care. Not about the office or its politics, at least not as much as she'd thought she would. What she cared about was her books. Not the ones that might be, but the ones here with her now. She hung up and spent the rest of the day in bed, then on the couch, moving slowly from level to level, story to story. Not reading, just looking at the shelves.

She found a listing on the local university online bulletin board—*Looking for work: Companion. Babysitting. Organization.* Madeline didn't want the first and hadn't ever needed the second, but like Goldilocks, the third one seemed about right to her. She set up an appointment for Saturday morning, two days from then.

The girl rang the bell promptly at 8:30 A.M. and was just turning away when Madeline got to the front door. The wrist was feeling much better, but it was still a four-story house, after all.

Not a good sign, Madeline thought. *She's impatient.*

But in fact, the girl looked more curious than anything, staring up the tall, thin length of Madeline's home.

"Is that you?" she asked, pointing at the building. Not *yours* but *you*. And while Madeline thought the answer should be obvious, she also liked how accurately the question was phrased.

"Yes," she said. "I'm Madeline."

"Nola," the girl said, holding out her hand, as if she had been taught to in one of those seminars on how-to-land-a-job. Madeline raised her casted wrist and Nola blushed.

"Sorry," she said, and then, more firmly, "nice to meet you."

Madeline led the way up the stairs to the living room. She'd made tea—that's what characters in novels did, when they were old and looking for assistance, or just wanting to make their cultural superiority known. Nola sipped from her cup thoughtfully, looking about. She was maybe twenty. Pale, dark hair. Eyes that stayed busy, checking doors, windows.

Interesting, Madeline thought.

"What are you studying?" she asked, to get things started.

"Biology," Nola said. "Animals, specifically."

"Why New York City, then? All we have are pigeons and rats."

"I know, right? But there was a scholarship and I thought—when else am I going to live in a city like this? Plus, the program has an internship with the Bronx Zoo. It's not exactly animals in the wild, but I like it. I mean, not the cages, but the way you get to know the animals."

She stopped, seeming to realize she had wandered a bit.

"So," she said, "what do you need?"

It was such a quick conversational turn that it took Madeline aback. There were so many potential answers. *Twenty years. A good scotch. That carpenter back in my bed.*

"I need to sort through my books," she said.

Nola cast her gaze across the shelves covering the walls.

"There are four floors," Madeline added.

"I'm in," Nola said quickly, as if it was up to her. As if she'd had to get used to grabbing what she needed. As if, perhaps, what she'd needed had not been just earrings or a cell phone, but something far more elemental.

"So, are you remodeling?" Nola asked. "Downsizing?"

Madeline pictured an urn and nodded, then gave herself points for dark humor.

"How many can you take with you?" Nola asked.

The age-old question. The age-old answer: none.

"Let's try to get it down to a couple hundred," Madeline said.

"Wow." Nola looked at the shelves around her, but she appeared more excited than daunted. "How soon do you want to do it?"

"How about now?"

"Good thing I'm on break," Nola said. "I've got all week."

For someone interested in animals, Nola had a remarkable affinity for books. More than once, Madeline caught sight of Nola's fingers gently touching the spine of a novel before moving it onto a stack on the floor.

"They aren't alphabetical," Nola noted that first morning.

"Chronological," Madeline said. Nola shook her head, confused.

"I'm a literary agent," Madeline explained. "So, order of publication. Mostly."

"Are these all *your* books?" Nola looked around her.

Now she'll ask, Madeline thought. That question people who weren't in the business always asked: *Which one is your favorite?* Meaning *the best.* As if she could ever separate the story from the conversations with the author, the dinner she was eating when she read it for the first time, the negotiation of the deal, the first sight of the cover, the reviews, the book events, the faces in the audience. The thought, *I made this happen,* even if none of the words were ever hers.

But Nola just smiled. "So, you're the head zookeeper," she said. "What a cool job."

They fell into a routine with surprising speed. At the end of the second day, Madeline gave Nola a key so she could let herself in easily in the morning. Nola agreed to pick up meals on her way, and that, combined with her presence in the house, meant Madeline could keep the worriers at bay. Within a few days, the calls from friends and the office slowed, then, for the most part, stopped. Savannah still texted, as did Lara—both subtly checking that Nola was not some scam artist there to get bank account info—but it was disconcerting how quickly most other people were willing to check her off their list. Her invincibility had been a vision she'd curated aggressively throughout her life, so perhaps she could see it as a compliment.

"How are you really, though?" Lara asked on the phone. If anyone at the office understood her, it was Lara. Lara, who had gone from half-crazed young mother to a strong and capable agent. It was Lara who had covered for her more than once recently, discreetly editing her most important emails before they were sent. Catching the switch of a title, a confusion with an editor's name. Saying nothing.

"I'm doing what I need to do," Madeline said now. It was a line she'd use with new assistants who liked to spin in anxiety circles as the work piled up around them. *Just do what you need to do.* The underlying message *and please shut up in the meantime.*

"Okay," Lara said. "But I'm here if you want visitors. I could bring you manuscripts." She held out the offer like candy.

"Maybe in a few days," Madeline said. Then she heard the door open downstairs and Nola's voice calling "It's just me," and her thoughts returned to the books on the shelves.

Initially, it was all about speed and organization. Madeline approached the task as she had her life—with a measurable goal that, if necessary, meant one worked through lunch. But on the third day, she asked Nola if she wanted to break early and stay for dinner.

It was warm for late September, and they sat on the patio, the last of the sunlight filtering down through the wisteria. Madeline negotiated her food with her left hand while Nola gazed at the foliage around her.

"I've never been anywhere like this," she said.

"It's small, but I like it," Madeline said. It was what she always said.

"This isn't small." There was an edge to Nola's tone that made Madeline look over.

At times, Madeline thought, Nola was like one of those too-subtle-by-half manuscripts that needed an insightful editor to bring the whole story to light. But manuscripts contained stories that wanted to be told, full of hints dropped to entice a reader's interest. With Nola, the hints seemed to originate more from an inability to hold inside something that was too big for the space. Madeline knew the effort it took to keep a container intact, however, so she didn't push, letting Nola's comment mingle into the wisteria.

"Wine?" she asked, holding out the bottle of white. The girl was almost twenty-one, and something told Madeline it would not be her first glass in any case.

By the end of the week, they'd gone through the first two floors and the office at the top. All that was left were the shelves in Madeline's bedroom. This was where Madeline kept the special books; the ones that weren't just a quick political or celebrity tell-all, a how-to on a zeitgeist topic. The books in this room were ones she'd fought for, changing a life in the process. Taking more time than she should have given, probably, for almost none of them had been big moneymakers. But these were the ones she slept with at night.

"Hey, I read this one in high school," Nola said, taking down a book.

Madeline recognized the distinctive blue-and-yellow cover. *Theo.* It had been almost ten years, but she still remembered Lara sending her the manuscript, her advocacy impassioned—maternal, you might say, although Lara would have hated that description. Madeline had read the manuscript, going farther than she might have because of Lara's insistence, and eventually she found herself sucked in, inhabiting this boy's universe. Wanting him to understand the gift that grew out of his brokenness. To see that he had been given not just a hell to live in, but the road out.

She'd thought the author would be older, but Alice Wein hadn't even been thirty, a thin, pale thing, made of nerves. Madeline expected her to vomit in the middle of her first book event and sent Lara to hold her hand. *Would this girl-writer be a one-and-done?* she'd wondered. *Would this story, so obviously carved from her own guts, be all she had to say?* Madeline had hoped not, but by now it appeared that might be the case. Five years ago, she'd passed Alice on to Lara, stating that the connection between the two of them might prove fruitful.

"What did you think of it?" Madeline asked Nola now.

"I liked it," Nola said, leafing through the pages. She paused. "So, what do you think happens at the end?"

The ending, Madeline thought. With every book, it came down to this. Endings had been another specialty of Madeline's. She didn't write them, but she'd had an unerring instinct for the good ones—all the elements of a story coming together like an Olympic gymnast sticking a landing. Boom. The way a reader would put down a book like that and instantly turn to social media. *You've got to read this.* From such endings were bestsellers born.

Theo's ending, on the other hand, was a walk off into the sunset with no particular destination in mind. Lara had liked it; Madeline had wanted more. She'd had discussions with Alice about reader expectations—but Alice had been adamant.

"What do you think?" Madeline asked Nola now. Deflection was always a good strategy.

Nola shrugged. "We had a big debate in class. There was this girl, Tina, and she *really* needed to know what the author meant."

"What about you?"

"I just don't think life gets tied up with a bow very often."

No kidding, Madeline thought. *Even when they tell you, standing there in their white coats, you still won't know. Not the when. Not the how. And definitely not the after.*

"Maybe that's why people want it in a book," she said. It was basic marketing—give readers what they don't get or can't have in regular life. A safe brush with evil. A flaming romance. Certainty.

Nola thought for a moment, then shook her head. "I guess I just like the idea of possibility. Like an invitation, not an answer, you know? It gives you something to think about later."

What an unusual young woman, Madeline thought, looking at Nola. It was strange, but this was exactly the kind of conversation she might have had with Alice, back in the beginning. In fact, now that she thought about it, Nola reminded her more of Alice than anyone had in a long time. Not just what she said, but how she said it. Something broken. The origin would never be divulged out loud, you could tell. But if you looked closely—at the words on a page, the expression on a face—you might be able to read it.

Madeline hadn't had time for any of that back when she first met Alice. Her job was to sell a good book. But now she looked over at Nola, who was standing quietly, the copy of *Theo* in her hands.

"Would you like to keep it?" Madeline asked. Nola looked at her, startled.

"Really?" she said. She opened the cover, looked at the first page. "But there's something written to you."

All Madeline's books had inscriptions. Most of them said the same things. *Thank you. I couldn't have done it without you. You're the best!*

Alice's inscription had been different: *Take care of him.*

"I'm sure," Madeline said.

Nola touched the inscription with her finger. "Thank you," she said. Madeline relaxed, suddenly feeling tired.

"Lunch?" Nola asked. "Shall I bring it to you?"

Was it that obvious? Madeline raised her cast. "Wrist, not legs, Nola. I'm perfectly mobile." She paused. "But thank you for the offer, anyway."

Nola headed downstairs. Madeline looked around the bedroom, taking a moment before she followed. On the other floors, the books were organized in categories, still on the shelves (she couldn't stand the thought of them empty) but labeled for future exits. Gifts to friends. Donations to libraries. And yes, some for used bookstores.

There was only this floor left. She was almost done, she told herself. She would call Lara tomorrow. Start passing the baton. It was time.

She awoke the next morning to an astonishing pain behind her left eye. *Pick, pick, pick your pickax,* she thought, the words sloshing, slow and heavy. *Pick. Pick. Ouch.* Eyes still closed, she went to reach her right hand toward the bottle of pills near the bed, then remembered the cast, then realized she was on the floor and couldn't lift her arm at all.

Strange, she thought. *It's only cracked. I should . . .*

What a funny word, she thought. *Should.* Like someone telling you to be quiet before you even started. *Shhh. Shhh. Shhhh.*

She decided she would open her eyes, see what was going on. The light in the bedroom was bright, a beam of sunlight coming in through the sheer curtains. Ridiculously immortal thing, the sun. Not immortal, the scientists would say, but when time was measured in such infinitude, it didn't matter. Time, seen from such a distant perspective, just came apart.

Apart. A part. She was coming apart. She closed her eyes again. She could feel the boundaries of her body beginning to dissolve, and she wondered why she'd ever needed them in the first place.

Focus. Her mother's voice, coming from some deep and ancient part of her brain, and Madeline wondered *Why are you here?*

Her mother hadn't focused—the original Did Not Finish. Not marriage. Not parenting. Not work. A pirouette of a woman, gone by the time Madeline was thirteen. *Off on a jaunt*—that one another DNF, if by finish you mean come home. Leaving Madeline with a father who thought love was boarding schools, the best colleges. Shut little boxes. Neat little bows.

Madeline's brain sloshed companionably around her memories, like waves on a beach. Not an original simile, Madeline thought, or even an appropriate one for a woman who never went on vacation. *Make the metaphor fit the character,* Madeline always told her authors.

More like bourbon in a glass, then, she decided. The gentle back-and-forth as you pick it up, gold catching the light as you toast the next deal, let the liquid slide down your throat.

How many deals? How many stories? *As many as the sun,* she thought, letting her mind slide toward the books on the shelves.

I was going to call someone this morning. The thought came into her mind, but the waves pushed it away and she found she didn't mind because she was rocking along with them. *Gently out to sea.*

Far off in the distance, she heard the front door open, a voice calling. Low, but young. Rhythmic sounds, coming closer. Feet? On stairs?

Why were they so loud?

The sounds came into the room, became a body, bending down, a face. Someone familiar, female. Madeline looked up at her mouth, which was saying something. Words, maybe.

I used to love words, Madeline thought.

The voice was asking a question, several of them, it seemed, the sounds trending upward at the end, over and over. How many authors had Madeline retrained to speak so that every sentence didn't end in a lift, carrying away the meaning on a gust of breathless indecision? Still, this voice—*Nola, was it? Yes. Nola*—seemed to want actual answers. It was important; Madeline could tell from the expression in her eyes. And suddenly it was Nola's face that was the marvelous, informative thing. No need for words.

Just read the face.

The eyes, brave and scared. The mouth, firm on one side, bitten down on the other. This was not Nola's first crumpled body on a floor, Madeline understood. Not the first time she was too young for what was happening.

Ahhh, thought Madeline, *there's the broken part.*

Then suddenly there was resolve on the girl's face, a decision she was making. Her hand pulling a phone from her pocket.

Focus. It was Madeline's own voice in her head now, because suddenly she knew this next part mattered.

Nola was going to call for help—and in a sudden flash of clarity, Madeline understood what that call would mean. Hands, handling; a world of beds and trays. A half-life that would take twice as long to live. Words that would be not stories, not joy, not brilliance, but sharp little objects that made no sense and must be picked up, put in the right box.

No, Madeline thought.

But there was another option on today's tray.

What had that essay called it—*the least painful exit?* Too bad she'd never learned to drive, Madeline thought, and chuckled, or at least she thought she did. Nola's expression said the sound might have been a little different. She'd turned back to her phone, started making the call.

Madeline realized she needed to do something, soon, but time was turning to water, to blood, to the gentle sloshing in her brain.

Now, Madeline, she told herself.

She searched in her mind for the words, but they had all disappeared. And so instead, she reached out with her left hand, and grabbed Nola's wrist. The girl looked at her, startled, but Madeline held her gaze until Nola's face went deeply sad, then finally cleared.

"Okay," she said.

Madeline closed her eyes with a sense of profound relief. For a moment she hung there, suspended in not-time, and then she relaxed into the waves. The room around her expanded, its boundaries, her boundaries, unweaving with a soft laugh into everything. She could hear a rustle as the stories in the books began to move, too, slipping out of their pages, finding their way back into the air, drifting, exploring, losing themselves in one another. Simple emotions now. Pain. Joy. Excitement. Terror. And beauty—because yes, she was understanding, beauty was an emotion, too. She'd gotten that wrong. Thought it was a thing, but it wasn't. It was this motion, this wandering. This finding.

Then, because she understood as well that this story was not meant to be kept to oneself, she made a herculean effort and opened her eyes one more time. Looked into Nola's. Let her see.

"Oh," Nola said. "Ohhh."

Madeline smiled and left the page.

New York City,
December
2019

Epilogue

Alice was hiding. At thirty-four she was a bit old for that, but she'd needed the quiet. She could hear the noises from Madeline's memorial reception down the hall in the big, domed room of the New York Public Library, rented for the occasion. Glasses clinking, now that the big words had been said, the memories trotted out like elevator pitches for new novels. *She changed my life when . . . I remember the time she . . .*

Good stories, all of them, well delivered, but what else would you expect? Madeline's stable of authors was legendary, luminous, and many of them were in attendance, scattered among the agents and editors and publishers like human versions of the sparkling white lights hanging from the ceiling.

Alice was not a luminary. Barely a spark, she thought as she hid in the small reading room. She'd contemplated not coming, playing the introvert card, the author-as-recluse, tucked away in rural Maine writing the next great book. The only problem was, there was no great next book. Hadn't been for nine years.

What if I was only supposed to write his story? she'd asked Professor Roberts, and he'd said *I don't believe that, not for a moment,* but he'd died as well, three years ago.

It didn't help that her father had refused to speak to her after the book came out.

People think it's me, he'd said.

It's all of us, she'd replied. *A book always is.*

The only reason she was at the reception at all was Kit. He'd seen the email she received from the agency, and those booklover eyes of his had lit up.

"Just imagine who will be there," he'd said. And she couldn't say no, even though she'd been to group author events before, knew how the one-trick ponies were treated.

If it were up to her, she'd never leave Maine. One of her fantasies was getting snowed in for an entire year, with food but no expectations. No people. Kit said human beings went crazy if they couldn't see other people at least some-times, but she wasn't sure that applied to her. Unless it was Kit, who'd come into her life like a great warm sun. Who made the not-writing a puzzle instead of a wall.

What do you want to say? he'd ask her as they lay in bed at night.

But the problem wasn't having something to say. Alice

could feel things simmering inside her, amorphous, powerful things. The problem was the *how*. It was the *who*. She'd
pick a different perspective each morning—a girl, a boy,
a dog, a river, old, young, straight, slant—just to see what
might jog something loose. But she knew it didn't work
that way. You didn't come to a story; it came to you, a million little things that fell together like cells turning into a
body. You just needed the image. The question. The door to
set it free.

Where are you? she'd ask the air. *Why are you waiting?*

Down the hall, someone must have told a good story because laughter billowed up to the domed ceiling, playing off
the walls. She heard the click of high heels clipping down
the hall, heading toward the bathroom, probably. Whoever
it was would pass right by the open door of the reading
room. Alice looked about, saw a book lying on the table
nearby. It should have been reshelved but staff was short in
libraries these days. She went over, ready to pretend to be
reading, engrossed, and saw the title: *Found Art*.

She remembered the moment when the boy came to her
in the water, that feeling of being found as well as finding.
Her fingers dropped to the book, opened the cover, leafed
through the pages. Photographs. A nest made of curving
metal spoons. An urban landscape created from frosted
glass bottles and jars. The *Mona Lisa*, re-envisioned in
beads and buttons and shells.

And then, she saw it.

It was the hair that caught her eye—wooden slats, flying out from the head like speed itself. The photograph was black and white, but Alice could tell there had been color in the drawers that made the mouth and nestled between the hip bones, color in the V for Victor emblazoned across the rat trap on the forehead.

It was angry as hell, but also—what? Joyous?

Because there were wings, spreading out behind the body. Alice leaned closer to the photo and saw markings on the feathers. Impossible to read, but clearly words.

What would that woman say? Alice wondered. *With that drawer of a mouth? With those wings?*

She looked at the title of the sculpture: *Woman in Pieces.*

And for just a moment, the world stopped. *There you are,* Alice thought.

She stood in the reading room, the noise of the memorial service and the woman walking down the hall and even her own fears well and truly forgotten. Because this was a door, and she was going in.

Acknowledgments

No Two Persons was written during a pandemic. I've always said my fictional characters keep me company—this time they kept me sane. So, my first thank-you is to the characters on these pages. They kept me learning, exploring, feeling, thinking, and I am grateful for every minute with them.

There are some very real people who made sure that what was in my head made it onto the page in words you might want to read. Thank you to the team at Writers House—Amy Berkower, Genevieve Gagne-Hawes, and Meridith Viguet. A bow of gratitude to my writing group, Louise Marley and Anna Quinn. To my early readers, Adrienne Brodeur, Nina Meierding, Jennie Shortridge, and Marjorie Osterhout. To Hedgebook, for providing a peaceful place to think. To my editor at St. Martin's, Leslie Gelbman, for believing. To the dedicated folks in marketing and publicity at St. Martin's—

Marissa Sangiacomo, Dori Weintraub, and Brant Janeway. And as always, thank you to Ben Bauermeister, for listening, and for understanding that sometimes a woman just needs to go write in a shed.

This book covers a lot of ground, and the inspiration and research for these chapters came from a wide variety of places and people. One day, wandering William James Books in Port Townsend, I spotted the gorgeous blue cover of Adam Skolnick's *One Breath*, and then got sucked into its riveting descriptions of free diving and one diver who went too far. Jill Bolte Taylor's *My Stroke of Insight* took me inside a brain that was losing itself (and, as I read it in the days following a concussion, it was a two-fer, so I am doubly grateful). Chelsea Pace's *Staging Sex* was invaluable in understanding the fascinating job of intimacy coordination. Cassandra Campbell and Tavia Gilbert generously gave me the benefit of their expertise in audiobook narration. *Atlas Obscura* is a constant source of brain-spinning ideas (here's looking at you, leap seconds). And a story in *The New York Times* about Brent Underwood got me started on William's story. Brent and William are remarkably different, but that's the magic of fiction. You read an article about a young man who got stuck in a ghost town during a snowstorm and you end up with a story about a sixty-two-year-old widower who learns a completely different lesson.

Because *No Two Persons* is also about the serendipitous routes a book can take, not just to readers, but to publication, I want to take this moment to thank Josh Getzler. Fifteen years ago, he read my first novel when he was a literary assistant at Writers House. Without his passionate advocacy back then, I'd probably still be writing manuscripts that ended up in my filing cabinet.

And while we are looking back—each writer takes their own path to this profession. Mine was made clearer by Holly Smith—reader, writer, bookseller, friend—who some three decades ago taught me that a great book is one that you love.

May you find many.

Author's Note

The epigraph that begins *No Two Persons* is generally attributed to Edmund Wilson (1895–1972), a well-known
American literary critic. You can find "no two persons ever
read the same book" credited to Wilson on blogs, stickers,
frameable artwork, and Twitter, along with pages and pages
of Google links. Because I was curious, I tried to find the
original source. I could not. In an introduction to *The Triple
Thinkers* in 1938, Wilson did write the thought-provoking
statement: "In a sense, one can never read the book that the
author originally wrote, and one can never read the same
book twice." This comes close, but both of those scenarios
are different—one talking about the difference in interpretation between author and reader, and the other referring to
the same reader encountering the same book multiple times.
Not to mention that it's not the actual quote.

You *can* find the words "No two persons ever read the

same book, or saw the same picture" in *The Writings of Madame Swetchine*. Madame Swetchine (1782–1857) was a well-educated Russian woman who spoke several languages and spent much of her growing-up years at the court of Catherine the Great. In 1815, she moved to Paris, where for many years she had a well-known intellectual salon that was frequented by Alexis de Tocqueville, among many others. Her writings were gathered posthumously by Count de Falloux in 1860 and 1861. An English version of *The Writings of Madame Swetchine* was published in Boston in 1869.

If you are a close reader, you have already figured out that 1869 was twenty-six years before Edmund Wilson was born.

Mind you, I'm not saying Wilson claimed the quote for himself. We in the internet age are quick with our attributions, and not always accurate. In my search, however, I did find Wilson's savage review of Tolkien's *Lord of the Rings*, in which he calls the trilogy "juvenile trash," and comments "Dr. Tolkien has little skill at narrative and no instinct for literary form."

So this one's for you, Alice and Peter. And Madame Swetchine.

Reading
Group
Gold

NO TWO
PERSONS
by Erica Bauermeister

About the Author

- A Conversation with Erica Bauermeister

Behind the Novel

Keep On Reading

- Recommended Reading
- Reading Group Questions

A
Reading
Group Gold
Selection

Also available as an audiobook
from Macmillan Audio

For more reading group suggestions
visit www.readinggroupgold.com.

 ST. MARTIN'S GRIFFIN

A Conversation with Erica Bauermeister

The title No Two Persons *comes from the quote "No two persons ever read the same book." Your book is a novel about a novel, which we follow from its creation and then through the reactions of a disparate group of readers who encounter the book in various ways across the span of almost a decade. How did the idea come to you? Why do you think it's important?*

No Two Persons was inspired in large part by talking with book clubs. As an author, it was initially disconcerting to see how one novel could be interpreted in such a variety of ways. I soon became intrigued by the discussions, however, and I loved how books created a safe space to talk across and about differences.

We need those discussions, because—just as no two persons will read the same book—no two siblings, or spouses, or friends, or enemies will view the same event in the same way. What we see has everything to do with who and where we are in our lives at that time. Books are a microcosm of the world in that regard. And yet, the beautiful thing about books is that in the end, no matter our interpretations, we still share the common experience of reading.

I wanted to write a book that would celebrate differences while reminding us of our shared humanity. I chose to focus on reading and books because that is where my heart lives, but I hope its message will be taken in a wider sense as well.

There's the old saying "form follows function." No Two Persons *has the arc of a novel, but its chapters could also easily stand alone. How does the form of your novel affect the story?*

No Two Persons is really what I would call interconnected short stories. Each chapter focuses on one character, a deep and immersive dive into a particular life. There are connections between the characters, but they may never know them. It is the reader who sits above the page who gets to put all the pieces together.

For a book about readers and the shared experience of reading, it is a perfect form, as the structure subliminally reinforces the message. Because the stories are self-contained, there is a little jolt when each chapter ends, and the reader must move on to the next character. That moment is a reminder that each of these characters is an individual—separate, never completely knowable. But the structure also gives us connections between the characters, slipped into one chapter after another, made even more exciting because they help us cross those boundaries and create a whole where before there were parts. The ending brings it all back around, not just to close up shop, but to encourage us to rethink all that came before—which makes the plot not a straight line but a circle, encompassing all the characters, and us.

Your characters range widely—a free diver, a homeless teenager, an intimacy coordinator for movies, a literary agent, the caretaker of a ghost town. Where did these characters come from? And what is your research process like?

I love research, and that moment when a fictional story shimmers up out of an odd fact. Sometimes it feels like fishing. I wander the nonfiction sections of bookstores, and read everything from *The New York Times* to *Atlas Obscura* each morning. You just never know where a character is going to come from—and in *No Two Persons* I had a lot of characters to create. One day in a wonderful, old used bookstore, I saw a book about free diving. The cover was a mix of deep, intense blues, and in its center was a slim line of a human, no tanks or gear, swimming headfirst down into nothingness. I looked at that diver, and I wondered, *Who the hell would want to do that?* And suddenly, there was Tyler. Then I read an article about intimacy coordinators, and it got me thinking: What would intimacy mean for someone whose job was making it look real? I came across a book of strange animal facts and that inspired Nola, a homeless teenager who uses those facts to make a difficult world a little easier. An article about leap seconds turned into Annalise—who would never read fiction, so it only made sense that she was the girlfriend of the quirky bookseller. And what a pair they turned out to be.

Once I had the characters, the fun and challenging part was figuring out how each of them would end up reading the same book, what they would learn from it, and how they were connected. Because they were, and it seemed as if they knew it even before I did.

*In one of the chapters, a bookseller is having a
debate about the value of fiction with his
fiancée, a scientist who studies leap seconds.
He thinks to himself, "And that, perhaps, was
the difference between the two of them. Science
heard that fragment of a second and wondered
how to make it fit into a whole. Fiction wondered
what hearing it felt like" (page 206-7).
What do you see as the power of fiction?*

I grew up the daughter of a scientist. I watched his
fascination with technology, but I was always more
interested in the cultural and emotional effect of
each innovation. I think it was one of the reasons
I was drawn to writing, because fiction was all
about exploring those more subliminal issues.
Rather than asking, "*Can* we go to Mars/track our
child's every move/change a photo so we take out
the parts we don't like?" fiction asks, "How will
that change us?" and "Who do we want to be?"

These are critical questions, and they are what
makes fiction such a powerful and necessary part
of our lives. Sometimes a fictional character can
teach us things a real person cannot—in part
because that character is not constrained by a life
already lived. Fiction, like science, looks at what
might be, and we need both those kinds
of imagination.

*No Two Persons ends in December of 2019,
at the beginning of the pandemic. How did the
pandemic inform your book?*

I don't believe it's coincidental that each of the characters in *No Two Persons* is relatively isolated, and sometimes remarkably so. I didn't set out to make that happen, but what is occurring in the larger world usually creeps into our writing in one way or another.

And yet, I think the beautiful thing about *No Two Persons* is how, in the end, these characters are not alone. They are more connected than they will ever know, just as we are. And I think this, too, came from the pandemic, and those moments when a meme, or a book, or a social movement brought people together. Even in the midst of our isolation, there was still a collective desire to connect.

You wrote for over twenty years before your first fiction was published. How did that affect you as a writer, both before and after?

I'll be honest, those years were terribly difficult. It is hard to be rejected, manuscript after manuscript, year after year. And yet, I will always be grateful to those books. They taught me the craft of writing. How to hear the rise and fall of a sentence, or a word, or a plot line. How to open your mind to a new image. How to listen to characters and let them in.

Those years also taught me that the story is always more important than the author, and that good writing starts with a question, not an answer. When you're young, you often think you need to have an answer if you want to be taken seriously. But an answer is already finished. It lies there flat on the page. A good question, on the other hand, is open-ended, light on its feet. It takes you places you didn't know you needed to go. And that's where the interesting stuff is.

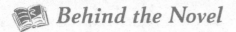 **Behind the Novel**

We live in an era of social media, where news comes to us in bits and bites, and we might have hundreds or thousands of friends we will never meet in person. But humans desire connection, the kind that makes us feel as if we are part of humanity.

I see interconnected stories as a response to that cultural need. They provide us with the intimacy of deep dives into individual characters, while giving us the pleasure of seeing the connections between them. The connection can be obvious and central: a cooking school, a group of friends. But in the case of *No Two Persons*—where the characters are strangers and mostly remain that way—the connections are more gossamer, and finding them becomes a grand Easter egg hunt. Do you have to do it to enjoy the book? No. Will it enrich your experience to try? Absolutely.

So here are some hints to get you started:

1) Each character in *No Two Persons* is connected to at least one other character in the book. Sometimes this connection is quite direct and obvious (a character from one story shows up in another). Sometimes it can be as subtle as a poster on a wall.

2) Want a little help? Pay attention to the graphics at the beginning of each section and chapter. They are like road maps—the first circle is the story itself, and as each character is introduced, so is their circle in the design, which will also tell you where the overlaps are.

3) Reading an ebook or an audiobook where you don't have those graphics? You can find them on my website: www.ericabauermeister.com.

4) Have fun! And tell me what you find! :)

Behind the Novel

Recommended Reading

I love the intricacy of interconnected stories. I get to feel like I am both reader and detective, seeing things the characters themselves might not see. Here's a list of some of my favorites. . . .

Girl in Hyacinth Blue by Susan Vreeland

Gorgeously written, this novel-in-stories follows a fictional Vermeer painting back in time through its various owners to its creator. It's fascinating to see what this one painting can mean to different people in different times, and each chapter is an extraordinary re-creation of its time.

The House on Mango Street by Sandra Cisneros

A classic. Through a series of quick, vibrant vignettes of twelve-year-old Esperanza Cordero and her neighbors, Sandra Cisneros immerses us in the life of the Hispanic quarter of Chicago in the late 1960s. The writing is so alive, I swear I saw colors in the words.

Olive Kitteridge by Elizabeth Strout

Strout really pushed the boundaries here—the connection between the stories is a prickly older woman named Olive, who may be the central character of a story, or so minor as to be a moment in the background. In the end, we get a rich composite portrait of both Olive and her town.

I Am, I Am, I Am: Seventeen Brushes with Death by Maggie O'Farrell

I read *Hamnet* and loved it, but Maggie O'Farrell's memoir-in-essays stunned me. She uses the unusual frame of surviving death to take us deep into questions of living. The writing is honest and beautiful, sometimes heartbreaking, and always powerful.

Blackbird House by Alice Hoffman

Most people don't associate Alice Hoffman with short stories, but *Blackbird House* is my favorite of her books. She displays her classic skills of magical realism and quick, quirky character development as we read our way through the generations of owners of one house in remote Cape Cod, starting in the early 1800s.

*Keep On
Reading*

Reading Group Questions

1. The title *No Two Persons* comes from the quote: "No two persons ever read the same book, or saw the same picture." What does that mean to you? Have you experienced this yourself?

2. The opening line of *Theo* is: "Wandering is a gift given only to the lost" (page 49). What does the phrase mean to Alice? Lara? The Cultus book reviewer? Miranda? Have you ever felt like a wanderer?

3. In "The Writer," Professor Roberts says: "If you think about it, every story—even the most fantastical—is grounded in things we already know" (page 12). How do you think Alice's life informed the novel she ended up writing?

4. Why do you think Lara, the literary assistant, has such a strong response to *Theo*?

5. What do you think Tyler gets from free diving?

6. Which characters in *No Two Persons* elicited the strongest reactions in you? Why do you think that was?

7. In "The Bookseller," Kit says to Annalise: "I'm just saying that a character can be as real as a person. Or teach you as much, anyway" (page 206). Do you agree? If so, what fictional characters have been meaningful in your life?

8. In "The Caretaker," Abigail's margin comments in her copy of *Theo* draw a connection between Theo, William, and the mules in the mine. What do you think she was seeing?

9. In "The Coordinator," Juliet's experience of *Theo* is affected because she listens to an audiobook. How do you think audiobooks affect us as readers?

10. There are almost no quoted passages from *Theo* other than the first line. We learn his story in bits, given to us through each succeeding character. How does that affect your understanding of *Theo*?

11. In "The Agent," Nola and Madeline have a conversation about what kinds of endings they like in books. Nola likes to be left thinking, while Madeline believes things should be more nailed down. What kind do you prefer?

12. What do you think about Madeline's choice for her own ending?

13. Initially, the characters in *No Two Persons* seem unrelated to one another, but as the book progresses, connections begin to surface. How many connections can you find? Which ones surprised you the most?

14. At the end of the book, Alice finds inspiration in an unlikely place. Where have you found inspiration?

About the Author

Susan Doupé

Erica Bauermeister is the bestselling author of five novels, including *The Scent Keeper* and *The School of Essential Ingredients*, as well as the memoir *House Lessons: Renovating a Life*. She has a PhD in literature from the University of Washington and is the coauthor of two readers' guides: *500 Great Books by Women* and *Let's Hear It for the Girls*. She currently lives in Port Townsend, Washington.